A Lake District
Christmas Murder

By Rebecca Tope

A Lake District Christmas Murder

REBECCA TOPE

Allison & Busby Limited
11 Wardour Mews
London W1F 8AN
allisonandbusby.com

First published in Great Britain by Allison & Busby in 2024.

A CIP catalogue record for this book is available from
the British Library.

First Edition

ISBN 978-0-7490-3169-5

Typeset in 11/16 pt Sabon LT Pro by
Allison & Busby Ltd.

By choosing this product, you help take care of the world's forests.
Learn more: www.fsc.org.

Printed and bound by CPI Group (UK) Ltd, Croydon, CR0 4YY

In fond memory of Sally Laird (1945–2024)
My friend for almost 60 years

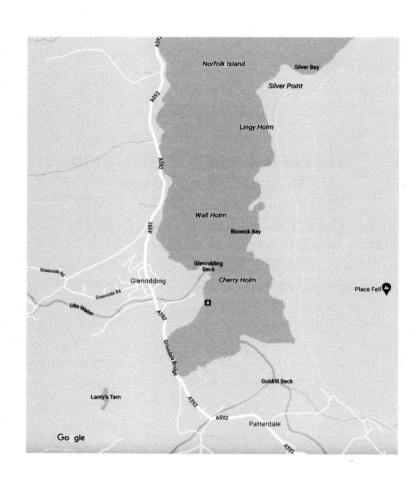

Author's Note

As in previous titles, this story is set in real villages. Some liberties have been taken with precise layout and distances to fit the storyline. The White Lion Inn in Patterdale is now under new management. It appears in the story as it was until recently.

Chapter One

'We have no idea what they're like,' Simmy worried. 'What'm I going to *wear*? How long do we have to stay?'

'There'll be loads of other people there. Nobody's going to take much notice of us. If they do, it'll be Robin they talk to, not us. It's just a nice village get-together for Christmas. Don't get all obsessive about it.'

'It's not our village, though, is it? We're not part of Glenridding society – or do we say "community"? That sounds nicer, somehow. Whichever it is, it's not us. I wouldn't mind if it was people we know here in Hartsop. Why have they even asked us?'

'Because we go to the shop there, and people know us, whatever you think. They're only being friendly. Why're you being so weird? I'd have thought you'd be thrilled at the chance of meeting more people. You're always saying you wish you'd got a friend within walking distance.'

Simmy paused, trying to analyse her own response.

Christopher had dropped the news of the invitation only ten minutes earlier, and her instant reaction had been resistance bordering on panic. A couple slightly younger than them, named Dan and Fran Bunting, had approached Christopher in the Glenridding store and invited the Hendersons to a late-afternoon get-together in two days' time – which would be 21st December, a Friday. 'It's a solstice party. We're asking everybody,' said Dan. 'Really going the whole hog. Kids, dogs, grannies – the works. Sausages, punch, mince pies. We won't turn down any contributions, but it's not obligatory.'

'You've got a little boy, haven't you?' put in Fran. 'I bet he's excited about Christmas. I'd love to meet him.'

'He doesn't really understand what's going on, but we think he'll enjoy it this year. But I don't think we'll bring the dog,' said Christopher cautiously. 'Thanks for asking us – it sounds great.'

'I don't know,' said Simmy now. 'I feel overwhelmed for some reason. I like people in small doses. I'll be stupidly shy.'

'I doubt if there'll be all that many, when it comes to it. Not a lot of people live in Patterdale, after all, and some of them are bound to be otherwise engaged. Think positive. It sounds pretty good to me.'

'You just said there'd be loads of people there,' she accused him. 'Make up your mind.'

'We're going, Sim – and that's final.'

'I know we are,' she sighed. 'I didn't doubt it for a moment.'

* * *

They arrived early, on the basis that this meant they could leave early, too. 'I bet everyone'll be gone by seven,' said Christopher. 'They obviously don't intend to give us much food. Although he did mention sausages and mince pies.' They'd used the village car park a short way below the designated house.

'And it'll be Robin's bedtime. They must realise that.'

The house was one of the oldest in the area, made of the typical dark grey slate that characterised Lakeland. 'What do they do?' Simmy whispered belatedly, as they were almost on the doorstep.

'No idea,' Christopher replied, before turning a wide smile on Fran Bunting, who had thrown the door open for them. 'Here we are,' he added fatuously.

Their hostess was thin, with make-up worthy of a film star. She wore tight leggings and a long red top with sparkly bits in it. 'And this is your little boy!' she trilled excitedly. 'Remind me what he's called.'

Simmy responded gratefully, aware that this was a ploy to make her feel welcome, rather than any genuine interest in the child. In the turmoil of releasing Robin from his buggy, getting into the living room and trying to focus on the three or four faces already there, any lurking shyness was dispelled. The doorbell rang again, and Fran sped off to answer it, leaving guests to introduce themselves.

'Drink?' asked a man Simmy vaguely recognised. He watched Robin's sturdy march across the room with obvious enjoyment. 'They look like drunken sailors at that age, don't they?'

Simmy laughed. It might be a cliché, but it was no less true for that.

'This is Dan,' said Christopher to his wife. 'What drinks have you got?'

'Gin. Wine. Sherry. Juice. Punch.' The last was uttered with special emphasis, suggesting that there really was little or no choice.

'Punch, then,' said Christopher. 'Right, Sim?'

'Lovely,' she said. 'What's in it?'

'All the usual. Most of the alcohol's boiled off, according to Fran, if that's worrying you.'

'Not really,' said Simmy. She looked at him more closely, trying to identify what he reminded her of. She thought it might be a vicar. There was something in his manner suggestive of solicitude, an excessive attention to her feelings and wishes that felt intrusive. 'It smells gorgeous,' she added.

The room was decorated with swags of greenery: mostly sprigs of fir, holly and ivy, with pine cones added here and there. As a florist, Simmy felt obliged to give a further inspection, although she had already ascertained at a glance that it was all home-made. A small Christmas tree stood in a corner, looking oddly irrelevant. Christmas carols were playing in another room.

Robin shared none of his mother's discomfort amongst strangers. At twenty-one months, he was walking and talking with confidence, accustomed more to adults than other children and alarmingly enthusiastic about dogs. Dan Bunting rapidly provided punch, and Simmy drank half of it right away. 'Hello, little man,' a youngish woman greeted Robin, ignoring his mother. 'Shall I give you a cake?' Without glancing to a parent for permission, she handed the toddler a large mince pie.

'Ah . . . um . . .' Simmy managed. 'Well, I suppose it's all right. He'll make an awful mess.'

'Oh – sorry,' said the woman unapologetically. 'He's not allergic, is he?'

'I shouldn't think so. He's never had a mince pie, so we're probably about to find out.'

The woman laughed much louder than was appropriate and Robin gave her a sideways look before sinking his teeth into the pastry. His face was instantly besmirched with crumbs.

'I'm Aoife,' said Robin's new friend. 'It's Irish for Eva. Don't even try to spell it.' She then proceeded to do exactly that.

'You don't sound very Irish,' said Simmy, trying with difficulty to avoid any stereotypes. Irish people did feed their infants on sweet unsuitable food, she suspected.

'Well, yes – I mean, no. I've been here most of my life, as it happens. Since I was nine, in fact.' Her eye caught another woman, and she grinned. 'If you're looking for funny names, how about Diellza? She's Albanian. I've just been getting to know her, but I didn't get very far. She's quite exotic, don't you think?'

A large female approached warily. 'Hello,' she said in a musical voice. 'My English is not too good. Sorry.'

'You're doing brilliantly,' Aoife assured her, with a patronising smile. She waved at the Hendersons. 'Some local people for you to get to know. They'll tell you their names.'

'Christopher and Simmy,' said Christopher. 'We live in Hartsop.'

'Oh? You are . . . *Simmy?*' She was obviously querying the name, not the individual.

'Short for Persimmon. Tell me your name again.'

'Di-ell-za,' came the answer, slowly, separating the syllables.

Before any more could be said, Fran Bunting appeared waving an envelope. 'Hey, Diellza – this came for you this afternoon. I forgot to give it to you. Looks like a Christmas card.' She handed it over and moved quickly away. Diellza put it in a pocket.

Robin was standing close to his mother, gazing up at the new person towering over him. She was wearing an all-enveloping kaftan-style garment, made of a heavy material that hung from her substantial figure. She had to weigh sixteen stone, Simmy assessed, and she had a sweet face. 'It's a pretty name. Like Demelza. That's Cornish, I think.'

'Names are interesting. My husband is called Alexander. He's Scottish.' She rolled her eyes. 'You say "Scottish" not "Scotch". I have to take care to get that right.'

'Your English is really good,' said Christopher. 'How long have you been here?'

'Oh, quite a long time. But I don't think I will ever get to know all the idioms. I take everything much too literally.'

'It must be awfully difficult,' said Simmy. 'And the English are so bad at other languages. We just expect everyone to learn ours. It's awful, when you think about it.'

The Albanian's jaw tensed, her teeth clearly clenched. 'Ooh,' she gasped. 'Sorry.'

'Are you all right?' asked Simmy.

'Yes, yes. Bad tummy,' Fran said. 'Mince pies. Cheese.' She gave a rueful smile. 'English food can be hard to digest at times.'

The conversation was turning out to be harder going than Christopher for one was prepared to put up with.

He drifted away, holding his glass of punch, and Robin followed him. Simmy let the toddler go, confident that nothing much could happen to him. His hands and face were revoltingly sticky. If there was any justice, he would wipe himself all over Aoife, but she had disappeared from view.

She turned back to Diellza, with a sense of obligation. While she had more patience than her husband, it was limited. However curious she might be as to the reasons for an overweight Albanian finding herself in Patterdale, the prospect of forming the right kind of questions and perhaps being regaled with too much information as a result was not enticing. 'Go and sit down,' she advised, and then added. 'Are you living nearby?'

Diellza hesitated, making no move to find a seat. 'I'm living here. Dan and Fran have let me have a room for a time. They are kind. I'm trying not to bother them too much.' Something guarded in her expression made Simmy wonder what the precise relationship might be. 'Christmas is a strange time for everyone, in different ways,' Diellza went on. 'Ordinary life is paused for a few days.'

In spite of herself, Simmy felt curious. The Albanian was young – probably under thirty – and her English was really not so bad. 'That's true,' she said. 'Although it really boils down to just *one* day. When you get to Boxing Day, the whole thing's pretty much over. I always find Boxing Day a bit depressing.'

Diellza smiled fleetingly. 'It's very strange,' she said again.

Simmy wanted to ask more, while avoiding any appearance of undue curiosity. Her complete ignorance of Albania made it difficult to frame casual questions, but

15

she gave it a go. 'I expect all the rituals are different in Albania,' she tried.

'We don't think of them as rituals,' came the slightly frosty reply.

'No – wrong word. I mean—'

'I know what you mean. But really it is not so different. We have the food and the music and the gifts, just the same as you.' Again, the rictus of discomfort. 'I'll sit down, as you suggest,' she decided. 'I'm sorry. You find me at a difficult moment. It's nice of you to talk to me – Simmy. I will remember your name. Perhaps we can see each other again after the Christmas days. I think Dan will agree to that.'

Uh-oh, thought Simmy. Was she imagining an implication that Dan Bunting was not the simple benefactor she had assumed? Was Diellza in some way an unwilling recipient of his largesse? There was no avoiding the idea of 'human trafficking' or 'modern slavery', merely by learning the woman's nationality. Suddenly it felt horribly possible.

Her instant inclination was to back away from this sort of trouble as fast as she could. She looked round for Robin, as a handy excuse, but he was across the room with his father. At least four more people had arrived in the past few minutes, not counting two children aged about six, who were quietly fighting in the doorway. Someone had turned up the volume of the carols and 'Hark! The Herald Angels Sing' was belting out.

'Go and sit down,' she said loudly. 'Before people grab all the chairs.' There were two armchairs near the fireplace, and a scattering of upright dining chairs obviously brought

16

in from another room. Diellza did as suggested, sailing across the floor as if it was empty of people. Her bulk ensured a clear passage. Simmy smiled slightly to see it. Then she turned away, slightly ashamed of herself for her cowardice. But after all, you were supposed to circulate at a party and talk to everyone there. If Diellza was being exploited in some way, others could see it and deal with it, rather than her. She could hear voices in other parts of the house, which had at least three big downstairs rooms, and concluded there was a table somewhere bearing sausages and other seasonal fare. She would find someone else to talk to, and then go and explore.

But nobody offered themselves as a likely conversationalist. Simmy stood beside a small table, checking one face after another. There was a woman with very short pink hair she had seen before in the Glenridding shop, and an older one who was excruciatingly thin and who sometimes jogged determinedly through Hartsop and off towards Crookabeck. A man with a gingery-grey beard was also faintly familiar.

Simmy's thoughts remained stubbornly with Diellza, who was now seated regally on a rather small chair, one hand on her stomach. She could hardly be an illegal immigrant if the Buntings were happy to expose her to all their friends and she had been in the country for a while. Where was the husband called Alexander, who was Scottish? The very fact of his existence further reduced any suspicion of illegality. But equally pertinent was the fact that he was not spending Christmas with his wife who was staying in a tiny Cumbrian village with an apparently charitable couple. It made her realise how sheltered and spoilt she had always been, when such matters as Albanian politics and displaced migrants were so far beyond her understanding.

Dan Bunting came smoothly to her rescue, the perfect host. 'Hey – Simmy, right? You look as if you might need more punch. Come and talk to Louise. She's expecting her third and feeling hot. She's been admiring your Robin. Her second one is just his age.'

Simmy already hated Louise for having the babies that she herself had wanted. With every passing month it became more obvious that Robin was never going to have any siblings. 'I met Diellza,' she said, hoping for some explanation.

He nodded cheerfully. 'She's a sweet girl. Very well educated, actually, but got herself in a bit of a mess these past few weeks – well, months, actually. Badly treated by her husband. We've taken her in until after Christmas. Well – wouldn't you? Poor thing had nowhere to go.'

Simmy sighed, knowing that she was really very unlikely to have offered a roof to a troubled Albanian. 'That's very good of you,' she said.

'Well, we've got the space, and far too much food. It's making a nice change, and she's no trouble. Stays in her room most of the time. Doesn't even hog the bathroom, which was Fran's main worry. We've only got one.' This oversight was evidently a cause of some regret. He went on, 'She didn't want to come down to meet people, but we persuaded her. I hoped she'd make one or two friends.' He pulled a face. 'Although we don't expect her to be here for very long, so it wouldn't be a very good idea to get too rooted.' He was watching Simmy for her reaction, which gave rise to a degree of resistance. Again, there was the hint of hungry attention that sometimes imbued a vicar's conversation. She had no intention of repeating anything Diellza had said to her.

'It was very nice of you to invite us to the party,' she mumbled instead, noticing that the carols had gone quiet again. 'I feel awful, not knowing more people. But it's always so busy with Robin and the shop and everything. It's all we can manage to walk the dog and see family. Christopher's got brothers and sisters he likes to keep up with.'

'Shop?'

'Oh, yes – didn't you know? I've got a florist shop in Windermere. I'm back there three days a week now. Robin goes to my parents. It's a real hassle getting him to them – they're in the exact wrong direction. I should be full-time, really, but that's just too much.'

'He's still very young,' said Dan Bunting, with the same sympathetic understanding as before. *This man is too good to be true*, thought Simmy, again with a flicker of shame. 'And yes, I remember now about your flower shop. Silly me.' He gave a self-deprecating laugh.

Simmy waved this away. 'The punch is delicious,' she said.

'So I'll fetch you some more.' And he went off with her empty glass, having mercifully forgotten all about the pregnant Louise.

At six o'clock, Dan appeared and loudly clapped his hands. 'Happy solstice, everyone!' he shouted. 'Now it's time for a few little rituals.'

Simmy had been talking to the woman with pink hair, who knew just who she was and wanted to pick Simmy's brains about plants. Her name was Celia Parker and she lived in Patterdale all the year round and never rented out rooms to holidaymakers, winter or summer. 'I like to be mistress of my own destiny,' she said obscurely. 'And I often go off on a whim, leaving everything to fend for itself.' She also confessed to having a thing for hellebores, which Simmy found easy to understand. Catching a glance at the hair, Celia laughed. 'I did it deliberately to confuse people. It tempts them to put labels on me that are actually quite misplaced. Anyway, I decided I liked it, regardless of my original reasons. I was going grey and couldn't stand the prospect of becoming invisible.'

Simmy had been finding grey hairs herself lately and inwardly sighed. It was not clear what the woman did for money, but it sounded as if she had some at her disposal.

'Rituals?' Simmy murmured now, looking round for her husband in mild panic. He was last seen by the sausages with two other men.

'Don't worry – it's all very simple. More like a party game than anything else,' Celia reassured her.

'You've done it before?'

'Oh, yes. We're all a bit pagan around here. Hadn't you noticed?'

'Not really,' Simmy admitted. 'Although Dan comes over as a bit like a vicar.'

Celia Parker laughed out loud. 'So he does,' she said, with an amused shake of her head.

The first 'ritual' entailed writing down everything from the previous year you were glad to be rid of, Fran Bunting having distributed slips of paper and pencils. It was then thrown on the fire, which Dan had stoked up to a satisfying

20

blaze. Simmy could not think what to write, and eventually managed *Feeling isolated, with not enough friends.*

'Don't worry,' Dan called. 'Nobody's going to read what you've put. It's between you and the fates, or gods, or whatever you like to believe in.'

'He's always so inclusive,' Celia whispered. Simmy smiled. She had caught sight of Diellza throwing her paper into the flames and wondered what she'd written. Whatever it was, she had taken no time at all to record it. Most other people were still tapping their pencils on their teeth and scratching their heads.

When it came to her turn to burn her words, Simmy felt a strange sense of power in the simple act. She really was going to ask the fates or gods to lend a hand in improving her social life. And there were people right here in front of her who were offering themselves as material. Aoife seemed approachable; the pregnant Louise was an obvious pal; and Fran Bunting herself seemed worth getting to know a bit better. But they were all a lot younger than her. Celia, on the other hand, was quite a bit older. Simmy had never regarded herself as stand-offish, but being an only child meant she sometimes had a shaky grasp of the necessary processes that went into forming a friendship. She had had a few good friends at school, but not many since.

'And now the second part,' called Dan. 'Write down what your hopes are for the coming year.'

'And burn that as well?' murmured Simmy. 'Isn't that a bit counterproductive?'

'No – listen,' Celia told her.

'Then pin it onto the tree. There are little pegs in a box.'

'Such efficiency!' said Celia.

Simmy had even more difficulty with hopes for the future. She wanted to put *Another baby*, but that felt oddly dangerous. *Beware of what you wish for*, came a voice in her head. The overattentive fates might respond with twins, or a child with extra needs that she and Christopher would be unequal to. Simmy Henderson had reason to mistrust the fates, after all. They definitely should not be tempted. So she wrote *Good health* and felt pathetic.

'Are you doing anything tomorrow?' asked the pregnant Louise, ten minutes later, during which Simmy had meandered around both rooms and eventually ended up with the one person she had rather hoped to avoid. 'I thought you might like to bring Robin round to mine tomorrow. We should have done it before this.'

'Oh – well, thanks, but I'm at the shop all day, actually,' she said, thanking her stars that it was true. 'It's been terribly busy and tomorrow's the last day for Christmas things. Table centrepieces, mostly.'

Louise waited calmly for the excuses to run out, then said, 'Well, couldn't you leave Robin with me, and then stay for a drink or something when you fetch him? What do you usually do with him?'

But I don't even know you, Simmy silently protested. 'My parents have him. They've got all sorts of plans. Thanks for the idea. Maybe after Christmas . . . ?'

'Okay,' shrugged the woman. 'But I warn you, I won't give up. You haven't spent a proper winter here yet, have you? You'll soon see you need people, sometimes a lot more than you think.'

'Actually, we were here the whole of last winter. We know what it's like.'

'You have no idea,' Louise contradicted her. 'Haven't you seen the forecast?'

Chapter Two

Neither Simmy nor Christopher had registered the fact of an ominous weather forecast. 'We've been too busy,' Simmy admitted. 'Why – what's going to happen?'

'Ice. Minus twelve. Christmas Eve's the worst.'

'Better than snow, then,' said Simmy, who had no more than a mild sense of excitement at waking up to a white wonderland. Her mother's loathing for any inconvenience had passed onto her. Without siblings, there had been no sledging or snowball fights, although her father always built a snowman.

Louise pulled a face. 'I'm due on the sixteenth of January. I want to be sure I can get to Carlisle quickly when the time comes.'

'Why not have it at home?' asked Simmy, who had romantic ideas about natural home births.

'You're joking! What do you take me for? Some primitive earth mother?'

Oh dear, thought Simmy, relinquishing any idea of adopting this person to be her new friend. 'Did you have trouble with the others, then?'

'It was *agony*, both times. But they wrote me up as "straightforward", which made me laugh. The whole thing's a nightmare.'

Simmy had had enough. 'At least the babies survived,' she said quietly. 'My first one was stillborn.'

'Oh!' said the pregnant Louise, recoiling. Simmy could see that the conclusion was mutual that no friendship was imminent. 'How awful.'

'Yes,' said Simmy. 'It was.'

The party was starting to wind down by seven. Children had to be taken home, and the punch was all gone. It had been dark for hours, giving a sense of late night-time and an obligation to be safely home. 'Have you seen the stars?' someone cried. 'It's a glorious night.' Several people went outside for a look, leaving the front door open. Christopher and Robin rejoined Simmy and they began to hunt for their coats. 'The car windscreen's going to ice up at this rate,' said Christopher. The distance between car and house had been just great enough for them to need the buggy. Robin had recently become too heavy for comfortable carrying, and his walking pace was annoyingly slow.

The Buntings could not conceal their relief at the departures. The Christmas carols had begun to repeat themselves for a third time, the atmosphere somehow less festive and harmonious than might be ideal. Simmy sensed some kind of rift or divide between two sets of guests. Maybe it was solstice versus Christmas, she thought, looking forward to debating the issue with her father. Or local politics, of which she was blithely ignorant. Living in Hartsop set the Hendersons apart from the more populous Patterdale and Glenridding. Despite the plethora of holiday homes of varying sorts, there were still a good number of permanent residents in those two settlements. Roughly a thousand in total, she thought, having checked it when they'd first moved in. Hartsop itself couldn't manage more than about fifty.

Simmy would have liked to have seen Diellza again before leaving. She had spent the past forty minutes vaguely trying to find her and learn more about her. After failing with Louise, she wanted to assure herself that she was capable of forming a bond with at least one woman – although the Albanian was an unlikely candidate. Too young, too foreign and too transitory. And her needs were obviously being met by the Buntings. Even so, Simmy felt compelled to try again, if only because there was a novelty to the idea and Diellza herself had suggested a further meeting.

'Where's Diellza?' she asked the hostess. 'I wanted to say goodbye to her.'

Fran Bunting blinked. 'Did you? She's gone to her room. She's quite shy, poor thing. It's a sad story. It's nice of you to show an interest.' The last words were thrown over her shoulder as yet another party guest approached with thanks and farewells.

Robin was drooping, sitting on his father's arm. 'Come on,' said Christopher. 'This boy's heavy. Where did you put the buggy?'

'I didn't put it anywhere. I thought you had it.'

It was soon located, and they walked the few yards down the hill to the car park. It was almost empty, since the other partygoers mostly have walked. There was no chance of parking closer to the Bunting's house with double yellow lines everywhere.

'It's cold. Apparently, we're due for a big freeze in the next few days.'

'So everybody kept saying. I expect they're exaggerating,' said Christopher.

'Are you hungry?' Simmy asked an hour later, after Robin had been put to bed. The child had shown no interest in food after two mince pies, several crisps and a sausage. 'I didn't eat very much, did you?'

'It wasn't very appetising. My sausage tasted of cardboard. I think I accidentally chose a vegetarian one.'

'I had quite a nice mince pie. I'll do some soup, then. Carrots, onions, parsnips.'

'It'll take ages.'

'Half an hour. I'll do them in milk, like my mother does. It'll be just the thing.'

'Lovely.'

'What did you write for that solstice business?' he asked her, ten minutes later.

She flushed. 'I'm not telling you. They're supposed to be secret, like wishing on a wishbone.'

'Well, I put "High business tax and cruel salmon farming". It was all I could think of. Fiona's been ranting about the salmon for weeks now. She's got us all converted.' Fiona was a work colleague at his auction house.

'I don't think you quite got into the spirit of it.' She felt

27

oddly let down. 'It was meant to be something personal.'

'Business tax *is* personal. Feels like it, anyway. So, what about that Albanian woman? Did you find out any more? I saw you talking to her.'

'Not much. The Buntings came to her rescue somehow, but she's only staying a little while – it sounds as if she has plans. She's got a husband who's been nasty to her, according to Dan. Who were you talking to?'

'A farmer from up on one of the crags. He was really interesting. Diversified, of course, with two barns converted for visitors, and his wife making mutton pies and wine. But he's got five hundred sheep and keeps the farming going as well. They've got three sons. One of them works with Dan Bunting, apparently in the social services or something. They're all connected, one way or another – the permanent residents, I mean.'

Simmy felt another surge of loneliness. 'I didn't really find anybody I liked much. The best one was Celia – with the pink hair. But she must have gone home early or something, because I couldn't find her when I got away from Louise. She was the pregnant one. We didn't like each other. She wanted to mind Robin when I go to the shop.'

Christopher stared at her. 'For free? God, Sim, why didn't you jump at it?'

'I don't *know* her. I didn't like her attitude. I don't think she even likes children very much.'

'Fran Bunting's all right, isn't she?'

Simmy shrugged. 'I suppose so. But she probably works full-time and she seems a bit nervy. I was hoping to find someone with free days now and then, so we can go for walks and chat, and have pub lunches, and take the kids to the sea, and gossip about our husbands and parents . . .' She stopped, hearing herself. 'Yes, that's what I want. A friend. A proper old-fashioned best friend.'

'Maybe Santa Claus will bring you one, then.'

'Santa might not get through this year, if the weather forecast's right. The reindeer will freeze to death.'

'Reindeers are used to cold.'

She laughed.

Christopher was not giving up. 'No, but you should try again with Louise. It would make a huge difference if Robin could go to someone local.'

'It wouldn't work,' said Simmy decisively.

Over the soup they tried to plan the coming week. Simmy was going to the shop the next day, which was a Saturday, and then not again until Saturday 29th December. Christopher had an even longer break, having closed his auction house for a full ten days. 'I might go in and do a bit of tidying on Thursday or Friday,' he said carelessly. 'I'll be stir-crazy by then.'

'We need to take the weather into account,' she cautioned. 'It might affect everything we wanted to do. Tomorrow looks all right for me to get to Windermere, but what about my mum and dad getting here on Monday and back on Wednesday? They might not come if they think they'll be stranded.'

Christopher shrugged. 'We'll have to see. I can't believe it'll be all that bad. They can come on big roads for most of the way. I don't think it freezes too badly along the Ullswater road. The lake affects the temperature, apparently.'

'I need a whole lot more shopping yet. I was going to storm the supermarket in Keswick on Monday. Along with everybody else, probably. Stuffing, crackers, cream—'

'You've got all the basics,' he interrupted. 'And your mother's bound to bring a whole lot of stuff. Including stuffing,' he added with a laugh.

'It'd be terribly dull for Robin if they don't manage to come,' she worried. 'My dad's so good at Christmas. Games and songs and everything.'

'Well, maybe I'll take him up to his cousins tomorrow. They'll give him all the excitement he can handle. And he had a wildly sociable time at the party. He's certainly not shy.'

'Miraculously.'

'He prefers adults to other kids. That's supposed to be a sign of intelligence.'

'I think it's because he never *sees* other kids. He doesn't understand them.'

'Oh well,' said Christopher vaguely. 'It is what it is. And he likes it when Hannah's two make a fuss of him. Pity all the cousins are older than him.'

'Mm,' said Simmy.

Just after nine there was a call to their landline. 'It's Celia here,' came the voice. 'From the party just now.'

'How did you get this number? I didn't give it to you.'

'In the olden days I could just say you were in the book, couldn't I? Everything so simple and open. As it is, I copied it down a few months ago, when you put that card in the shop about babysitting. Did that ever get anywhere, by the way?'

Simmy's mind was working slowly. 'Have you got a baby?'

'Don't be daft. I'm fifty-six. I just thought it might be handy to keep the number. It's called networking. Anyway, I'm calling to ask if you're doing anything on Sunday. I thought a few of us could get together for a Christmas lunchtime drink. And food, of course. Maybe at the White Lion. Just girls.'

'Oh.' Simmy had a sense of being dragged into something that she knew she should welcome. 'Well, thanks. I'll walk up with the dog, maybe.'

'Good. And did you find a babysitter?'

'There's a girl here in the village. She walks the dog as well as babysitting. Not that we need her very often.' Less than once a month, in fact, she acknowledged to herself. The Hendersons did not go out very much.

'Of course! Lily – that's her name, isn't it? She's perfect. Well, see you on Sunday, then. About twelve-thirty.'

'All right,' said Simmy. She put the phone down and told Christopher what had been agreed. 'Why do I feel so nervous?' she wondered.

He shrugged.

Because I'm getting what I wished for, she thought. It was almost as if the pink-haired Celia had managed to read her slip of paper before she burnt it.

They went to bed early, aware that another try for a second child was on the agenda. Simmy did her best to enjoy it for its own sake, but the fact of a purpose behind the act itself took a lot of the shine off it. Too much disappointment was wearying, getting in the way of natural spontaneity. What was the point? And weren't they too old, anyway? What if the child had Down's syndrome? What if Angie or

Russell fell ill and Simmy was torn between her duties as a daughter and mother? Did she *really* want another baby now? None of this could be said to Christopher, who tended to live for the moment and push future worries aside.

Chapter Three

On Saturday morning Simmy made an early start for her shop in Windermere, leaving husband and son to sort themselves out. 'I'll close by one,' she said. 'Home by two at the latest. Save me some lunch.' There had been talk of Christopher going up to Keswick for the morning, checking on his saleroom, but it had come to nothing. 'There's really no need,' he decided.

In Windermere, young Bonnie Lawson, one of Simmy's two full-time assistants, did not arrive until half past nine, leaving Simmy time to go through everything on the computer, straighten quite a lot of mess in the back room and turn up the heating. Verity, her other employee, did not work on Saturdays, but had left a long note listing all the deliveries she had done the day before, and wishing Simmy a wonderful Christmas. There was also a little package and a Christmas card. 'Drat!' said Simmy to herself. 'I never got her a present.' The oversight was embarrassing, and guilt-inducing. Verity was a reliable worker, on shamefully low pay. She was good-hearted and generally cheerful. She drove Bonnie mad with unceasing inane chatter and local gossip. It was too late to do anything about a present, or even a card. The only option was to send a lavish e-card, if she could work out how to do that.

Most of the plants were looking decidedly chilled. Poinsettias, lilies, indoor hyacinths – the customary Christmas flowers, all of which would be redundant if they didn't find new homes this morning. Except the hyacinths, in fancy bowls, which would be welcome for another month or so. Some had been forced and were in full bloom, but others had scarcely started.

'Hey!' Bonnie greeted her. 'How's things?'

'I forgot to get Verity a card, or a present. She's left something for me, look.'

'No worries,' breezed the irrepressible girl. 'I did it for you.'

'What?'

'I realised you'd forgotten, on Thursday, so I wrapped up something from one of Corinne's boxes of car boot crap. It was nice, actually – a little cut-glass vase. I pretended it was from you.'

'Bonnie! That's amazing.'

'Same thing happened last year, if you remember.'

'Did it? Really? I should pay you, then, or Corinne.'

Bonnie shrugged. 'It probably cost about 15p. Did you go to that party?'

Simmy followed the change of subject with little difficulty. 'We did and I have instantly become part of the

Patterdale social set as a result.' She explained about Celia and Louise and Aoife. 'Christopher thinks I should let Louise look after Robin.'

'She'd want paying.'

'She didn't say anything about money.'

'Well, you'd owe her in one way or another, wouldn't you? She might want you to have her three for a whole month in the summer.'

Simmy shuddered and then laughed. 'She's going to be busy with her new one for a while, anyway. I think Robin's safe for a bit.'

Bonnie cocked her head. 'You didn't like her – right?'

'Right. I thought she was a bit lacking in maternal instinct, which sounds awfully judgemental, doesn't it.'

'First impressions are always right,' said Bonnie with utter certainty. 'It's been proven.'

Simmy laughed. 'I thought it was the opposite – don't they tell you not to judge by first impressions?'

A small group of customers interrupted the chat and the morning began to get busy. Christmas cheer was there in abundance, with wide smiles and sincere good wishes on all sides. Bonnie had decorated the shop with holly, ivy and mistletoe, as well as silver bells and sparkly chains. 'Not long now,' people kept saying. 'Only two more days.'

'I make it three,' Bonnie muttered, every time. 'Counting today. And not counting the Day itself, of course.'

'Better to say "three sleeps",' said Simmy. 'Although a lot of people assume it all starts on Christmas Eve. They're still very traditional up here.'

'Not you, then?'

'Filling Robin's stocking. Putting parcels round the tree.

Eating mince pies. My parents will be there already, so we might play some games. Did you hear about the scary weather forecast?'

Before Bonnie could reply, a customer interrupted. 'Minus fourteen, I heard. Starting tomorrow night. They'll close the passes.'

Simmy felt a quiver of apprehension. 'I expect we'll be okay. Christopher says it's not so bad alongside Ullswater. They'll keep our roads clear.'

'You hope,' said the customer with relish. 'We haven't had a decent winter for a while now. It's overdue.'

'Haven't you heard of global warming?' came a man's voice from near the door. 'No more deep freezes and blizzards.' The tone was sceptical, and nobody knew how to respond.

Bonnie broke the silence. 'Did you say ten or a dozen?' she asked the person she was serving, turning to Simmy. 'Have we got that many left?'

'What?'

'Red roses. The lady wants them.'

'I'll go and see.'

It was twenty minutes before the shop was empty, and then only briefly. 'Ben should be okay, even if it does freeze,' said Bonnie. 'It's a main road all the way between here and Keswick, more or less.'

'Where is he now?'

'Still in his digs. He's coming home this evening. Staying until Thursday, I think. The trouble is, he says the exhaust on his car is making a noise and he's not sure he ought to be using it.'

'Oh dear,' said Simmy inattentively. Any risk of being

drawn into giving lifts to the young couple was best avoided by failing to show much interest.

Bonnie was thumbing her mobile. 'I'm going to look at the forecast for myself. It can't be as bad as the woman said.'

'Let's hope not.'

'Oh! They've found a body in Glenridding.'

Simmy still found it surprising the way all kinds of news popped up on Bonnie's phone without any warning. There was an uncanny sense that the phone knew exactly what would interest her. 'A hiker, I suppose?'

'Maybe. A man – no further detail. The police have not ruled out foul play. Hey – you've got a Christmas murder, right on your doorstep. And Ben won't be able to get there if they close the pass at Kirkstone, or his exhaust falls off. Unless he goes today, which he'd better not.'

'Check the forecast,' Simmy reminded her.

Bonnie swiped briefly. 'Minus ten on Monday night. That's pretty bad. No snow, though. Everybody's pipes are going to freeze.'

'Warm woolly jumpers coming out of the cupboards. Has Corinne got enough firewood?' Bonnie lived with Corinne, who had been her foster mother until she reached eighteen, and had since mutated – in theory – into landlady, friend and confidante. In practice, very little had changed.

'She got Eddie round last week, as it happens, and he lopped off a couple of dead branches from the end of the garden. Cut them into logs, so we've got enough for a month at least.'

Another surge of customers took them almost to midday. 'I think I should go to the supermarket now, in case I can't get out again on Monday,' said Simmy.

'You could go tomorrow. Everything'll be open.'

'I suppose I could. I only need a few final things, really.' She heaved an exasperated sigh. 'It's all so silly, when you think about it. There's a horrible sense of obligation to get everything right. Even when nobody really cares. All that food and work getting it cooked.'

'We've said this before,' Bonnie reminded her. 'Why d'you go along with it? Nobody's forcing you.' Bonnie had her own aversions to the excesses of Christmas dinner, after several years of severe anorexia.

'Social pressure,' said Simmy darkly.

'Plus, you like it really,' the girl teased. 'Sitting round with your family, drinking fizzy wine and guzzling all that turkey. Shutting out the world and pretending you're safely hiding away in your cave.'

'I don't think cavemen did Christmas.'

'They did the solstice, though, I bet you. And it's pretty much the same thing.'

'Which brings us back to last night's party,' said Simmy. 'Did I tell you about the rituals they made us do?'

They closed the shop before one and wished each other a happy Christmas with hugs and presents exchanged, but not opened. Simmy had found a sky blue top made of soft jersey that would reach down to Bonnie's hips, which she hoped the girl would like. Buying clothes for other people was always fraught, but Bonnie's slim figure and pale colouring made it relatively easy. Cheerful colours and smooth lines suited her beautifully. She handed it over, carefully wrapped and added an envelope containing a

38

hundred pounds as a Christmas bonus. In exchange she received a rectangular packet that could only contain a book. 'How exciting!' she smiled.

'That's for Robin, really,' said Bonnie. 'But you're supposed to like it as well.'

Neither of them had forgotten the fact of a dead man in Glenridding, although each one pretended that she had.

Simmy phoned her mother before embarking on any shopping. Angie and Russell Straw lived in Threlkeld, close to Keswick and had much better opportunities for buying things than Simmy did. 'Have you got stuffing and crackers?' she asked.

'Among a hundred other things, yes. We made a list a week ago, remember?'

'Have you seen the weather forecast. Everybody's panicking about it.'

'Your father did the winter tyres a fortnight ago. And there's not meant to be any actual snow. It'll be perfectly all right, you see.'

Simmy and Christopher had never got the hang of winter tyres, agreeing that they sounded expensive and bothersome. 'Oh good,' said Simmy. 'Although I'm sure I should be buying *something*. What about Boxing Day?'

Catering came naturally to Angie, after years spent running a B&B. She laughed impatiently. 'Leftovers. Salad. Cheese. I've got a nice Stilton. And a bottle of port that went with it. Nobody's going to be hungry.'

'You must have spent a fortune,' worried Simmy.

'It's only money,' said her mother.

'I'll go to Ambleside on the way home, and get some

bits,' she decided. 'You never know – people might drop in.'

She bought two bottles of red wine, a tin of Quality Street, a large net of satsumas and a dozen eggs. Then she drove bravely up the steep road known as The Struggle, over the Kirkstone Pass and was home shortly after two o'clock. The sun was already low in the sky, but not enough to dazzle her. *It's Christmas!* she reminded herself, trying to generate the childhood magic that she was sure she must have experienced. An only child, living in Worcestershire next door to an orchard, she had found the whole thing mostly confusing. Angie tended to the cynical, even in her younger years, mocking the excesses of neighbours who hung fairy lights around their gardens. Russell did his best to make it special for his little girl. He dressed in a red hat and watched her avidly as she opened her parcels. He organised games in the afternoons. He insisted on a big tree with an angel on top. Nobody said anything much about Jesus, although at school they made up for that. Simmy was afraid that her own child would have a similarly ambivalent response to it all as he grew up.

And after the sudden influx of potential friends, it did seem possible that someone might indeed drop in at some point over the coming days. There would be a test of community spirit if freezing weather caused pipes to burst and batteries to die.

'Did you have lunch?' asked Christopher, hearing her come in. 'We've not long got back ourselves.'

She shook her head. 'No. I think I told you I'd be wanting something.'

'Aren't we supposed to starve ourselves before the big

event? Work up a good appetite for all that turkey.'

'I'll just have bread and cheese, then,' she said peaceably.

'No problem. Plus coleslaw, of course. And that pickle Hannah gave us last Christmas. We still haven't finished it.'

'Thanks.' All the talking and thinking about food was starting to irritate her. 'You've had yours, then?'

'Ages ago. Robin's just gone for his nap. He's been reading the Christmas cards. He likes the ones with robins on best.' He laughed. 'Everyone said that cards would have died out by now, but I think we've got more than ever this year. Amazing, when you think what stamps cost.'

'Right,' said Simmy. Then she looked up. 'Did you hear they found a dead man in Glenridding? Not ruling out foul play, apparently.'

Christopher's expression turned wary. 'No, I did not hear that,' he said.

41

Chapter Four

Only one person called during that Saturday afternoon. Seventeen-year-old Lily brought a Christmas card and a tin of mince pies. 'Mum always makes far too many,' she laughed. 'There's only four of us.'

Simmy ushered her in, where the wood burner was doing an excellent job of heating the big main room. 'Four?' she queried.

'Right. My big sister's here. It's all a bit awkward, actually. She's walked out on her boyfriend after about six years together. These things always happen at Christmas, apparently. He's been cheating on her and my dad's all for going down to Sheffield and thumping him. He can be a bit like that sometimes.' Lily gave a brave smile. 'My brother could tell you.'

Brother and sister? Simmy felt ashamed of her ignorance. Lily lived three doors away and had walked the dog for most of the year now, and still the Hendersons knew almost nothing about her. 'What's your sister's name?'

'Nicholette – with an h in the middle. She's twenty-seven. I'm the afterthought. Mum was forty-three when she had me. Theo is even older. We haven't seen him for two years now. He lives in Germany.'

Simmy suppressed the flicker of hope that this raised in her. She was still a little way short of forty-three. Why, she wondered, did everything anybody said to her connect to babies and older mothers and the whole frustrating business?

'They must have been thrilled,' she said.

'They made the best of it. Have you got people coming for Christmas?'

'My parents. They'll come on Monday, weather permitting. The mince pies will come in very handy – thanks.'

'So you won't be needing me for Cornelia, then?'

'Not for a bit, no, thanks. I'm taking her all the way to the White Lion and back tomorrow, which'll wear us both out. She'll get spoilt all over Christmas, I expect.'

The dog had greeted Lily with an enthusiasm born of a misplaced expectation of a walk, but had settled for a cuddle instead. 'Let me know, then,' said Lily, clearly in no hurry to go home. 'Mum sends her love. She's not doing cards this year. We haven't had many. It's a pity because they're useful for making things. Did I show you the little boxes? I love doing them.'

'You did. They're brilliant.'

Lily was a genius at a variety of craftwork. Every time Simmy saw her, she had embarked on yet another project. Recently the girl had discovered that Christopher Henderson's auction house often had large bags of fabric and other materials salvaged from house clearances and had persuaded her father to take her to Keswick at least once a month to snap them up. Her excited enthusiasm made everyone smile. She carted home boxes of coloured card, ribbons, silver paper, bags of tangled knitting wool and much more besides.

'I put chocolate money inside the little boxes. They're great for stocking fillers.'

'I'll have one or two for Robin, then. I should have thought of it sooner.'

'Too late – they're all gone. I had a stall in Pooley Bridge last weekend and sold practically everything.'

'Well . . .' said Simmy, 'they'll be wondering where you are, won't they? What's Nicholette doing today?'

'We were going to have a driving lesson, with her teaching me about parallel parking. She's super good at it, and I can't get the hang of it at all. My test is only three weeks away now.'

'It'll be dark in an hour,' Simmy pointed out.

'I know. And icy, according to Dad. We probably won't go. Mum's got a cold and the boiler's misbehaving. It's all a bit chaotic, actually.'

'Oh dear.'

'Sorry. I need to get out of your way. Everybody's busy these days, aren't they?'

'Not me, really. But it sounds as if you're needed at home. Thanks for the mince pies. I'll see you later in the week. I'll phone you.'

'Text. Send a text,' said Lily. 'The phone always

rings when I'm trying to do something complicated. I'm teaching myself to make lace, and it needs every bit of concentration.'

'Right,' said Simmy.

Bonnie had no such reservations about phone calls. At half past four, Simmy's mobile jingled with a call. 'Ben says the dead man in Glenridding has not been identified, but it's definitely foul play. He thinks you should be taking an interest, seeing as how it's so close to you. You might know him.'

'Really?' said Simmy with as neutral a tone as she could manage. 'We don't know many people, actually.'

'You do after last night,' Bonnie argued. 'You must have met half the population.'

'Hardly. Just some of the ones our sort of age, mostly. And we didn't talk to many of them. Why didn't Ben call us himself, instead of getting you to do it?'

'He thought it'd come better from me. The thing is, he's going to be down here in Bowness, so he can't easily be there himself. He's worried about the car, but I think he'll risk it if he sees any chance of finding out what's been happening.'

'For heaven's sake!' Simmy flared. 'What makes him think he could come over here with any hope of getting involved? He can't just go barging in because he's feeling nosy. It's nearly three miles from here to Glenridding; it's not as if it was on our doorstep.'

'I said you'd say that.' Bonnie's voice was soft and placatory. 'But he thinks it's all rather providential, the way you were on the spot last night, probably at the same time as the man was getting killed. He thinks it would be a waste not to make something of that.'

'It's *Christmas*, Bonnie. Why can't he just enjoy himself and forget all about this sort of thing?'

'Good question,' said Bonnie with a little laugh. 'But Christmas is lasting a long time this year. He's worried he'll get bored.'

'There's no harm in being bored,' said Simmy prissily. 'And I bet it'll turn out that the man was a hiker who fell off a crag and bashed his own head in on a rock.'

'I don't think so,' said Bonnie. 'I gather there was a weapon. Some sort of knife.'

'How in the world do you know that?'

'The thing is, you see, Ben knows someone in the mortuary where they took him. It's a girl called Nancy. She was at school with him, a year or two above, but he helped her with her A levels or something – him being so clever. I know her a bit, as well. She's on some long training course, which has secondments. I don't understand it all, but they kept in touch, and she's told him a bit about the body. That's how he's got so interested.'

Simmy had no doubt she was being manipulated, having learnt to recognise the danger signs. 'I'm starting to understand,' she said slowly. 'But I still don't like it.'

'Sorry. I knew you wouldn't. It's not very Christmassy, is it? And Nancy's not really very nice. She's annoyed with Ben for dropping out, and keeps trying to get him to go back and do some proper training. I think she sees him as a sort of protégé, although he says she's not terribly bright and doesn't have any idea how he feels about anything.' There was satisfaction in the last few words.

No need to feel jealous of Nancy, evidently. Bonnie's capacity for jealousy had become apparent when Lily put in an appearance. In many ways, Lily had several of the same virtues as Bonnie herself did. The worry was, at least in Bonnie's mind, that Ben might one day notice this fact.

On leaving school, Ben had gone to Newcastle University in triumph to take a place on a forensic archaeology course. Very soon, he discovered that student life was not for him, and he retreated in ignominy after less than a year. Instead, he took up work for Christopher, applying his forensic skills to the provenance of antiques.

'Tell him to forget all about it,' Simmy repeated sternly. 'He won't get any co-operation from me.'

'Okay, I will. And Corinne says Happy Christmas. Again.'

'Same to her. Make sure you both have a really lovely time.'

Christopher had been in the kitchen for much of the afternoon, with the door firmly shut. 'I've got to do some last-minute work on a present,' he said. 'Neither of you can come in.'

Simmy and Robin contentedly played by the open fire, making a model village out of a large collection of stone bricks. Christopher had bagged them at the auction some months earlier. They were in their own wooden box, with a diagram inside the lid showing how they should be arranged. They came in six different sizes and three different shapes. Simmy loved them. 'Here's the pub,' she said. 'And what do you think that is?'

'Shop,' said the child promptly. 'Beans.'

'Right. Beans and peas and broccoli.'

Robin pulled a face. 'No broccoli,' he insisted.

Simmy tried not to laugh. She did not like broccoli either. 'Tomatoes, then. And pineapple.' She offered small bricks to represent each item, and Robin stacked them carefully. It was absorbing her as much as her little boy, neither of them showing any sign of wearying. Phone calls and visits were mere irritating interruptions. The happy sense of lazy days ahead of her was barely dented by Lily or Bonnie or a woman called Nancy. Christmas should not be a time of hassle and schedules and worries about suitable presents. Coming from a very small family had always meant that gifts and food were of minor significance, all dealt with quickly and easily. This, however, did not apply to Christopher, who had two brothers and two sisters, all with offspring and partners. He also had employees who expected to be remembered. Simmy had made it very clear to him that all this was his department, and she was not prepared to do any shopping, labelling or wrapping for him. 'I'm hopeless at all that,' she insisted, playing a game she had learnt from her father. Claiming incompetence was an effective way out of awkward tasks.

And yet there was a persistent lurking awareness that somebody had died from violence barely three miles away. Virtually on their doorstep, in fact, despite her claiming otherwise to Bonnie – which had never happened before. This time there was no connection with Simmy's work as a florist; none of that tenuous feeling of guilty involvement that had come in Ambleside and Coniston and other places. The flowers themselves had sparked a series of emotions and events that led to murder – or so it had seemed to Simmy. This time it was Christmas, and she had resolved to be more sociable, to get more involved with the local population. But if the locals were going to start killing each other, she might do well to keep her distance. The faces of those she had met the previous evening floated before her. Were any of them close to the murdered man – or his killer? Celia with the pink hair, or very pregnant Louise? Or even the too-good-to-be-true Dan Bunting?

And what about that big Albanian with the upset stomach?

'Car?' said Robin, trundling a middle-sized brick down their imaginary high street.

'Oh yes, we should have some cars,' his mother agreed. 'What about giving them a nice car park?'

'Still at it?' came Christopher's voice from the kitchen doorway. 'You've been playing with those bricks for nearly two hours.' There was admiration in his voice, partly, Simmy suspected, at his own good sense in finding the bricks to start with.

'And we're nowhere near finished,' said Simmy.

'You've let the fire die down.' He crossed the room and added three logs to the smouldering embers. 'I'd better go and fetch some more.' Which he did.

The day drifted on, with a modest evening meal, Robin's bedtime, and a game of canasta, which they had played together many times before, in their teenage years. Christopher always won.

Simmy's phone hummed politely, to indicate an incoming text, at nine o'clock. *'See you tomorrow, about*

12.30. Looking forward to getting to know you better. Celia,' it said.

'I did tell you, didn't I? I won't be here for lunch tomorrow. You and Robin can have sausages or something.'

He shrugged. 'No problem. We're saving ourselves for the Christmas turkey. And we've got Lily's mince pies. Although I did think they look a bit *dense*. The one Robin had at the party wasn't like that.'

'Flaky pastry,' Simmy nodded. 'Makes an awful mess. I prefer them a bit dense.'

'More filling, anyway,' he agreed.

Simmy looked again at her text. 'Does it strike you as ever so slightly *controlling*?' she asked. 'Making sure I don't forget.'

'A bit, maybe. Is she a schoolteacher or something?'

'I don't think she said. Or maybe there was mention of being self-employed. I never remember what people tell me about their work. I was too flummoxed by the hair to listen properly. I thought she was nice at the time, though now I'm not so sure. At least she's a bit different, I suppose.'

'I thought all the women seemed unusual. Not a farmer's wife or a software analyst in the place.'

'Fran Bunting's pretty normal, and I bet she does software,' said Simmy. 'Louise might, as well, come to that. Neither of them struck me as at all unusual, actually.' She sighed. 'Heaven save me from Louise.'

Christopher cocked his head at her. 'You're nothing but a helpless victim, let's face it. Once those females get their claws into you, you won't stand a chance. You'll have social lunches and day trips and babysitting swaps before you know it.'

'What's the matter with me that none of that sounds appealing?'

'I blame your mother,' he said, and they both laughed.

Chapter Five

'If I'm walking all the way to Patterdale, I need to set out at about eleven,' Simmy realised next morning. 'And I won't be back again until it's nearly dark. Maybe I should go in the car, after all.'

'I'll come and fetch you,' offered Christopher. 'Although it won't take you more than an hour each way. It's probably less than five miles, round trip.'

'I suppose that's not far, really. The weather's perfect for it. Look at that sky!' They both looked out of the back window where Hartsop Dodd was outlined in perfect detail against a cloudless blue. 'Who cares how cold it gets, when everything looks so lovely?' she went on. 'I wonder if the beck ever freezes?'

'It will if the temperature goes as low as they say. We'll have to find someone who's lived here for eighty years and can tell us tales of real weather in the olden days.'

'There'll probably be one in the pub,' she said. 'And

don't come for me. I'll set out at two at the latest and be back in time for tea. You can play with the bricks. Try building a castle or something.'

He gave her a look. 'I think we can work out our own amusements, thanks. I thought we might do a bit of cooking together if all else fails.'

'He's too young,' Simmy objected. 'What sort of cooking?'

'Biscuits,' said Christopher airily. 'He can do the decoration.'

Simmy and Cornelia left at ten past eleven, stepping into a world that was at least eight degrees colder than the previous day. Hat, scarf and gloves were all required. 'Is it silly to walk in this weather?' she wondered to the dog. 'What if I slip on ice?' Was it not neglectful of her husband not to try to stop her? But then she reproached herself for wimpishness. There were other people out, and a car went past. There had been no rain for some days, which meant the road itself was not slippery. Plants had a sheen of ice on their stalks, making everything look pretty. 'Come on, then,' she said to Cornelia, who understood the words perfectly. They turned up the little road that led towards Ullswater, past the holiday lodges and into the fields alongside the beck. It was a familiar path, with stiles and gates and a few stony slopes all the way to Crookabeck. There were sheep, but no other livestock. Cornelia, being of retriever stock, did not incline to chase them unduly. As a puppy she had given it a try, but stern reprimands had soon changed her ways. Now she could lope contentedly amongst them, ignoring them. The sheep threw nervous glances and tended to huddle defensively, but there were no great stampedes.

On the ridge of Dubhow above and to her right she could see walkers, too far away to tell exactly what they were wearing, but woolly hats were discernible. She had only been up there once, marvelling at the view. Views were common across the region, of course, but no less uplifting for that. At first, she had tried to rank them in order of magnificence, but soon abandoned the attempt, which seemed rather childish after a while. Even so, whenever she thought of views, her mind conjured images from the Castlerigg stone circle near Keswick. From there one could see landscape that defied belief. Timeless, gigantic, dominating any silly little human endeavours – so overwhelming that she only went there occasionally.

Now, as she approached the Beckstones Farm, with its famous old buildings, she could hear voices and a dog barking. 'Better come here,' she told Cornelia, and attached the dog's lead as a precaution. 'Just until we get into the trees.' Shortly before Crookabeck, the path led under a stretch of gnarled trees for a little way. Simmy calculated that the walk was more than half done by this stage, with the road only another ten minutes or so away. There was suddenly a cluster of houses, the ground more level and the river more evident. Goldrill Beck ran into the southern tip of Ullswater, having seeped out of Brothers Water and then gathered momentum by the time it reached Patterdale. The cold was finding its way through her boots and gloves, as well as nibbling at her nose. The ground crunched beneath her feet, but there had been very little actual ice to threaten her balance. The bright blue sky and the long shadows from the low winter sun gave everything a heightened focus. Some people might think that a good covering of snow would enhance the fairy-tale appearance of the fells and woods and gardens, but Simmy could not imagine anything lovelier than what she was seeing.

Breaking her promise, Simmy kept Cornelia on the lead for the rest of the walk. In Crookabeck – a tiny settlement mainly given over to holiday lets – the lane turned sharply to the left, then over a bridge and onto the A592, which headed northwards on the edge of Ullswater. The pub was soon visible and Simmy consulted her watch. She was ten minutes early.

For most of the walk she had given almost all her attention to her immediate surroundings. It had been necessary to keep watch over her feet, as well as the dog; any spare mental capacity had gone to admiring the ever-changing scenery and making tentative plans to follow some of the lesser paths that connected to the one she was using. Only now, when her goal was so close, did she start to think about the forthcoming gathering. The pub landlord knew her and Cornelia, which was a plus. He probably also knew the others, and would draw conclusions as to budding friendships and alliances. 'I see that Mrs Henderson is getting to know the locals, at last,' she could imagine him saying.

The bar of the White Lion ran along the front of the building, its windows looking out onto the road. Had Celia reserved a table? Simmy wondered. The Sunday before Christmas was likely to be unusually busy – or was it? Were people being abstemious in preparation for the festivities, or did the Christmas season extend backwards to at least a week before the day itself? Angie was always saying that the whole thing started somewhere around the middle of November these days, with parties and decorations and panic-buying in full swing by then. Simmy herself had never entirely got the hang of it, imbued with her mother's cynicism and her father's tendency to dwell on the pagan origins. 'It's all about the winter solstice,' he insisted. Dan and Fran Bunting would probably agree with him.

There were voices and music coming from the pub, as well as flashing lights from the big Christmas tree when she walked in. Cornelia hesitated, pulling back. The sudden drastic change of atmosphere alarmed her. 'Come in, quick,' said a man. 'You're letting the cold air in.'

'That's your table,' the barmaid told her, indicating with her chin, both hands holding a tray full of drinks. 'You're first to arrive.' She eyed the dog. 'Nobody said there'd be a dog. We've put you in the dining area. They're not meant to go in there – but I don't think it'll matter for once. It's all chaotic today, anyway. Just make sure she behaves.'

'She's been in there before,' Simmy protested.

'Yeah, but some bloke complained last month about a poodle. It was so smelly it put him off his grub.' The woman laughed. 'He was right, as it happens. The thing was a real stinker.' They were walking between tables as they talked. 'So we started telling people to keep dogs out of that bit. It's not working out very well with the locals. Ah, there's one of your lot, look.'

The door had opened again, and pink-haired Celia came in. She spotted Simmy instantly and waved. Moments later they were both sitting at the designated table. 'Aoife's always late,' said Celia. 'And I don't know about Fran.'

Simmy had a sense of drowning in all the new information she was about to receive and probably convey. Getting to know new people was hard work – remembering details about where they grew up, how many siblings they had, the current state of their relationships, how they felt about climate change or Donald Trump. All the basics that people felt were important. She thought wistfully of the customers in her shop, dozens of them regulars known by name. All she needed to remember about them was whether they preferred pink or red roses, and how well they understood the need for fresh water.

When Celia had phoned to suggest this get-together, she had not specified which 'girls' would be included. Simmy had assumed three or four, all from the Buntings' party, but somehow she had not expected Mrs Bunting herself. She was braced for the importunate Louise and perhaps the intriguing Diellza, but had mainly fixed on Celia as the pivotal point, and the one she felt most drawn to.

'Is Diellza coming as well?' she asked.

Celia rolled her eyes. 'Who knows? Last I heard she was in bed with a bad tummy. That was yesterday morning.'

'Poor thing.' Simmy was opening her mouth to ask more, when two more women came stamping in, clapping their hands together and blowing out their cheeks. *Anyone would think they'd walked five miles*, Simmy said to herself. Her own walk had been a lot longer than that from Glenridding.

'There they are,' said Celia unnecessarily.

Aoife and Fran Bunting came rapidly along to the table, pausing briefly to ensure the barmaid had seen them. 'We'll come and order drinks in a minute,' Fran called to her.

When they took their seats with Celia and Simmy, they were still exclaiming about the cold. Fran noticed Simmy's expression and said, 'It's much worse where we are, you know. We're a lot higher than you, down in cosy little Hartsop.'

'It's so beautiful, though,' said Simmy. 'So crisp and bright. We don't get many days like this, do we?'

'You're right,' said Aoife. 'But my nose is not so happy. It's lost all feeling.'

'Hello, dog,' said Fran. 'What's your name, then?'

'This is Cornelia. She's had a lovely walk.' Simmy sounded stiff in her own ears, and wished she felt less self-conscious, monitoring her own words and tone far too carefully. 'Hadn't one of us better go and order drinks?' she went on, before worrying that she was poaching on Celia's territory. 'I can do it if you like. And what about food?'

They all opted for half pints of the local ale, Aoife making hers a shandy. Simmy took the order and went up to the bar, having started a tab. 'They want to know what we're eating,' she reported when she returned with a tray of glasses.

'No food for me,' said Fran vehemently. 'We're saving ourselves for the excesses of Christmas. I've lost seven pounds this year and I don't want to wreck it now.' Simmy cast a discreet eye on the slender frame and thought of Bonnie Lawson's dysfunctional relationship with food. Fran appeared to be on the same trajectory.

Celia nodded understandingly. 'It's the same every year, isn't it? All that pigging out undoes the good work of months. Ridiculous, really.'

'Well, I'm hungry,' said Simmy. 'I need to gather strength for the walk home.'

'All the way to Hartsop?' gasped Aoife. 'That's *miles*.'

The others laughed. 'It's barely two and a half,' said Simmy. 'And it's a perfect day for it.'

'God! You are a little Pollyanna, aren't you. Doesn't anything annoy you?'

'Shut up, Aoife,' said Celia peaceably. 'Don't be so aggressive.'

'Never start a sentence with "you",' said Fran, like a teacher. 'It always sounds like an attack.'

Simmy had never thought about that before. She reran Aoife's words. 'You're right,' she realised. 'It does. I must remember that.' She smiled in a general sort of way, hiding the hurt feelings. 'And I'm still hungry.'

'I could fancy a lasagne,' said Celia. 'I'm too old to worry about my weight.'

'What about you?' Simmy asked Aoife.

Decisions were eventually made, with Fran compromising to the extent of ordering soup. 'It's Diellza who should be fasting,' she said darkly. 'I'm not surprised she made herself sick after Thursday. She went out and got herself a great bag of crisps, cheese, mince pies, chocolate and I don't know what. Said she didn't want to sponge off us – words to that effect, anyway – so she'd get her own food. Silly, really.'

'Is she still poorly, then?' asked Simmy.

Fran shrugged. 'Apparently. She's locked herself in her room and won't talk to us. It's quite rude, actually, but she has had a bad time, I suppose, according to Dan. She just needs to stay quiet and get Christmas over with. Dan's terribly patient with her. She's his pigeon, anyway. I'm staying out of it as far as I can. At least she won't starve, with all the food she bought herself.'

Aoife was quiet, looking out of the window at the crags above Glenridding and the blue sky beyond that. 'It *is* a lovely day,' she said thoughtfully. 'I was too busy all morning to appreciate it, and then too cold walking down here. I should have added another layer.'

'Where do you live?' asked Simmy, hoping to convey forgiveness.

'One of the cottages under the Rake, if you know where that is.'

'Not exactly. I need to learn much more about all the fells and crags right here on my doorstep. It's been a bit difficult with the baby. He's still not quite ready for serious fell walking.'

They clearly all remembered little Robin from the party, and laughed. 'A fair few years yet,' said Celia.

There followed ten minutes of general chat about Christmas, covering family obligations, forgotten presents and the price of Christmas trees. The food arrived and another round of drinks; conversation briefly fell into abeyance.

When Aoife went to the ladies, Celia leant across to Simmy and said in a low voice, 'In case you're wondering, Aoife's husband is in the grip of a debilitating depression. He hardly gets out of bed these days. She's putting a brave face on it, insisting on carrying on her own life, but if she's a bit snappy, that's why. You need to keep that in mind and make allowances.'

'Oh.' Simmy wondered whether she had been unduly

cool with Aoife. 'Thanks for telling me.'

'She's a great person, believe me. You've just caught her at a bad time.'

'Right,' said Simmy, taking a defensive swig of her beer. 'I'll remember.'

A minute or so later, when Aoife had come back, she caught a glance between Celia and Fran, followed by Fran taking a deep breath. 'We're assuming you heard about the dead man in the beck at Gillside. You'll know more than us about it, most likely.'

Here we go, thought Simmy. 'I heard something, yes,' she said vaguely. 'Have they identified him?'

'If they have, they're not disclosing it yet. Finding his next of kin, presumably, before telling the media.'

'The place where they found him isn't far from me,' said Aoife. 'We saw the kerfuffle yesterday.'

'They're saying there's a group of men staying in an Airbnb right there, but he's not one of them,' said Fran.

'Where's Gillside exactly?' asked Simmy.

Fran sighed impatiently. 'How can you not *know*? It's just beyond Glenridding – the path that goes up to Helvellyn. There's a farm with basic accommodation for walkers. There's always someone staying there.'

Celia smiled at Simmy. 'The police are going to be asking if anyone knows of a missing man before long, most likely. It'll be all over WhatsApp and Facebook – as usual, with a description. That's what they usually do, isn't it? I assume you know the routine.'

Simmy shrugged. 'Not exactly. I'm pretty rubbish at all the social media stuff. And I have to say I'm not really interested. All I can think about is Christmas, and keeping the house warm. It can't possibly concern me.'

'And yet somehow these things so often *do* concern you, don't they?' said Aoife. 'Sorry if that sounds nasty, but somebody has to say it.'

'I have got involved sometimes, yes,' Simmy nodded. 'It's been different with each one, though. Mostly it came through the flowers somehow. After all, people get flowers sent to them at the big moments in their lives – weddings, funerals, anniversaries. There's lots of emotion swirling around, which can get out of control. And lately, there've been ructions at the auction house – which is another place where feelings run high. There's often a lot of money involved.'

'Antiques,' Celia nodded knowingly.

Simmy could not resist saying, 'He can't be a local, can he? They'd know right away who he was, if so. When was the body found?'

Fran took a swig of her ale, rather as Simmy had done – as a way of hiding her thoughts for a moment, before answering with a little shrug, 'Just as it was getting light, they say. Hey – I thought you weren't interested!'

'I'm trying not to be. It must be habit. It's only human to wonder.'

'Like people gawping on motorways, holding up the traffic on the other side of the carriageway,' said Aoife. 'Everyone sneers, but we all do it.'

'My father says it's actually showing humanity, wanting to know what's happened. Much worse just to sail past and pretend it's nothing,' said Simmy.

'And a murder's far more exciting than a road accident,' said Aoife with a grin.

Simmy considered the woman with the Irish name, trying to assess her response to her in the light of Celia's information about her husband. Clearly the determination to 'live her own life' was real. She had been at the Buntings' party, and here she was lunching out. Did the depressed husband get his own meals, or was he too disabled to eat? Despite Celia's assertions, Simmy could not recapture her initial impression that Aoife was 'nice'. She was direct and intelligent and occasionally witty. Cynical too, for sure. And perhaps slightly too fond of Fran for an ordinary friendship. They sat close together and seemed to read each other's minds. As far as Simmy could work out, they lived barely a quarter of a mile from each other.

Then Celia's phone demanded attention. 'Who's this?' she frowned at the screen. 'Sorry, everyone.'

Aoife laughed. 'Don't mind us,' she said.

Celia appeared to consider getting up and walking away, but changed her mind. Her food would get cold, and she was crammed in too tightly for a quick or easy escape. 'Hello? . . . What? . . . No, I don't think so. Are you sure? . . . it sounds very odd. . . . Oh, right. . . . Okay, then. Thanks. I'll be back in about an hour. It'll have to wait till then. I've just started eating.'

Everyone pretended not to be curious, in the accepted protocol around calls made on a mobile while in a group having a meal. Celia quickly satisfied their ill-concealed desire for enlightenment. 'That was the Felton man, from the green house on the corner near me – you know?'

Fran shuddered dramatically. 'Oh yes. Awful creature. Always spying on everyone. What does he want?'

'Some story about hearing funny noises when he passed

my house just now. Thought I should know, in case I'm being burgled. Wanted to know if I'd left my door unlocked. He's done it before, actually. Got my number the same way I got yours' – she looked at Simmy – 'and thinks he can change the habits of a lifetime. The fact is, I hardly ever do lock the door, especially out of season. There's nothing in the house worth stealing, anyway.'

'I don't always lock ours, either,' said Simmy. 'I've never heard of any burglaries here since we came.'

'Take no notice,' Fran advised Celia. 'That man's a real pain. Wasn't Louise moaning about him a while ago? The trouble is, he can see nearly all the village from where he lives. I think he spends all day at the window with binoculars, watching everybody.'

'Not me,' said Aoife. 'Nobody can see my house from anywhere. I've got a very useful crag blocking everyone's view.'

Simmy was intrigued, not just by the nosy resident but the positioning of Aoife's house. 'Have you really?' she said.

The others all nodded. 'It's been there nearly a century now,' said Aoife. 'Everyone said it would be hell to live in when we first considered it. I found some old newspaper cuttings about it. It is rather dark in winter, being in shadow all day, but it has fabulous views over to Ullswater. We think it's wonderful.'

And completely wrong for anyone subject to depression thought Simmy, who knew about the utter necessity of light, for people as well as plants.

Under the table, Cornelia stirred restlessly.

Celia had finished her lasagne some minutes ago and

kept glancing at her phone. 'The trouble is, he said he heard *noises*,' she said. 'He was out, walking past my house. I think I really ought to go and investigate. I might have a burst pipe or something.'

'I don't want to go home yet,' sighed Fran.

'Scared you'll find Dan and Diellza in a compromising position?' teased Aoife. *She really isn't at all nice*, Simmy confirmed to herself.

'Hardly,' said Fran stiffly. 'If I thought that could happen, I wouldn't have left them alone, would I? Anyway, Dan's gone off to Penrith for something. She'll be there on her own.'

'So why don't you want to go home?' asked Celia.

'Because the woman annoys me. It's all very well being so charitable and accommodating and taking in distressed migrants, or whatever she is, but the reality can be very wearing. Dan's doing his best to keep us both happy, and I know he's doing it for all the right reasons, but he never properly explained the situation. He keeps saying it's complicated and we need a nice quiet time for him to make it all clear to me, as he knows he should have done at the start. Fat chance of that when we're throwing a party and doing Christmas, and there's never a spare moment. I've been working flat out since Friday – hardly been in the house.'

'Is she a distressed migrant, though?' asked Simmy. 'Or what?'

Again, all three seemed to gather together in a union that excluded her. 'I just said – I don't exactly know *what* she is,' said Fran. 'Dan just says she landed in his lap two weeks ago and he couldn't think what to do with her. She isn't a migrant or a refugee. She's got money, according to Dan, and when the husband sees sense, it'll all be okay. Or something,' she finished with a dramatic sigh. 'It makes no more sense to me than it does to you. I'm hoping we can get a bit of time this evening for it all to be spelt out.'

'It seems to me it's the same story all over Europe now,' said Aoife. 'Everyone running away from somewhere and foisting themselves on willing do-gooders in a new place. But I thought we'd decided that Albania was perfectly all right to live in, and nobody needed to go anywhere else.' She frowned. 'Does that sound heartless?'

'A bit ignorant, perhaps,' said Celia, with an air of restraining herself from saying what she really thought. 'I don't think you can generalise. Besides, she says the husband's a Scot. That must make a difference.'

'Yes, she told me that,' said Simmy. She turned to Fran, 'What's your job? I don't think I've got round to asking you that.'

'Oh – financial management. That's the short answer. High-pressure stuff, even up here where it's meant to be less cut-throat than London. The sort of thing normal people never need to think about.'

That explained the nerviness and the absence of body fat, Simmy concluded. 'Sounds exciting,' she said.

'No two days the same, and not a lot of time off,' Fran agreed. 'I give myself another year before burning out and doing something completely different. Dan says that's much too optimistic and he can't see me getting past Easter.'

Cornelia had had enough. There was very little space under the table amongst all the feet and bags. She heaved herself up and pushed her head onto Celia's lap, confident of a friendly reception. Which she got. 'Hello, pooch. You've been a good girl, haven't you.' She fondled the soft ears. 'Has it been very boring down there?'

'She's been fast asleep,' said Simmy. 'Now she's all raring to go again.'

'Nice company for the little one, I dare say,' said Celia.

'So long as she doesn't eat him,' said Aoife. 'Give me a cat any time.'

'Or five,' laughed Fran. She addressed Simmy. 'She's got five cats, did we tell you?'

'Gosh,' said Simmy, who had never seen much virtue in cats. She was trying to ascertain the time without being obvious about it. The pub was full to capacity, but no new people had come in for a while. It had to be approaching two o'clock. She looked at the three women, one by one. She felt warmest towards Celia, who did at least pay attention to how a person might be feeling when she was speaking to them. Considerably older than the others, she was settled and sensible by comparison. Simmy could not remember what her job was – if she had ever known. And she still hadn't found out what Aoife did with her days, either, other than share a house with a depressed husband and a lot of cats. Which took her to thoughts of the absent Louise. Presumably Sunday lunchtime was not free for a woman with a husband and two small children.

'I'd better go,' she said after a few more minutes. 'I told Christopher I'd be back before dark.'

'Dark! I should hope so!' scoffed Aoife. 'It's only quarter to two. How long do you think it'll take, for heaven's sake?'

'Over an hour,' said Simmy mildly. 'It's not the terrain for fast walking.'

'Which way do you go?' asked Fran.

'Through Crookabeck and Beckstones. It's a lovely walk, but I wouldn't want to do it in darkness.'

'Where *exactly* do you live?' asked Celia. 'I haven't been to Hartsop for years.'

Before Simmy could reply, Fran jumped in. 'It's that converted barn – surely you know it? Pretty much in the middle of the village, such as it is.'

'You're not scared, then?' said Celia lightly. 'With a murderer on the loose?'

'I think I would be,' said Fran.

Simmy just smiled faintly and said nothing. Aoife spoke for her. 'Don't be daft. It's much too cold for anyone to be hanging around out there in case a likely victim comes by. That's the stuff of fairy tales. It always makes me cross when people talk like that.' She patted her friend's hand. 'Even you can annoy me sometimes.'

'I think, my love, that that's your problem,' said Fran with a fond smile.

Simmy got up. 'Can I leave cash for my food?' she asked. 'How do we want to do it?'

Celia took charge. 'Cash is fine. Leave it to me.'

'I've only got a card,' said Aoife. 'Nobody uses cash any more, do they?'

Before it could become acrimonious, Simmy threw down a twenty-pound note, and made her escape. Her calculations had convinced her that she had overpaid by fifty pence. 'Put the change towards a tip,' she said blithely.

Outside it was noticeably colder. The walk home felt dauntingly long and uncomfortable. Before she reached the bridge near the big B&B place, she realised she ought to have gone to the loo before leaving. The prospect of baring her nether regions in sub-zero temperatures was not appealing. 'Not much choice,' she muttered to herself, hoping there would be no loitering hikers in the stretch under the trees past Crookabeck.

Chapter Six

'Had a nice time?' asked Christopher, when she finally got in at twenty past three. 'I thought you might be sooner than this.'

'I fell over,' she said. 'And bruised my knee. And I peed on my boots.'

'Blimey! You sound like Robin. He peed on himself as well. That potty is all the wrong shape.'

'I thought we decided we wouldn't even start trying to use it until he was two.'

'I thought it was worth a try,' shrugged Christopher. 'I remember my mother saying we were all trained by our second birthdays.'

'Times change,' said Simmy vaguely. Then she added, 'Cornelia's happy, anyway. She chased a red squirrel for about half a mile up the fells. It was deliberately teasing her. She wouldn't come back when I called.'

'*We're* happy,' he corrected her. 'Young Sir and me. Is your knee seriously hurt?'

'It was agonising at first, but it works all right. It's absolutely perishing out there.'

'Minus four,' Christopher nodded. 'Dropping to minus nine by midnight and even colder tomorrow night. Let's not go anywhere.' He looked at her more closely. 'I would have come to find you, if I'd known. Why didn't you phone me?'

'You couldn't take Robin out in that. And you might have missed me somehow. And what could you do? It's not drivable.'

'True. So how was it?' he asked again.

She wanted to give a comprehensive reply, if only to help her to process the whole experience, but Robin was also demanding her attention, and her first priority was to get warm. 'Give me twenty minutes,' she said. 'I'm going to change into a bigger jumper. Have we got enough logs in?'

'Plenty. We can hunker down for the duration and never go outside until Boxing Day. Maybe not even then.'

She knew he was exaggerating. The logs went down at an alarming pace, despite the state-of-the-art stove that was said to be so efficient. 'My dad's going to want to take us all for a walk,' she warned.

'Oh – that reminds me. He phoned and said they'd leave about midday tomorrow, when the sun was highest. He thinks the roads will be okay.'

'Does that mean they'll want lunch?'

'Probably. But they're bringing stuff, aren't they?'

'Who knows?' sighed Simmy wearily. She went upstairs for a fresh set of clothes, wanting to shake off the sense of being tainted somehow by events of the day. Nothing bad had happened, no fights or tragedies or scares, and yet she had not enjoyed herself. Even the walk back had been a struggle, with Cornelia ignoring her shouts when she dashed off after the squirrel. It was Aoife, she knew, who had spoilt things. Her remarks were like a nasty sharp little knife, always ready to prick and twist for no reason at all. What had been the point of that lunch, anyway? Is that what normal people did – just gather together for inconsequential chatter? Yes, she supposed it was. Somehow it had passed her by, and she knew she was missing something in finding it disagreeable when she did make an effort to conform.

But a man *had* been killed, close to that place and only a day earlier. Was there some opaque agenda underlying the chit-chat? Had those women been testing her, or trying to tell her something? If so, then Celia was the one doing it. Fran had seemed detached, with her own thoughts and an interesting affection for the spiky Aoife. There was obviously history between all three of them, as well, probably, as Louise. A little gang of local women, lunching together, knowing each other very well and experimenting with inviting a newcomer into their midst. And perhaps it had been entirely well-intentioned. The Hendersons had, after all, been asked to the Buntings' party, and welcomed in unreservedly.

And what about the Albanian? Where did the mysterious Diellza fit into the picture? Fran's almost total lack of information had been frustrating and mildly peculiar. Such trust in her husband could have been misplaced – although she could imagine how it must have been. With Dan's kindly manner, conveying that he knew best and had everyone's interests at heart, why would Fran see any reason to resist? Perhaps it had happened before – the social worker husband offering sanctuary to waifs and strays. Perhaps especially at Christmas. Fran went out and earned the money, mixing with hyperactive fund managers or whatever, while he immersed himself in the poor and needy, taking more than his share of household matters onto his shoulders, as well. What would happen, Simmy wondered, if and when Fran really did 'burn out' and opt to reduce the stress by working part-time and tending the garden?

Christopher would be wanting to hear some of these musings, and Simmy was perfectly willing to share them with him. But it was past four o'clock on the Sunday before Christmas. They had planned a return game of canasta or possibly Scrabble, with Lily's mince pies and some ginger wine. It would be the last hours of normality before the onslaught of Christmas was upon them. Did she want to bring the females of Patterdale into that island of cosiness? Would it not be preferable to discuss the Henderson family, most of whom had been visited the previous day, with a distribution of Christmas presents and a chance for Robin to romp with his cousins? Simmy was very familiar with all her in-laws, having grown up sharing summer seaside holidays with them. She liked to keep up with all their doings, symbolically reinforcing the prime importance of those connected by blood. Simmy and Christopher had known each other's families from their first day of life – the same day in the same hospital. Since Simmy and Christopher had finally got together officially, they would all phone each other on Christmas Day, and meet up in a big gathering on New Year's Eve. Christopher had been accumulating quirky gifts for them all year, bagging appropriate – and not so appropriate – items from his auction house. Games, ornaments, vintage linens and blankets. He paid a fair price for them, as a rule, but contrived to prevent anyone from putting in a higher bid. There were tricks that he was still acquiring to create an invisible barrier against competitors. It was unfair practice and he kept it small scale, but it happened, nonetheless.

And then there was Robin. He understood that something unusual was going to happen. There was a tree in the house, for one thing, covered in sparkly garlands and baubles. Bright cards showing a man in red clothes, and birds and a lot of white stuff on everything, were slung right across the main room, on a string that stretched from corner to corner, over their heads. He was aware that his grandparents would be showing up sometime soon, and there would be a lot of food. His day at home with his father had gone well, on the whole. They had looked at a lot of books, and then gone to Auntie Hannah's for a bit. That had been quite good fun. She had given him a sausage roll to eat, and then they came home again. Everything was really cold. He was not entirely pleased that his mother and dog had gone off without him. Daddy had been silly with the potty, as well, so the wee had gone all over the floor. Robin did not really understand the potty. They never made him use it when he was at Granny's house.

'There's ice on the windows, look,' said Christopher at six o'clock.

'Not the inside?' Simmy recalled her mother's stories of early years in a draughty old house where the bedroom temperatures could fall below freezing – although she sometimes wondered whether the stories actually belonged to her *grand*mother, and Angie was exaggerating her own hardships.

'Of course not,' scoffed Christopher. 'Not with double glazing. Why – do you think it's cold in here?'

'Not really. No – not at all. It's just the *idea* of what it must be like outside. Think of all those poor sheep and rabbits and things.'

'They're fine. That's what wool's for. They bring most of them in these days, anyway.'

'Not the rabbits,' she pointed out.

'They're far under the ground. It's hares you should worry about. But they've probably got it taped. Everything has, one way or another.'

They drifted into an easy silence, staring at the logs in the cast-iron stove that dominated the room and threw out exactly the right time-honoured sort of heat. But Simmy had not quite finished with her thoughts of the inhospitable conditions just outside her door. Cars that broke down on little fell-top roads, the sudden inescapable need to go out, pipes bursting and ankles breaking. 'I suppose snow would be worse,' she murmured. 'Then we really would be stranded.'

'We're not even slightly stranded,' he pointed out. 'Why? Where do you think you might want to go?'

'Nowhere. But my parents are coming here, aren't they? What if they skid on ice? What if the car hasn't got enough antifreeze? How many days do they say this is going to last? What if they can't get home again?'

'The last is the biggest worry,' he joked. 'But I think it's going to warm up again by the weekend.'

'Oh.'

'You're avoiding the dead elephant,' he accused. 'As Bonnie might say.'

'Was it Bonnie? I thought it was my mother. Not that it matters. I suppose I know what you mean. The murdered man.'

'Precisely. Don't tell me the subject wasn't mentioned over your girlie lunch.'

'Much less than you might think. Some hikers found him in a beck, just above Glenridding, apparently. They were a bit vague about the details, but I gather Aoife lives close by and knows the spot. It was funny, really – they thought I'd know all about it, and could tell them the gory details. It seems I have a reputation.'

'Of course you have. Was the dead man local, then, or what? Do they know who he was yet?'

'Seems not. Not staying there and not identified.'

'Was the place buzzing with police? Must be, presumably. Where's the incident room?'

'Get you – all up to date with the jargon,' she teased. 'Ben would be impressed.'

'Rubbish. I've always known about incident rooms – since the thing in Grasmere, anyway. Probably before that. I admit I'm not too keen on the stuff Ben and Bonnie get up to, but I've had more than my share of police involvement, don't you think?'

'We all have,' she sighed. 'And no, I didn't see a single police person. Maybe they've decided to do it all in Penrith.'

'It must be a mile from Patterdale up to the place they're talking about,' he said slowly. 'I don't think you can drive it, if I remember rightly. Just a footpath for hikers and their backpacks. Tricky for the cops and the people who have to remove the body.'

Simmy shrugged. 'I made sure I didn't say anything about the knife, anyway. I'd be in trouble with Moxon otherwise. Bonnie should never have said anything about it.'

'What knife?' said Christopher.

'I forgot to tell you. It doesn't matter. Let's talk about something else.'

Which they did, sporadically, for the next hour or so. After that, the whole subject of the dead man was forgotten for quite a long time, because they had a visitor that threw everything else into oblivion.

Chapter Seven

Celia Parker was standing on the threshold, wearing a big black woolly hat and carrying something bundled into a brown furry wrap. 'Let me in,' she said, almost pushing Christopher out of the way. 'Where's your wife?'

'Here I am,' said Simmy. 'What's the matter?'

'You're the only person I could think of. Have you got baby formula?'

'What?'

'I thought you might. Your kid's not very old, is he?'

'Why?'

'Why do you think?' Celia threw aside one fold of the blanket to reveal a small crumpled face. 'This'll need feeding any time now.'

It was surreal. Simmy leant over the little creature in utter disbelief. 'A baby?' she queried, not believing her own eyes.

'Right. And I can't have him. I'd never keep him alive.

All I've got is a bit of old powdered milk I used for lambs two years ago. Cow's milk would be better than that.'

'Which everybody has in their fridge,' said Christopher. 'Why come to us? Whose kid is it, anyway?'

Robin was not yet in bed. He pushed his way between the adult legs, craning his neck to see whatever the woman was holding. Simmy automatically picked him up. 'It's a baby,' she said. Her insides were jumping all over the place, including her breasts, which tingled with the memory of milk. It was less than a year since she weaned Robin. Probably the system could be restarted without too much trouble. For months after weaning her own child, the mere sound of a baby in a supermarket could do the trick.

'Look. This note came with him. It explains the basics.' Celia fumbled in the pocket of her thick padded coat and produced a sheet of paper.

His name must be Jerome. I have given him life, from here it is all in the hands of fate. Do what you believe to be best.

'That Albanian woman,' said Christopher superfluously.

'She was in labour,' Simmy realised. 'But when . . . ? How . . . ?'

Celia sat down on the sofa and laid the baby on her lap. 'She must have given birth sometime in the night, I suppose, either during yesterday or last night. Fran said she'd kept to her room all day yesterday and this morning. She'll have walked down to my place while we were at the pub and left him under my back porch. That's what old Nosy Parker Felton must have heard.'

'He could have frozen to death,' said Simmy.

'He was well covered up. Babies are tough, apparently.'

'He's only one day old,' said Christopher wonderingly. 'But if you know who his mother is, why not simply call the police and get them to sort it all out?'

'I nearly did. I'd tapped two nines before I had second thoughts. I mean – what'd happen to him? They can't *force* her to take him back.'

'A proper foster mother,' said Christopher. 'There are procedures.'

'It's Christmas,' said Simmy faintly. 'And cold. And I'm guessing Diellza isn't at the Buntings' any more.'

'She must have good reason,' said Celia with a frown. 'I daren't talk to Fran about it – do you see? If Diellza trusted her and Dan, she wouldn't have struggled down to me, would she? She's obviously scared of something.'

'Why leave him with you?'

'She liked me. We had quite a long chat on Friday afternoon, when I took some glasses round to the Buntings.'

'Did she know she was pregnant? Obviously, she must have done. Is it ever possible *not* to know?' Simmy wondered. 'She told me she thought she'd eaten something that was upsetting her.'

Celia let a small silence develop before saying, 'Sometimes people won't let themselves know, if that makes sense. It would be too much on top of everything else. What's more to the point – did the *Buntings* know? If they did, then Fran was lying her head off just now in the pub. You saw the size of Diellza. It would be easy to hide a pregnancy – possibly even from herself. She's quite young, and I think her life has been all about politics, science – things that ignore the physical.'

'What's *your* line of work?' Simmy asked suddenly.

'What was that about lambs just now?'

'I teach psychology,' said the woman with a wry smile. 'For the OU, so it's mostly from home. And I do a bit of counselling on the side. I've got a bit of land over in Bannerdale and let it to people's sheep. Or I did. They let me help with the lambing when it got busy. All hands to the pump, sort of thing. *Have* you got any formula?'

Simmy shook her head. 'I never used it.'

'We did get a packet, though,' Christopher interrupted. 'For emergencies.'

'Did we? Where is it, then?'

He looked sheepish. 'Actually, I might not have told you. I just thought – what would I do if you couldn't feed him – if you fell downstairs or had a stroke or something. It's under the kitchen sink.'

'Good God! Is there a bottle as well?'

He shook his head. Celia produced a canvas bag from under the baby. 'There's one in here. It's not very clean – the teat's a bit cracked as well. But it might work.'

The baby had not stirred. Celia had slowly unwrapped him, as the warmth of the room made itself felt. 'Did she feed him at all, I wonder?' said Simmy. 'He doesn't look hungry – but then they don't need much for the first couple of days.' It was all coming back to her – the half-hearted acceptance of nourishment by the newborn, and the terrible oversupply that caused such agony in those first days. Her thoughts flew to the new mother. 'She'll be getting all engorged in another day or two. Where can she have gone? Has she got a car?'

'I don't know. I mean – no, she hasn't got a car. But she's got some money, I think. And a phone. I guess she might be looking for her husband.' Her expression was one of absolute puzzlement as she looked from Simmy to Christopher and back. 'Although I've no basis for thinking that. He just came to mind for some reason.'

Simmy was barely listening. 'She can't possibly be wandering about in the open. That would be tantamount to suicide. It's terribly cold and dark out there. We have to call the police. She might be dead.'

Beside her, Christopher stood tall and assertive. 'And get this wretched kid some proper care,' he said flatly. 'It's madness to bring him here like this.'

Celia faced him from the sofa. 'No, I can't do that, if you mean I should call the police. It's too dangerous. Don't forget a man's been murdered about half a mile from where she was staying. Dan Bunting must have had a good reason for bringing Diellza home with him in the first place. We could try talking to him, perhaps, before doing anything else, just to see if he knows where Diellza might be. But I really don't think we should tell *anyone* about the baby, not even Dan or Fran. Nobody at all. He'll be safe down here with you. You're not going anywhere, are you? You understand babies. It's *Christmas*, for God's sake. Nobody's going to want to take him on now, are they? Everything's closed down until Thursday at the earliest. If it helps, I can go and find some formula somewhere.' She groaned. 'There are times when living out here feels as if we're in the Middle Ages. Especially when there's *weather*.'

'You make it sound simple,' Christopher grumbled.

'Well, perhaps it is,' said Simmy softly. She and Robin were sitting next to Celia, bending over the tiny face in her lap, watching all the little twitches it was making. 'He's terribly sweet, isn't he? Jerome,' she murmured. 'I wonder why that's so important?'

'Named after some Albanian drug lord, probably,' said Christopher darkly. 'We're getting into something way beyond our comfort zone. Dangerous is hardly the word. It's madness. Even if there hadn't been someone killed three miles away, it'd be insane. As it is, it's totally and completely out of the question.'

'I could ask my mum to get some formula and a bottle,' said Simmy, ignoring him. 'She can go into Keswick tomorrow.'

'I don't think the drug lords will be looking for him,' said Celia, with a smile. 'I have a feeling it's all a lot more *domestic* than that.'

'What makes you think that?' Christopher was growing more subdued in the face of two implacable females. You couldn't make women see sense where babies were concerned, anyway. 'You said yourself it was dangerous.'

'I know I did. And maybe it is. But we're stereotyping, aren't we? All I know is that Diellza has qualifications, and is no hapless refugee brought here by traffickers. It's nothing like that. She's been married to a man called Alex for nearly two years, and she thinks all their papers are legal and valid. She has a perfect right to be here in this country.' She was speaking slowly, feeling for the words – which closely echoed those that Diellza had spoken to Simmy at the party.

Christopher tried again. 'So why did Dan Bunting have to rescue her?'

'Who knows? He never said. He's always been rather close, according to Fran. Didn't she say at the pub that he had never properly explained what Diellza's problem was? He hasn't even told her, let alone anyone else.'

'Because it's sure to be on the wrong side of the law,' Christopher said. 'Fiddling benefits, or working at something off the grid. Black economy sort of stuff. Maybe even drug trafficking.'

Simmy remembered her own suspicions about modern slavery. 'She seemed to need Dan's permission before she could go anywhere,' she said. 'I should probably have tried harder to find out what that was about.'

'He's always seemed pretty soft and easy-going to me,' said Celia, with the clear implication that she knew him a lot better than Simmy or Christopher did.

'But none of that ties in with the fact of a new baby,' said Christopher.

Simmy could resist no longer. Without asking, she scooped the baby up and held him to her face. 'Oh, he *smells* so lovely,' she crooned. 'There's nothing in the world like it.' She could feel hormones dancing in her bloodstream. 'We'll keep him here over Christmas. What harm can it do? We've got clothes and the little cot and everything. It's all in the cupboard in Robin's room.'

'Get us sent to jail, probably,' said Christopher sourly. But he bent down to inhale the baby smell, unable to resist. 'It does take you back, doesn't it,' he whispered.

'But what are we going to *tell* people?' Simmy wondered, wide-eyed. 'My parents. Lily. Bonnie and Ben. We can't say we've suddenly decided to become foster parents overnight.'

'Well, you *have*, in a way,' said Celia. 'Just say it was a Christmas emergency. Don't mention Diellza, but say it's a neighbour in crisis or something. How many people are we talking about?'

'Just those,' said Christopher. 'My family don't have to know anything. That's assuming we hand him over to some proper authority the day after Boxing Day.'

'"I have given him life, now he's in the hands of fate",' Simmy quoted softly. 'But *why*? What's the matter with her? She's got to be terrified of something – someone – fearful for the baby as well.' She tried to think herself into Diellza's mind. 'If she didn't know she was pregnant, she must have had a dreadful shock. Imagine it! All that bewildering pain, your body acting all by itself, entirely outside your control – and then this strange living thing comes out of you. It's like science fiction. She must have panicked.'

'If that's how it was, she probably did panic for a short time, yes,' said Celia. 'But then it looks as if she had enough self-control to keep herself and the baby quiet, write that note, wrap him up, clean herself. All in twenty-four hours, at most.'

'Where's the placenta?' Christopher asked, looking pleased with himself. 'It's too big to flush down the loo.'

'Not if you cut it up first,' said Celia, which made both the Hendersons flinch.

'You've never had a baby, have you?' said Christopher. 'If you had, you'd understand why that's such a sick idea.'

'Just lambs,' said Celia with a tight smile. 'But I have heard that in some societies the woman eats the placenta. It's full of minerals and things – right?'

'Fried in butter,' said Christopher. 'That's what they say in Guatemala, but I think it's a joke.'

'She probably did cut it up,' said Simmy. 'Or maybe it's

85

under her bed wrapped in newspaper.'

'We really ought to tell the police,' Christopher insisted. 'Especially after last time. I don't want to get any more of a reputation than I have already, after the Borrowdale business.'

'But what law has she broken?' said Celia. 'Why is it a police matter? This is a private arrangement between you and the child's mother. I'm the agent, getting it all arranged. Nobody's done anything illegal.'

The others had no reply to that. Robin poked a finger at the baby's head, making it stir and start jerking itself awake. Simmy's hormones stirred in sympathy. 'Would it be gross if I tried to breastfeed him?' she asked. 'Because I think it might work.' She grimaced in embarrassment. 'Something's certainly happening.' The tingling was intensifying, sensations taking her back to her own child's first days.

'We're only keeping him a few days,' Christopher objected. 'If you start lactating properly, you'll be sore for ages.'

She threw him a grateful look. 'That's true. But we should concentrate on what's here and now. It's a baby in need of milk and I can actually feel myself making some. It's like magic.'

'Go on, then,' he said. 'Who am I to question the mysteries of the female body?'

'We had a dog once,' said Celia, 'that produced milk for an abandoned kitten. She hadn't had puppies for well over a year, but she fed the little thing for months. It's probably quite normal, if we weren't so puritanical about it.'

'It is the definition of a mammal, after all,' said Christopher.

Simmy picked up the baby and headed for the stairs. Robin tried to follow her and Christopher held him back. 'No, let him come,' said Simmy. 'It might be the only chance he'll ever get to see what a baby's all about.'

Christopher's face registered alarm. 'Oh God,' he groaned. 'You're never going to give him up, are you? They'll have to prise him away from you.'

'Jerome's a lovely name,' she said, from halfway up the stairs.

Chapter Eight

They had a carrycot, nappies that were much too big, and a good supply of little vests and leggings that Simmy had hung onto. And the out-of-date packet of baby formula under the sink. 'I think Diellza must have fed him already,' said Simmy. 'Which is good. He'll have got some colostrum – I always think that's such a nasty word. Anyway, he seems perfectly healthy, look, even though he's so terribly tiny. Much smaller than Robin ever was.' She had undressed the baby, giving his navel a thorough inspection. A length of dried cord still connected to it. 'Like a lamb, I suppose,' said Simmy. 'Robin had a nasty big plastic clip thing that got in the way of the nappy.'

'He's bound to keep us up all night,' said Christopher. 'I should be cursing that Celia. Why did she have to pick on us? Surely the Louise person was the most obvious one to take him – she wouldn't have noticed an extra kid.'

'She probably had a good reason. Maybe Louise's

husband isn't as nice as you.' She grinned at him. 'I still can't believe the way my boobs came to the rescue. It's miraculous.' The baby had been co-operative, clearly encouraged by the few drops that were already produced and suckling vigorously. 'Do you think there's a sort of little reservoir of emergency milk sitting there, even after all this time?' she asked. 'I'll have to get Ben to google it for me sometime.'

'Google it yourself. It's not difficult, and I'm not sure it's quite the topic for Ben to get into,' said Christopher. 'I do have to say, I'm really not sure any of this is a good idea.'

'It's not an *idea*. It's an emergency. I think we're doing pretty well so far. And Robin thinks it's wonderful.'

Christopher heaved a rueful sigh, knowing he was outnumbered. 'Well maybe someone should google Albanian politics, as well. Mrs Pink Hair was all over the place on that, wasn't she? First, she says it's dangerous in some way, then she backs off saying it's just something harmless and domestic. What about the Buntings? If he's a social worker or whatever, he's obviously got to be told about this little chap. He'll know exactly what needs to be done.'

Simmy chewed her lip. 'We don't know what he is, exactly. I got the impression he's with some less official outfit than the social services. He might have no idea what the proper channels are. And what about other people who were at the party? Aoife, for example, who obviously knows everybody. She's the one who was most interested in the murdered man this afternoon, and my reputation for getting tangled up in police investigations. We're embarrassingly famous, apparently.'

'If the body was found near Gillside, and she lives somewhere above the Buntings, she must be pretty close to where he was killed. Closer than anyone else we've met, anyway.'

'I wish I'd gone up there more often. I can't remember what it's like. It feels much further away than three miles.'

'Because we nearly always walk there unless we're just popping to the shop, that's why. There's nowhere to leave the car most of the time. We'd end up having to walk about eight miles if we went up onto those crags.'

Simmy was not really listening. Nothing seemed to matter very much compared to the amazing fact of a new little life dropped into her arms. 'He's very placid, isn't he?' she murmured. 'Must have been an easy birth. No drugs or intervention. Nothing to *recover* from, unlike most babies these days. He's like a puppy or a kitten.'

'Or a lamb,' Christopher added. 'Robin was like that, wasn't he?'

'More or less. I did have that gas and air, and they were very quick to grab him and make him breathe. I have a feeling this one was left to get himself together in his own time.'

'She can't *really* not have known, can she? I know she's big, and maybe the bump didn't show much, but all those *changes*.' He shook his head. 'It just isn't credible.'

'I think she must have been working on two levels somehow. Rational mind, focusing on the world outside herself, which sounds as if it was pretty all-consuming, one way and another. And then the subconscious stuff, which she probably blocked. People do ignore their bodies most of the time. It's in the culture now, isn't it? Who you really

90

are doesn't match what your body's like – that's what loads of people believe these days. So, it might not have been too hard to stick with the mental side, if you see what I mean.'

'Sounds a bit garbled,' he said doubtfully.

They settled down at last, the baby in the Moses basket on the floor beside the bed, Simmy wrapping herself in their winter duvet with a blissful animal sense of satisfaction. She had performed a little Christmas miracle, all by herself and everything felt right. Better than right – she gloried in her own femaleness, which had never been entirely secure since losing her first baby. She felt young and capable and oddly powerful. *Stop it*, she told herself. *It'll probably all go wrong from here on.*

And it did, to the extent that the baby cried insistently from 4 a.m. to first light on Monday. Simmy's confidence in her milk production took a knock, and Christopher was adamant that they phone Angie and ask her to buy a bottle and formula before coming over that afternoon. 'We'll be lucky to survive until then,' he glowered. 'Can we try spooning some of that stuff we've got into him?'

Robin was distressed, too. 'Baby cry,' he repeated anxiously. He had woken at five and clamoured to be taken into the parental bed. All four were gathered under the duvet. 'All we need now is Cornelia,' said Christopher.

Simmy was remembering the darker moments of new motherhood – the helplessness and panic; the perpetually lurking fear that the child would die; the projections into a future where there would be nothing but wailing demands that she could never meet. She fought back tears, telling herself not to be so stupid.

'We don't have to do this,' Christopher spoke sternly. 'It's not our baby.'

'But it *might* have been,' she said. 'Nothing would be any different if it was. At this precise moment, we have absolutely no choice but to get on with it.'

Christopher made a choked sound of disagreement. 'Rubbish,' he spluttered. 'We can call the police right now and get them to find a proper foster mother.'

Simmy clutched the baby closer. '*I'm* a proper foster mother,' she cried. 'It's too late for that.'

'What? What does that mean? We're not *keeping* him, Sim. Surely that's blindingly obvious. There are *laws*.'

'I know. I didn't mean that.' But countless nerves and cells and instincts inside her said differently.

Christopher followed up on his spooning idea, taking over completely. 'You'll choke him,' Simmy worried. 'Just a few drops at a time.'

'I know,' he said tightly. 'I've done this before.'

'When?'

'When we had that dog, remember? When I was about fifteen. She had puppies and rejected them, and we tried to feed them like this until we could find a small enough bottle.'

'And did it work?'

'More or less,' he said, unconvincingly. 'Jerome might be small, but he's bigger than a puppy, which helps.'

The baby was at least swallowing normally, his eyes wide open and fixed on Christopher's face. He seemed to grasp the general idea of what was going on and stuck out his lower lip co-operatively. 'Good boy!' said Christopher.

'Good boy?' said Robin, eyeing the baby suspiciously.

Simmy pulled him to her and laughed. 'Two good boys,' she told him. 'And a good daddy as well.'

Simmy phoned her mother at eight o'clock, hoping she wasn't waking her. The Straws had taken to lying in outrageously since they retired to their bungalow. 'Listen,' she said, when Angie answered, sounding fairly wide awake. 'This isn't going to make much sense, but do you think you could go to Boots or somewhere and get some baby formula and a bottle – and some size one nappies. For a newborn. I'll reimburse you.'

'No sense at all,' Angie agreed. 'I demand at least a minimal explanation. Did you neglect to mention that you were pregnant – or did someone leave a baby on your doorstep?'

'The latter, actually.'

'I don't believe you. That never happens. For a start, the poor thing would have frozen to death within moments. It's seriously cold out there. Your father's agonising about the car and the roads and the whole business of getting to you – and back again.'

'It'll be fine,' said Simmy dismissively, on the basis of no real knowledge. She had not even glanced outside, and the dog was still waiting to be let out. 'We'll tell you the whole story when you get here. It's quite Christmassy, in a way.'

'Huh!' said Angie. 'Why am I getting a bad feeling about it? It's not connected to that murder in Glenridding, is it? It was on the news last night. They've identified the body, apparently. Looking for next of kin. They didn't say much, just asking for information. Usual stuff.'

'Nothing whatsoever to do with that,' said Simmy with misplaced confidence.

The baby fell asleep ten minutes later. Simmy wondered if she had conveyed a sense of relief, having extracted a promise from her mother to buy the required items. 'We'll come earlier,' Angie said. 'So we can find out what this is all about. The curiosity is killing me. We're bringing lots of food, in case we get stranded up there. It's a long walk to your nearest shop.'

'Tell me about it,' Simmy agreed.

'It's *bloody* cold out there,' Christopher announced having taken the dog to the end of the garden and back, as the nearest either of them would get to a walk that day. 'Lucky the fire stayed in.' He piled more logs into the wood burner. 'It's working well, isn't it? Worth paying extra for a good one.'

'It's wonderful,' said Simmy. 'Best thing about the whole house.' Which was true. The efficiency of the stove was little short of miraculous. 'We had one in Worcester that was probably a hundred years old, and it never worked properly.' Simmy had grown up in Worcestershire, married a local man and studied floristry. 'That seems so long ago now,' she sighed. 'But it's only five years or so since I moved up here.'

'Mum said they've identified the murdered man,' she reported idly. 'Now they're looking for his next of kin.'

'Good luck to them,' said Christopher, equally idly.

'Right.' She watched Robin eating a banana and drinking milk from a spouted cup. Awareness of the baby upstairs was pushing everything else out of focus. Her breasts started tingling again, with an encouraging dampness a few moments later. 'I really am producing milk,' she said, still marvelling at the way it all worked. 'I only have to think about the baby and it starts. I don't know why I'm so surprised, really.'

'Social norms. Cultural pressures. We don't talk about human lactation, do we? Most people find it embarrassing or even disgusting. At best it's a study for anthropologists. I don't expect there's much research into it.' He smiled reminiscently. 'All they need to do is ask a Jamaican grandmother about it. And even they've probably lost most of their knowledge by now.'

'What?'

'The grannies feed the babies – or they used to. Even into their sixties and beyond, they could breastfeed. I don't know how I know that,' he frowned. 'Picked it up somewhere.'

Simmy had an idea it could have come from his first wife, who almost never got mentioned. She had been a charity worker somewhere in Central America, and had married Christopher on a whim, before deciding it had all been a foolish mistake.

'So who was he, then?' asked Christopher ten minutes later. 'The murdered man.'

'Oh, I don't know. I doubt if Mum even registered a name – or they might not have broadcast it. They're asking for information, so I suppose that means they would have named him. I thought you weren't interested.'

'I'm trying not to be.'

Simmy laughed, fully understanding his dilemma. 'I know. It niggles, doesn't it. Let's hope Ben hasn't heard the body's been identified or he'll make sure we pay attention.'

'He'll be too occupied with the Harkness family

Christmas, with any luck. Is Bonnie going to be with them as well?'

'I think so.' Simmy wrinkled her brow, trying to remember. 'I'm not sure what she said. You know the way people go on about which set of relations they've got to spend the day with. It was a bit like that. Something about Corinne's older sister putting in an appearance, and the Askham lot needing to be factored in.' Bonnie Lawson had recently been reunited with relatives in Askham, with unforeseen ramifications. 'I guess she'll creep down to Bowness to get away from all that.'

'Poor old Bonnie.'

Upstairs the baby woke up. 'Baby cry,' said Robin, nodding wisely to himself. He was starting to get the hang of this baby business, he decided.

Angie and Russell Straw arrived at an unprecedented 10.45 a.m. The plan had been for them to leave it until just before lunch, but Simmy's phone call about baby equipment had galvanised them. 'Where is it, then?' demanded Angie, before she was properly inside the house.

'Hello, Granny. Happy Christmas. How nice to see you,' said Christopher, ventriloquising for his son. 'Thank you for coming so early.'

Russell nudged his way in, past his wife, plonking a large cardboard box on the floor and then clapping his hands together and shivering dramatically. 'I can't remember it ever being this cold,' he said. 'Coldest for twenty-seven years, apparently. We were living in the soft south then.'

'What are the roads like?' asked Christopher.

'No problem. Lucky it's been dry for a bit – there's

hardly any ice, even down these smaller roads. All over the hedges and fields, of course. Looks lovely. I should be out taking photos, but I worry for my fingers. And the camera might not like it either.'

'Where is it?' Angie asked again. 'Assuming you really do have a baby and not some abandoned animal. In which case, I can't see why you'd need nappies.' She proffered a red tote bag. 'It's all in here. We've got to go back to the car for the food.'

'Isn't that it?' asked Christopher, pointing at the box.

'No, that's the presents. And some drinks.'

'Hello,' called Simmy from the top of the stairs. 'Come and meet Jerome.'

Chapter Nine

The Straws manifested a much deeper bewilderment than Simmy thought necessary. 'What don't you understand?' she repeated several times. 'It's all pretty straightforward.'

'It's not, though,' her father protested. 'Where's the mother? Who's going to register the birth? Why don't the people she was staying with have any part in the story? It is about as unstraightforward as anything possibly could be, if you ask me.'

'You're setting yourself up for misery,' said Angie. 'Look at you!'

Simmy was clutching the baby defensively. She had managed another session of breastfeeding, tempted to think it was going to work well enough to preclude the need for formula. The steadfast gaze of the suckling infant had melted her from head to toe, everything concentrated on producing sustenance for him. Surges of euphoria went through her, stronger, if anything, than when she had fed Robin. *It's just hormones* she told herself. *It doesn't mean anything.* But just then, hormones meant practically everything.

'He's a cute little chap,' said Christopher feebly. 'And it's only for a few days. You can't register births on Christmas Eve, anyway. Besides, they give you six weeks to do it. It'll all be properly sorted by then.'

'Says you,' muttered Russell, who had the same forebodings as his wife.

Angie busied herself with Robin, then laying out a plain lunch of cold meat and salad. She poured everyone a glass of sherry as tradition demanded. Christopher threw more logs into the stove and got the sound system playing carols.

Then Simmy's phone rang. 'It's Bonnie,' she said. 'She never uses the landline.'

'The dead man's called Alexander McGuire,' Bonnie said, after a few brief preliminaries. 'Have you heard?'

'So what?' said Simmy.

'So you should probably take notice, with it being right on your doorstep. Don't you know anybody called Alexander? They say he's from Glasgow originally but had worked for years in Manchester. I expect they've found people who knew him in both places by now.'

'Lots of people round here are from Glasgow,' said Simmy carelessly. 'He can't be local, anyway, because someone would have reported him missing, or realised who it was as soon as he was found.'

'It's no good, Simmy. You've been mixing with people who live in the exact place he was found, if I've got it right about that party on Friday. And you saw them again yesterday, didn't you? At the pub?'

'Bonnie, you're taking an unhealthy interest in my movements. I can't even remember where you're going to be tomorrow. It's not right. Where's Ben?'

At that moment little Jerome gave one loud wail as if he knew he should announce his presence. He was lying in an armchair on his furry blanket while Russell and Robin arranged parcels under the tree and Angie did something in the kitchen. 'Was that a baby? You've got visitors, have you? Sorry.' Bonnie sounded surprised. 'Who do you know with a baby?'

Simmy couldn't lie. 'We're looking after him for a few days. I'll explain it all to you after Christmas.'

'Is it Baby Jesus?' asked Bonnie, like a five-year-old.

'I wouldn't be very surprised if he was,' said Simmy. 'Although I don't think he was quite born in a manger.'

'You know you said I should back off and forget about you, and concentrate on my own Christmas and all that? Well, it's not going to happen. Because not only have you got a murder right there, but somebody's left a baby on your doorstep, and you don't know who. That's what it sounds like, anyway. So you've got to tell me the whole thing or I'll walk through the freezing fog and come and find out for myself.'

Simmy forced a laugh. The distance was ten miles – a perfectly feasible walk in acceptable weather. 'Is it foggy as well now?' she asked.

'It is down here. Don't change the subject. Just *tell* me.'

'I can't, Bonnie. I've just had to explain it all to my

100

parents and I've been awake all night with him, and I'm supposed to be doing complicated things to the turkey. Robin's getting all excited and Christopher keeps using up logs that are supposed to last three days.'

'Awake all night? He's been there since yesterday, has he?'

Bonnie could be very dogged at times. 'I met his mother at Friday's party. She must have been in labour then. Now she's gone missing – or so I assume – and a friend of hers got landed with the baby and she brought him here, thinking we'd have the equipment because she hasn't.' At the word *equipment*, Simmy's mind flew to her own breasts and she smiled at the little joke. She almost began to explain that aspect of it all, but bit it back. Too much information, she suspected.

'You *assume* she's gone missing?'

'Well, she must have, or we could just have taken the baby back to her.' And yet, she realised, they could not have done that, because Diellza had firmly rejected her child, for unknown reasons, and somehow the very idea had not arisen. 'She's in some sort of trouble,' she added weakly.

'Perhaps she killed that man, then,' said Bonnie as if this was an obvious theory.

A delayed connection took place in Simmy's fuddled head. 'Oh God!' she gasped. 'Did you say "Alexander"?'

'Yes. Why?'

'That's her husband's name. She's got a husband who's Scottish and they've fallen out, so she got taken in up here by a good Samaritan. That must be why he was here – looking for her.'

'And now he's dead and she's had a baby and run away,' Bonnie summarised. 'Leaving the baby behind.'

A ten-second pause ensued while Simmy's thoughts found entirely new tracks to run along. 'It might be a different Alexander,' she said desperately.

'Call the police, Simmy. I'm going down to Bowness now, to tell Ben the whole thing.' Another pause, then, 'I bet you were thrilled to have him, weren't you?'

'He's very sweet,' sighed Simmy. 'You have no idea.'

Christopher had heard bits of the conversation, noticing the change in Simmy's voice. He mimed curiosity and Simmy ended the call. 'The murdered man might be Diellza's husband,' she said. 'They've announced his name. Alexander McSomething.'

'How did they identify him?'

'I have no idea. Unlocked his phone, probably. Or found a wallet on him. Maybe they knew all along and only just decided to make it public.' She had a thought. 'They won't know Diellza's here, will they? Not unless the Buntings tell them. How would they?'

Angie and Russell had gathered round, anxious not to miss anything, insisting on hearing more of the known facts. 'Bonnie says we have to call the police,' said Simmy.

'And say what?' asked Russell. 'What can you tell them that would help their investigations? Are you saying they won't already know the man has a wife, and probably where she's been, who she's stayed with – all that?'

'I don't think they will,' Simmy said slowly. 'If nobody in Glenridding has come forward, they might not have any idea she was there.'

'They'd take the baby away,' said Angie, eyeing Simmy warily. 'How could they not?'

'We could make an anonymous call dropping the Buntings in it,' Christopher suggested. 'It's basically their pigeon, anyway. They brought the woman here. Can't have bargained for a surprise pregnancy, all the same.'

'They might already have come forward,' said Simmy. 'It's probably through them somehow that the man's been named. Dan's some sort of charity worker – he'll be in the system, with refugees and all that. Don't they all have to check with the police or something?' She shook her head. 'Why don't I know more about this stuff?' She plucked the baby out of his nest on the chair. 'And they can't possibly take him away now. It's Christmas Eve!!'

'They'll see he's doing fine here,' Russell soothed her. 'You're as good a foster mother as they're likely to find, let's face it. I think somebody might even give you a medal.'

'Nice try,' muttered Christopher. 'So – do we put it to the test, or what?'

'I thought you told us she wasn't a refugee. The mother, I mean,' said Angie. 'It's odd the way we haven't been giving her more thought. What must the poor thing be going through? Where on earth *is* she? She can't be anywhere outdoors in this. If she is, she'll be dead by now.'

Simmy flinched. Thoughts of Diellza had persistently slipped away, every time she made a half-hearted effort to consider the woman's fate. She didn't want a rival for the baby, she acknowledged. Let her get safely back to Albania, or at least resume her life somewhere else in peace and as much prosperity as could be achieved, cheerfully childless. Now she had to confront the likelihood of a dead husband, which could only change everything considerably. 'She couldn't possibly have murdered him,' she said confidently. 'She was busy giving birth at the time.'

'Who said she did?' asked Christopher.

'Who do you think?' said Simmy.

Nobody called the police, but they talked about it a lot. Simmy kept quoting Bonnie's definite assertion that the police should be notified, while trying to convince herself that there was no need for that. The dilemma was frightening. Questions outnumbered answers a hundredfold, with Simmy increasingly aware that there had to be far more knowledge and connection between the people she had only just met than she had first assumed. Celia, Louise, Aoife and the Buntings had history, and that implied that there could have been a degree of planning behind events that had felt spontaneous. 'You're getting into conspiracy theory,' Christopher told her.

'You don't think they all knew Diellza was pregnant, do you?' asked Russell. 'And had worked out exactly what to do with the resulting infant? And now none of them are saying anything to the police about her or her baby.'

Simmy tried to confront the depths of deception and manipulation that would have required. 'Oh, no. That would be awful.'

'It would mean every word they've said would be a lie,' added Christopher.

'Well, not quite,' Simmy corrected him. 'Not at the pub, anyway. There was a lot of general stuff. In fact, there was more of that than anything about the murder or Diellza.'

'Well, I bet at least some of them knew who the dead man was,' Russell persisted. 'One of them probably killed him.'

Everyone looked at him with varying levels of scepticism. 'How do you work that out?' asked Christopher.

'Stands to reason. At any rate, I'll bet you it was someone at that party. I bet you the whole event was a smokescreen, so everybody had an alibi, even though any of them could have sneaked off and done the deed just up the road, without being noticed.'

'Dad!' sighed Simmy, while full of admiration for his grasp of the whole business. He even had a better understanding of the geography than she herself had. But there was another person who had most of the story. 'You sound like Bonnie. I wish I hadn't told her so much.'

'I thought he was killed *after* the party,' said Christopher. 'Isn't that what they said?'

'They don't know,' Russell said. 'It's never easy to get an accurate time of death, you know that. He was last seen on Friday afternoon, is what I heard.'

'Read,' Angie put in. 'You read it on the computer. You didn't *hear* it.'

'Pedantry is usually my department,' said Russell mildly. 'What difference does it make?'

Angie shrugged. 'Looks to me as if you're all getting silly. Nobody's going to do anything, are they? We're not going anywhere or seeing anyone or making any phone calls. It's getting dark and probably even colder. Let's just settle down and amuse the children.'

'"Children",' echoed Simmy softly. 'That does sound nice.' She was yet again holding baby Jerome, his little body nestled into the crook of her arm as if rooted there. It had struck her that she felt no differently towards him than she had towards her own Robin at the same stage. Wasn't that a bit shameful? Wasn't it somehow almost *promiscuous* to take to any random baby with the full force of biological maternity that should be the sole birthright of the one that came from your own body? It clearly wasn't the same for Christopher, who was manifesting none of the pride and wonder and sheer delight that had come at the birth of his actual son. He could hardly be expected to, nor could he properly understand what was happening with his wife, although he knew enough to be worried about what would happen when Jerome had to leave.

'Robin must be wondering where this little man sprang from,' said Russell. 'But he seems to be taking it in his stride.'

'It's the same when a real baby arrives,' said Christopher. 'I remember when my brothers were born – they were suddenly *there*, with no warning. Or if there had been warning, it went over my head. I don't recall that I found it anything to get worked up about.'

'This is a real baby,' said Simmy angrily. 'What do you mean?'

'Not forgetting that both your sisters were adopted,' said Angie, also sounding cross.

'God – that came out wrong, didn't it? I didn't mean it like that. A *natural* baby – is that what I should have said?'

'You've got to relish the symbolism,' murmured Russell. 'It being Christmas and everything.'

Simmy smiled gratefully at him. 'That's what Bonnie said, sort of. She asked if he was the Baby Jesus.'

'She was joking, obviously,' said Christopher.

Russell shook his head. 'Stranger things have happened. "The Night Before Christmas", and all that. All we really need now is a nice big covering of snow.'

'He's getting all whimsical,' sighed Angie. 'Happens every year. Usually it's "Away in a Manger" that does it.'

'Oh Lord!' Russell jumped up. 'We've almost missed the Nine Carols from King's College. Quick – where's your radio?'

Simmy stayed out of the scramble to catch the first haunting verse of 'Once in Royal David's City', suddenly finding herself irresistibly sleepy. She put her head back and dozed, aware of the music as a kind of lullaby. When Robin crawled onto her lap, she automatically put her free arm round him and drifted back to sleep. *Children* whispered a voice somewhere.

Ten minutes later, the magic of the carols had faded, and Angie started to talk, enough to rouse her daughter from her nap. 'You're storing up trouble,' Angie was saying to Christopher. 'Look at Robin! He's going to be as bonded as Persimmon if you go on like this. How long did you say that baby's been here? Less than twenty-four hours? What do you think another two days is going to do? At least stop this ridiculous breastfeeding and give him a nice bottle of SMA. You haven't even opened the box I went to such trouble to get you.'

'Breast is best,' mumbled Simmy. 'I'll give him a bottle if he cries in the night.'

'There's very little choice now, anyway,' Russell pointed out. 'Circumstances ordain that he stays here at least for another thirty-six hours.'

'Right,' said Christopher. 'And we have absolutely no idea what happens after that.'

Simmy knew she was being lazy and self-indulgent. She should be in the kitchen peeling sprouts or making brandy butter. She had not just given birth, and had no reason to sit around like a Madonna cradling the baby. The others had just as much responsibility for him as she did. Russell enjoyed infants as much as anyone, and had not yet had his share of cuddle. Dragging herself out of the short-lived bliss of dozing with two small boys, she heard again her mother's gloomy predictions. Parting with Jerome now would hurt, not least because her breasts would take days to settle down again.

'Don't be too sure,' warned Angie, not yet finished. 'I get a feeling we're all skating on dangerously thin ice.'

'Not me. I'm too old for skating,' said Russell, aiming for a joke that fell sadly flat.

As if with a single mind, both Robin and the baby decided they'd had enough inactivity. Robin elbowed his way off Simmy's lap, just as Jerome began to jerk himself awake. The toddler managed to crush the infant's leg under his foot as he climbed down, giving rise to loud howls of protest. Christopher jumped to the rescue, lifting his son clear and then taking the baby in both hands. 'Uh-oh,' he said. 'No more downtime.'

Cornelia, who had been innocently dozing in front of the stove, mistook the sudden change of atmosphere for the promise of a walk, or at least a game, and began to jump at Christopher, pulling at what she thought was his pullover, but was in fact a corner of Jerome's blanket.

'Don't let her bite him!' shrilled Angie, who had never been altogether relaxed about dogs.

Robin pushed heroically at Cornelia, shouting at her to 'Drop it!' while Russell and Simmy dithered, unsure whether or not to be alarmed. 'Noisy lot, when they get going,' remarked Russell.

'Give me the baby,' said Angie with total authority. 'Calm down, everybody. The most sensible person just now is my grandson. Well done, Robin. Brave boy.'

It was all over in under a minute. Sheepish looks were exchanged, Cornelia pacified and Robin making the most of his moment in the spotlight. 'Drop it!' he said again irrelevantly. It was a game he often played with the dog.

'She's not holding anything now,' said Russell. 'Maybe we could find her something.'

'She's got a box of toys in the kitchen,' said Simmy. 'But I think she might need to go out. She hasn't been since before breakfast.'

'I'll take her down through the village, shall I?' Russell offered. 'Have a look at what the weather's doing and admire people's fairy lights.'

'Wrap up warm, then,' said Angie.

But before Russell could open the front door, somebody rang the bell. 'Wait!' cried Simmy, suddenly panicked. Whoever it was might have come for the baby.

She wrenched Jerome away from her mother and charged upstairs with him. Russell blinked, cast a quick glance around the room and opened the door.

Two people stood there, both female. 'Oh, hello,' said the younger one. 'You must be Grandad. I'm Lily and this is my sister Nicholette. Is Simmy here?'

Chapter Ten

'I was just taking the dog for a little walk,' said Russell. 'Go on in. Everybody's here.'

Cornelia gazed at her friend in puzzlement, pulling at the lead.

'She thinks I've come to take her out,' said Lily. 'I'm the one that usually does it. Well – when Simmy's at work, I mean.'

'Can we get in?' said the other woman. 'I'm freezing to death out here.'

'Yes, yes, come on in,' called Christopher. 'Simmy's upstairs. Shut the door.'

Russell and the dog made their escape and the visitors made for the stove. The front door opened directly into the big living room – something that both Simmy and Christopher were beginning to regret. It let the cold in, and provided an inadequate defence against invasions of their privacy.

'Happy Christmas!' said Lily, overbrightly. 'I've brought my sister to meet you.' She looked round the room, as if desperate for Simmy to materialise. 'She's staying a few days with us.'

'Pleased to meet you,' said Angie, stepping forward. 'I'm Persimmon's mother. Can I make you a cup of tea?'

'Or ginger wine or something?' added Christopher.

At that point Simmy came downstairs empty-handed. 'Hey, Lily,' she said, from the bottom step. 'I thought we'd already said Happy Christmas on Saturday. We've eaten the mince pies. You can have the tin back.' She looked at the stranger. 'Lily's sister – right?' The woman was four inches taller than Lily, with a long chin and dark eyes rather close together. She looked slightly Dickensian to Simmy. Miss Murdstone came to mind.

'Pleased to meet you,' said Nicholette. 'Ginger wine would be very nice, thank you.'

By the time everyone had found somewhere to sit, and Robin had shown the newcomers the Christmas tree, Russell and Cornelia were back. 'No need to go out again for a while,' he reported. 'It's arctic out there.'

Lily laughed ruefully. 'So we discovered. It's only about fifty yards from our house, and my nose almost froze off.'

Simmy wanted to ask again why they'd come, anxious that they'd hear the baby and make awkward enquiries. If Lily was tired of her sister's company, why would she bring her along on the visit? An answer soon came.

'Lily wanted me to meet you. She was talking about you – the auction house and the flower shop. Our mother thinks you're an asset to the village.'

'Oh, Nic – she doesn't!' Lily protested. 'She's still in

a state about that man from Borrowdale accosting me in the summer.'

'But she doesn't blame these people for that,' argued the sister. She gave Simmy a long intimate look. 'I'm a solicitor, you see. I find everything I've heard about you so *interesting*.'

'I didn't mean she doesn't like you,' Lily tried to explain, her face very red. 'But Nic isn't saying it right. She thinks it's great that I get to walk Cornelia and earn a bit doing it.' Lily's mother was sixty, a dedicated housewife who did not go out much. Her father was a civil servant, close to retirement. He enjoyed reading history and going on Mediterranean holidays. Their three children were a credit to them in different ways.

Christopher poured ginger wine and found some biscuits. 'We're all out of mince pies,' he lied. There was a whole tin of them yet to be broached.

Simmy's heart was making its presence felt, thumping a warning that she could not ignore. She was surely breaking the law keeping that baby hidden away upstairs. If anybody found out, they'd take him away. She felt like the people who'd hidden Anne Frank must have felt when anyone in authority came to the door. She kept wondering whether it was best to keep things noisy downstairs, to drown out any cries, or stay quiet for fear of waking him.

'A solicitor, eh?' said Russell. 'Well done you.'

'Don't be so patronising,' his wife reproached him. 'Where do you practise?' she asked Nicholette.

'Sheffield, actually. Family law. My brother's in Leeds. He's in management.'

'Management!' cried Russell inanely. Simmy realised

113

that he had understood her worry and opted for noisy distraction as the best strategy. She was also put in mind of Fran Bunting with her own branch of 'management'.

'I bet that covers a multitude of sins,' Russell burbled.

Lily had joined Robin on the floor close to the tree. 'What a lot of presents! And you'll be opening them tomorrow, won't you? Do you think there'll be one for Cornelia?'

Robin gave this intent thought and then shook his head.

'Maybe a bone? Or a doggie toy?'

'It's a shame when you've only got the one kiddie at Christmas, isn't it?' said Nicholette. 'I remember when Lily was little, and we were so much older – we all sat round with her in the middle opening her presents like a little princess. No wonder she got so spoilt.'

Robin was following this with moderate success. 'Baby,' he tried to explain. 'Robin and baby.'

Everyone looked at Simmy with a wide variety of expressions. 'We live in hope,' said Russell archly.

Simmy forced a smile. 'I think I'm getting past it, actually.' Cornelia, having got too warm by the fire, strolled over and climbed onto the sofa beside her mistress. Simmy put an arm around her, grateful for the support.

Robin was pleased at the effect his words were having. 'Baby cry,' he reported seriously.

'That's right, son,' said Christopher. 'Babies certainly do cry.'

Lily had not missed the strange atmosphere, and neither had her sister. 'Does he know any babies?' Lily wondered.

'He sees them around. And there's a TV programme we

watch, where people take their little ones and sit in a circle with them. It's one of his favourites.' Simmy inwardly cringed at her own behaviour. Lily did not deserve to be deceived.

'Are you married, Nicholette?' Russell asked, trying to see her left hand. 'Any prospect of making Lily an auntie?'

The woman shook her head firmly. 'Not me. I'm a career woman through and through. With the best will in the world, you can't pursue a real profession if you've got a child.' She looked at Simmy with far greater patronage than Russell could ever achieve. 'Don't you agree?'

'Probably,' said Simmy. 'Although millions of women seem to manage it. It helps if you can work from home, I suppose.'

'Huh!' sniffed Nicholette, as if that sort of thing was only for wimps.

'Well,' said Angie, actually making rolling-up-her-sleeves movements. 'This isn't getting the mushrooms stuffed – as I think Katharine Whitehorn might have said, before any of you lot were born. Nice to meet you both. I expect you've got a few more neighbours to drop in on? Let's not keep you any longer.'

Simmy had to bury her face in Cornelia's neck to hide her grin. *Thanks Mum,* she mouthed. *I owe you one.* The dog, feeling herself tickled, turned and gave Simmy a lick on the nose.

Lily and her sister had no choice but to drain their wine and get to their feet. 'Oh yes,' said Lily. 'You'll be busy. We might go and see Mrs Anstruther,' she said without enthusiasm. 'You know, Nic, the one who gives me old jumpers to unravel.'

'Why not?' shrugged Nicholette. 'It passes the time.'

They pulled on woolly hats and scarves and departed. Thirty seconds later, Jerome sent a reverberating wail through the house.

'Baby cry,' said Robin.

'He is definitely hungry,' said Angie, twenty minutes later. 'If you ask me, he's been getting almost nothing since he's been here. I am doing him a bottle right now.' Which she did with impressive speed. Simmy struggled with herself, knowing her mother was right, and she had been more than foolish to think there was any other way. Russell and Christopher both hesitated to comment on something so female, but it was clear that they were in accord with Angie.

'I know. It was ridiculous to think I could suddenly supply enough for him all by myself,' Simmy admitted.

'It was worth a try,' said Christopher. 'He was so co-operative, it seemed to make sense.'

'The thing is,' Russell said slowly, 'now we think we know who the murder victim is, we should probably face up to things a bit more. I mean, we're hiding this child, aren't we? We could be accused of *abducting* him.'

'Or we could be keeping him safe from unknown elements, that are highly likely to be dangerous,' said Simmy. 'What if it is Albanian drug gangs, and the dead man was involved – if they know he's got a baby son, they might come for him as well.'

'Steady on!' cautioned Russell. 'You're getting a bit carried away there. We ought to stick to known facts.'

'Which are in very short supply,' said Christopher. 'We

really don't know anything for sure.'

Russell gave this some thought. 'Well, who knew the woman was pregnant, for a start? Surely that couple who took her in must have noticed?'

Simmy answered him. 'It was easy to miss. I think she was actually in labour when I was talking to her, and I didn't suspect a thing. But I do feel bad that we're not more worried about her. Where is she? She must be sore and miserable and scared. And in the end, she'll probably want her baby back.'

'It would be the best thing for him if she did,' said Russell.

'I know. But the note seemed fairly definite that she was giving him up for good. I've been repeating it to myself ever since I saw it. "I have given him life, I can do no more". That's what it said. But she might not have meant it – or changed her mind since.'

'Indeed,' said Christopher firmly.

Simmy gave him a narrow look before going on, 'And she put his name in the note as well. As if she'd decided it a long time ago.' She cocked her head in thought. 'So maybe she *did* know she was pregnant after all. Maybe she knew exactly what she was going to do when he was born.'

'The woman who brought him here must know a lot more than she told us,' said Christopher. 'Don't you think?'

'I don't know. I think she probably decided to pass the buck to us in a panic. On the face of it, she seemed pretty shocked. She sat there in the pub all relaxed and friendly. It wasn't until she got a phone call from some nosy old neighbour that she tensed up a bit. And that was because she thought she might be being burgled, or so she said.'

The repetitive debriefing took them to teatime at half past four – a special Christmas Eve tea that had long been a tradition with both the Straws and the Hendersons, who had actually shared it a few times. The Henderson family, comprising parents and five offspring, had settled in the Lake District not long after their first son was born. Many years later the Straws had followed, minus their daughter, and established a B&B in Windermere. Throughout the intervening decades, the two families had enjoyed countless summer holidays together in North Wales. Once they were neighbours, this had extended to Christmas and even Easter gatherings at times.

'It was like having Anne Frank in the attic,' Simmy said. 'I was terrified.'

'We've burnt our bridges now,' said Russell. 'That solicitor woman will testify against us when it all has to come out.'

'What did we do wrong?' asked Angie. 'We didn't tell any outright lies. Don't you hate it when people drop in like that? It's so rude.' For a former B&B hostess, Angie Straw could be decidedly inhospitable. The baby had consumed half a bottle of formula and was now slung over her shoulder, his face against her neck.

'Poor Lily,' Simmy sighed. 'She's obviously being driven mad by that awful sister.'

'She would be a solicitor, wouldn't she,' said Christopher. 'Made me feel like a criminal just having her look at me.'

When Simmy's phone summoned her, she was relieved.

The conversation had gone on too long and was too full of forebodings for comfort.

'Ben,' she said. 'Happy Christmas.'

'Have you told the police about the baby?' he launched in, without preamble. 'Bonnie's just told me all about it.'

'Why did she leave it so long?'

'I've been out with my dad and Wilf. We went down to Newby Bridge and had a bit of a walk. It was too cold for the usual five miles, though.'

'Is Bonnie there with you now?'

'No. She's coming down tomorrow afternoon. Corinne wants her till then, apparently. There's a bit of a party with some of her former foster kids. But Bonnie's told her about your miracle baby, and she wants to know all about it. Did you tell the police? Have they come for him?'

'They won't do that on Christmas Eve,' said Simmy defiantly. 'And, anyway, we didn't call them. We're not breaking any laws, are we?'

'Actually, you probably are. Who's registered the birth? There has to be a medical attendant, by law – if not at the actual birth, then right after. The mother has to be checked out. Why did they dump him on *you* specifically? Who are these people anyway?'

'Ben – why don't you just forget about it and concentrate on Christmas? It'll all get sorted out later in the week when things get back to normal. The baby's perfectly safe here with us. We've got everything he needs and he's very contented. And nobody has to register his birth for another six weeks. It's all perfectly fine. We've talked it through a hundred times, and everyone agrees we're doing the best thing for him.'

'It's not fine, Simmy, and you know it. Where's his mother – and what about the fact that a man was murdered right there on your doorstep? Have you forgotten about that?'

'I'm trying to,' she snapped. 'It's nowhere near our doorstep, either. It's more than three miles away.'

'I think I ought to report it if you don't. But Bonnie won't let me. She says it would be a betrayal.'

'She's right. It's none of your business. You don't even know for sure that there *is* a baby. I could be inventing the whole thing.'

'Ha!' he scoffed. 'As if.'

'You have no idea what female hormones can do. I might be having some sort of episode where I conjure a fictitious baby to satisfy my craving for one. It happens.'

'It doesn't,' he said, not sounding altogether sure. 'Besides, you've already got a baby. Robin, I mean.'

'That's right. So just go away and stop bullying me. I've got both my parents, a husband and neighbours dropping in. I don't need your input as well.' Then she softened. 'Sorry – that was mean. But you did ask for it. Just enjoy the turkey and I'll see you in a few days.'

'Goose. We're having goose,' he said. 'And I still think you should report the baby to *someone*. Even Corinne thinks so.'

'Bye, Ben, and have a happy Christmas.'

The protracted 'tea' was still not properly under way when someone else came to the door, knocking with a strange, muffled rhythm. Angie still had the baby, trying to get him to take more milk. Simmy was offering Robin toast and Marmite. Cornelia was back in front of the fire

120

and gave a single defending-the-castle bark. Russell went automatically to open it before anyone could stop him – which nobody seemed inclined to try anyway. 'Who's that, I wonder?' said Christopher. 'Carol singers?'

'Good God, man! What happened?' they heard Russell exclaim. Cornelia barked again, for good measure.

Chapter Eleven

Simmy was the first to get from the kitchen to the living room, where she stopped and stared for several seconds. 'Of all people!' she gasped. 'What . . . ? How . . . ?'

'Don't just stand there, girl. He's hurt,' Russell snapped. 'Look at him.'

Detective Inspector Nolan Moxon of the Cumbria CID stood on the threshold, the door still open. A purple lump surrounded his right eye and his right arm was cradled protectively across his chest. He was shivering.

'Skidded on some ice,' he said. 'Just up at the junction. No other vehicle involved. Car safely off the road. Bashed against a stone wall, hit my head and arm.' He shivered. 'Thought I should find somewhere warm to wait for the recovery vehicle.'

'And you naturally thought of us,' said Simmy. 'My dad said the roads weren't icy, because there's been a dry spell.'

'Trust me to find the one patch between here and

Windermere,' the detective tried to joke. But something was clearly causing extreme discomfort, making speaking, standing or even breathing rather disagreeable. 'Might have cracked a rib,' he added apologetically.

'For heaven's sake, come and sit by the fire. Hot sweet tea as well,' Russell ordered. 'What a thing to happen!'

Simmy was still trying to make sense of it all. 'Why were you up here, anyway?' she asked. 'Not delivering Christmas cards?'

Moxon made no immediate reply. He succumbed to Russell's ministrations with meek gratitude, yelping as his arm caught the side of the chair he was given.

'Broken or dislocated,' Russell diagnosed. 'I'd guess the latter – which tends to be a lot more painful. Elbow, by the look of it. Nasty.'

'Did the airbag go off?' asked Christopher, who had joined them a moment before. 'That can break ribs, apparently.'

Moxon sat back very carefully and closed his eyes. 'That tea sounds good,' he said. 'Is somebody making it?'

'I'll go,' said Russell. 'Back in a minute.' He trotted into the kitchen where they all heard him telling Angie that there was a policeman in the house with a number of injuries, not necessarily minor.

'I've been here all day,' Moxon said, with audible breaths between words. 'A man's been murdered at Glenridding. I assumed you'd have heard.'

'Oh yes,' said Simmy, feeling immensely foolish. 'I forgot.' Which was true – the sight of her much-loved friend so bruised and battered had driven everything else out of her head.

'Door to door. All through Patterdale as well.'

Simmy had learnt not to even try to fathom the mechanics of the Cumbrian police districts and how officers were dispersed. Moxon lived in Windermere, and had largely kept to that area until Simmy had moved north, with murders dogging her every few months. Moxon had been called in by Penrith once Simmy had moved, with his special relationship proving helpful at times.

But Christopher was not afraid to ask: 'Rather far from your patch, isn't it?'

Moxon sighed. 'Skeleton staff. Wanted to get the legwork done before tomorrow.'

Suddenly there were numerous questions Simmy wanted to ask. How much did the police know about the dead man? What had they been told by the local people? How close were they to knowing who killed the man – and was Diellza anywhere in the picture? And what would the reaction be if they knew there was a baby?

But she couldn't ask any of them because the poor man could hardly speak. 'We'll have to call an ambulance,' she concluded.

Moxon did not argue. He merely nodded and said, 'I think the breakdown people might agree with you.'

Simmy frowned. 'What's it got to do with them?'

He pulled a mobile phone from his coat pocket awkwardly using his left hand. 'They were the only call I made. They'll phone any time now to say they're coming – I hope. I'll tell them I'm here. Someone will have to go and talk to them by the car.' Again, he was panting after every third or fourth word. 'I think I might be having a pneumothorax. Punctured lung from a broken rib.'

'Oh God!' yelped Christopher. 'Give me the phone.' He snatched it and keyed 999. It seemed a long time before he got to speak to anyone, and then he gave an impressively urgent account of the injuries, which seemed to be effective. He looked hard at Moxon and asked, 'Is there an open wound?' Moxon shook his head and Christopher reported this. 'All right,' he finished. 'We'll watch out for them.'

'Thirty minutes at least,' he reported. 'They were fairly concerned, I must say.' He was still scrutinising the patient. 'Can you take a deep breath?' he asked.

Moxon cautiously experimented, his left hand pressing tightly on his right side. 'More or less,' he said. 'But it hurts. It's very tight down here.'

Robin came wandering through from the kitchen at that point, and Simmy gathered him to her before he could climb on the injured man. The child gave an identical close scrutiny to the one his father had just made, and then said, 'Man.'

'That's right,' Simmy agreed. 'Poorly man.'

Only then, after a good ten minutes, did Simmy remember the baby. She looked at Christopher, wondering whether he had been actively trying to conceal Jerome's existence. Were her parents doing the same? Had her lapse actually helped the situation, making her behave normally, rather than the blushing and stammering there might have been?

There was a lull, in which she suspected everyone was holding their breath in case the baby started to cry. Then Russell appeared with a mug of tea. 'We called an ambulance,' said Christopher. 'We think he's got a punctured lung. They'll be half an hour or more.'

'Ah! In that case, we might have to keep him off any food or drink,' said Russell.

'Fluids are fine,' gasped Moxon, reaching for the mug.

'You don't actually seem to be in shock,' said Russell, giving it to him reluctantly. 'That's what hot sweet tea is meant to be for.'

'It helps,' Moxon insisted. 'And I expect I am in shock, actually.' He took several sips, and then set the mug down on the low table beside his chair. Then he deliberately inhaled again. 'It's no worse,' he reported. He looked around the room with greater attention than before, and then addressed Simmy. 'Where's your mother?'

'In the kitchen.'

'Doesn't she want to come and see me in my reduced condition?'

'"Reduced condition"?' echoed Russell with a laugh. 'Is that what this is?'

'Don't be mean, Dad,' said Simmy. 'He's in pain, and look at his poor face.'

'What's wrong with my face?' the detective asked. 'It feels all right.'

'You've got a black eye,' Russell told him. 'Purple, to be exact. And very swollen. I'm surprised you can see out of it.'

Moxon gingerly fingered his face, wincing as he touched the centre of the swelling. 'Ouch! I see what you mean. But I can see out of it, at least.'

'Could be a fractured occiput,' said Russell. 'Common result of road accidents, banging your head on the side of the vehicle, as you must have done. They'll be giving you multiple X-rays at this rate.'

Moxon's phone interrupted his final words and the patient handed it to Christopher. 'Can you talk to them? It's the Green Flag people. And it would be a kindness to go up and meet them. Sorry,' he added. 'It's cold out there.'

'Your breathing is a lot better,' Simmy observed, listening to him.

'The body heals itself remarkably at times,' said Russell. 'There'll be a whole lot of emergency responses going on in there, trying to seal the breach where the air's escaping. If there's too much, you see, the lung can't expand and you don't get oxygen and you die.' He spoke much too cheerfully for the subject matter. 'I did a first-aid course, you know, when we first had the B&B. It was recommended.'

'Yes, I'll come and find you,' Christopher was saying to the person on the phone. 'It's all rather complicated.'

'You've done everything in the wrong order, it seems to me,' said Russell, still in full flow. 'First you should have called yourself in to your colleagues. Then the ambulance and finally the car people. Don't you think?'

'The car's need seemed greater than mine at first,' said Moxon meekly. 'My legs were working, and my brain, as far as I could tell.' He breathed again, testing himself. 'And I just wanted to get home.'

'Here's your phone,' said Christopher, proffering it.

'Keep it. You might need it. When are they coming?'

'About five minutes, they said. I'll have to go.'

'Coat, gloves and scarf,' Simmy ordered.

Robin and Cornelia watched as their lord and father donned outdoor wear and went off into the darkness. They were both very conscious of a drastic change of routine. The whole day had been unusual, not least because neither of them got as much attention as they would have liked.

'Where's your mother?' Moxon asked again, with a much sharper enquiry than before. 'Is something going on?'

Simmy's conscience was entirely incapable of outright lying. 'Sort of,' she said. 'But I don't think you should worry about that now. It's nothing urgent.'

'Does it have anything to do with the murder at Glenridding? Anything at all?' The sudden intensity made him cough, and he shook his head impatiently at his own weakness. 'If it does, and I've been sitting here like a stuffed dummy ignoring it all, it's going to look bad, isn't it? For me, I mean.'

'You're hurt. Nothing's going to look bad. You'll be off in an ambulance any moment now.'

'Tell me,' he persisted.

As if in reply, the baby chose that moment to wake up and express discontent. The kitchen door was open and sound travelled easily. Angie would have heard every word that was spoken in the living room, and perhaps tensed at their import, thus disturbing the baby. 'Is that a *baby*?' Moxon asked, his good eye wide with surprise.

Simmy merely nodded. Then she called, 'Better come out, Mum. You must be fed up, sitting out there by yourself.'

There was no time for a single word of explanation. A vehicle could be heard outside the front door, and within seconds there was a loud knock. 'That must be the ambulance,' said Simmy. 'They've been quick.' Blessedly so, she added silently to herself.

It was not the first time she had witnessed the controlled bustle of paramedics following precise routines, muttering to each other, running back for equipment, elbowing relatives aside if they got too close. There had never been a time when she'd found herself actually liking them. Even their kindness, when it came, seemed scripted. There was an overarching sense of their own importance, an unassailable rightness in everything they did and said. They probably *were* right, most of the time, but they didn't know the whole picture. They didn't know what these particular individuals expected of them. And quite often they did not listen to important explanations.

Russell felt this even more acutely than his daughter. 'He's a police detective,' he announced. 'Skidded on ice. You must have seen his car up at the junction. We think he's got a punctured lung and a damaged elbow.'

'All right, sir,' said one of the two men, shining a small torch into Moxon's bad eye.

'And perhaps a broken rib,' Russell continued undaunted. 'You won't have the training or equipment to aspirate it, will you?'

'Depends on the severity,' snapped the man. 'This seems fairly stable. Can you take a breath for me, sir?' he asked Moxon.

Simmy was occupied with sweeping her child and dog to the far end of the room. Robin was transfixed by the commotion, and the uniforms. The men seemed to be bundled in more layers than usual, with heavy boots. Angie sat on one end of the sofa with the baby, saying nothing. 'Oh – what about your wife?' she asked as Moxon was at last being walked to the door, tightly held between the two men. 'We should phone her.'

'No rush,' was the reply. 'She knows to expect me when she sees me. I'll call her when I've got more news.'

'Christopher's got your phone,' she reminded him.

Moxon grunted impatiently. 'I'll ask these kind gentlemen to stop and get it back. We've got to pass my car, haven't we.'

In the open doorway, he hung back, and turned for a last look at Angie. 'That's a baby,' he said, as if only just letting himself notice. 'You're going to have to explain.'

'Don't worry about it,' said Simmy. 'Good luck at the hospital.' Then she had a thought. 'Do you want Christopher to go with you? He will if you ask him.'

'Come on, now,' urged a paramedic. 'No hanging about in the cold.'

And they were gone.

'Do you think we got away with it?' said Angie.

'Of course we didn't,' said Russell.

Chapter Twelve

Somehow it was still not much past six o'clock. 'Better get this boy to bed,' Simmy said, giving Robin a squeeze. This was her own precious child, she reminded herself. Was it treachery to become so enamoured of another woman's baby – or simply unavoidable biology? Robin seemed so big, all of a sudden, and relatively independent. Besides, he *liked* the baby, so there couldn't possibly be any harm – could there? She looked across at Angie, in full grandmother mode with the newborn, and forced herself to face practicalities. 'We might find none of us gets much sleep tonight.' Then she turned to her father. 'Dad – do you want to do Robin's story?'

Christopher had returned ten minutes before and was warming himself up with a mug of coffee. Russell had laid chestnuts on the flat top of the woodstove. 'I couldn't go with him to Penrith,' Christopher pointed out, when asked. 'How would I have got home again?'

'You could have followed in the car,' said Simmy.

'So could you,' her husband flashed back. 'The man's your friend much more than he's mine. He's in good hands, anyway, and the car's been transported back to the place in Windermere that does all his repairs. I don't think there was a lot wrong with it, actually. Nothing a good panel-beater can't handle.'

'It's much too cold for anybody to make any needless journeys,' said Angie firmly.

'Right,' Christopher agreed. 'It's barely a quarter of a mile to the T-junction, and I felt as if I'd been in Siberia for hours by the time I'd walked it. It's the wind. It's absolutely vicious.'

'I just know we'll have a whole evening of phone calls,' Simmy predicted. 'Bonnie, probably.'

'Or Ben again,' Christopher agreed. 'Who else?'

'Could be anyone,' she said. 'Don't you feel that everything's hanging by a thread, or teetering on a cliff edge? If we get through Christmas without some great drama, I'll eat my . . . I'll eat the entire Christmas pudding by myself.'

'You won't be able to, because if we've got through Christmas, the pudding will all be gone,' Russell said. 'And anyway, who's scared of a bit of drama? How bad can it be?'

'Stop it,' his wife ordered. 'Where a new baby is concerned, it's not safe to fly in the face of fate.'

'I nearly forgot about the baby,' he admitted.

Robin was in the bath, being supervised by his mother and grandfather, when another person knocked on the door and Cornelia barked. Simmy heard Christopher answer it and felt thankful that the baby was invisibly and silently in the big bedroom. Angie was yet again in the kitchen doing something that made a clatter. Her B&B years had taught her the virtues of preparation in advance when it came to large scale catering.

'Dan!' came Christopher's loud exclamation of surprise. 'Come in, man. Is that east wind still raging?'

'I'm going down,' Simmy told her father. 'Can you cope here? Nappy, pyjamas, story, drink? Shout if you need me.'

'Who's Dan?' Russell whispered.

'Tell you later.' And she was down the stairs almost before the front door was closed. 'This is a surprise,' she said. 'I wasn't even sure you knew where we lived.' In an effort to avoid sounding wary, she had slipped into something almost challenging.

The man looked more than wary himself. His gaze moved from one Henderson to the other and back again. 'You two,' he said. 'Hidden depths. Connections. I'm hoping you'll have some answers for me.'

'You sound like the KGB,' said Simmy.

'Do I? Sorry, if so. I'm here about Diellza. You know she's gone missing? Everybody's desperately worried about her, us especially. The *weather*.' He wiped a reddened hand across his brow. 'Not to mention Christmas.'

'Ah!' said Christopher, throwing a worried glance at his wife. 'Sit down. Have a ginger wine or something.'

Dan Bunting hurried to the fire, bending towards it and rubbing his cold hands together. 'Never thought to bring gloves,' he muttered.

'You didn't *walk*, did you?' Simmy asked.

'Hardly. I'd be dead in a ditch by now if I'd tried. But there's nowhere to park for most of your village. Had to go right down to the end and walk back. That was bad enough.'

'When did you last see Diellza?' Simmy asked. 'How much do you know about her background? Have you seen Celia?'

'Now who's channelling the KGB?' Dan tried to joke. 'The thing is, I had no idea you two were so thick with the police until today. They've been all over Glenridding and Patterdale asking questions, stopping traffic, causing all kinds of mayhem. The Instagram's gone mad, not to mention everyone crowding into the pub to talk about it. You wouldn't believe the rumours.' He paused and sat down in the big armchair that most people favoured. 'Why did you ask about Celia?'

By an unspoken agreement, Christopher was leaving everything to Simmy. He acknowledged her greater skill when it came to the subtleties. 'Ginger wine all right?' he asked, and at a very slight nod from the visitor, he went off to get it.

Simmy brushed aside Dan's question. 'It doesn't matter. Let's stick to the basics. We're completely out of the loop down here. We've hardly left the house all day. Even the dog's only been out for about two minutes. I don't understand why you've bothered to come. What do you think we can tell you?'

'It was Aoife's idea, actually. She came over, a bit ago – she lives just up the hill from us, as you might know. Anyway, she somehow got the idea that you had a hotline to the cops. Something about a string of murders in the area that you'd been involved with. Apparently, it's common knowledge – especially the one this year in Askham – and Fran and I must be living under a stone not to know about it.' He shook his head ruefully. 'I do work away quite a lot, and Fran's never been one for gossip. We don't really do Facebook and that sort of thing. But even we can't miss everything.'

Christopher appeared with a glass of ginger wine. 'This'll warm you up,' he said. His tone was verging on the unfriendly.

Simmy felt similarly ill-disposed. 'So you came barging down here to see if we know who killed that man, did you? Isn't that a bit stupid? Why is it so important to you? You didn't know him, did you?' She heard herself, and stopped. Something wasn't right. She tried to think logically. 'Have you heard who the dead man is?' she asked.

Dan drained the glass in seconds before replying. 'Well, of course. At least three people have told us today. Not counting the police, who are desperately hunting for Diellza. We feel so *helpless*,' he wailed. 'And responsible, of course. We should never have left her on her own.'

So the Buntings had not known about the pregnancy. But something still didn't fit. 'How did the police know that Diellza was here, staying with you? Even if they found people in Manchester who knew her and her husband, would they know where she was?'

'Someone in the village must have made the connection,' he said vaguely. 'I never thought to wonder about that. They just came to the door this morning and said they understood I had a Mrs McGuire as a house guest and could they speak to her. They wanted to tell her about her husband, of course. We had to admit we hadn't seen her since . . . well, we couldn't remember exactly. Sometime on Saturday, we think. But we did hear her early on Sunday. We've hardly been there ourselves, you see.'

'I bet it was Aoife who told the police where she was. It's the sort of thing she'd do.'

Dan looked shocked. Then he shook his head and took a deep breath. 'Let me explain. You've got it wrong about Aoife. She's genuinely worried about Diellza. We all are, of course. She wasn't well on Friday, after the party, and she huddled in her room all day Saturday and Sunday morning. Yesterday, that was. And then, when our backs were turned, she just vanished. Packed all her stuff and disappeared. And now the police have clocked that she was married to the dead man, they fancy her as prime suspect. Which means we got the third degree about her. Every word she ever said, every move she made, they wanted to know about. Plus, they wanted a list of everyone at Friday's party, which is when your names came up. And Celia's.' He frowned. 'What is it about Celia? Aoife seemed to think she might know something, as well. But she's not at home. I passed her house just now – the car's gone and it's all in darkness. Which looks bad, because Fran's sure she never said she was going away.'

'I doubt if she's the murderer, all the same,' said Christopher.

Simmy was working harder than ever to keep her thoughts straight. 'Yes, but *did* you know him? Alexander Whatever-it-is? Was he looking for Diellza? He'd got pretty close, if so. I'm trying to work out the timings – do they know when he died? When was he last seen?'

'They wanted everyone to account for their movements from the middle of Friday to the early hours of Saturday. I suppose that answers your questions. Not a very big window, as they say.'

'And had you ever met him?' prompted Christopher.

Dan shook his head. 'No, never. I even doubted if he existed, after knowing Diellza for a few weeks. I was never sure she was telling the truth about anything. She wasn't like most of the people I work with. You probably think it's very odd, the way we took her in. I only did it because she assured me it would be for a very short time. Fran left it all to me. She kept out of the way mostly. It's not the first time I've brought someone home with me. She says I'm hopelessly gullible, but there's never been any trouble before this.' He was prattling, talking quickly, rubbing his hands together and staring at the floor. 'So you haven't seen her?' he finished, raising his head. 'You don't know where she is?'

'Of course we don't,' said Simmy. 'She's a total stranger to us. Why would we?'

Angie had been in the kitchen all along, given a quick explanation of the visitor by Christopher when he went for the wine. Now she appeared, wiping her hands on a tea towel and looking very brisk. 'It's all ready for the morning now,' she announced. 'Your big roasting pan was in an awful state – can't have been used for months.'

'Not since last Christmas,' said Simmy. 'What was the matter with it?'

'You can't have cleaned it properly. It had some sort of mould in one corner.'

'Well, thanks for doing that.' Simmy turned to Dan.

'This is my mother, Angie Straw. Mum, this is Dan Bunting, where we went to the party on Friday.'

'Pleased to meet you,' said Angie carelessly. 'I'd better go and see if everything's all right upstairs.' There were sounds of footsteps overhead.

'Sit down, for goodness' sake,' Simmy ordered. 'You're doing all my work for me. That wasn't the idea at all.'

'I warn you – Russell's no good at nappies. Especially not the night-time ones.'

'He hasn't had much practise, has he?' defended Christopher, who was also liable to the same accusation.

Angie hovered indecisively, trying to catch her daughter's eye without the visitor noticing. The atmosphere in the room had changed with her entry, growing more spiky and suspicious. 'Nasty weather for paying a visit,' she observed. Dan had shifted to the edge of his chair, as if wondering whether he should stand up on being introduced. 'Did you want something in particular?'

'I did, actually,' he said, refusing to be intimidated. Angie Straw could wither most people with one of her looks or sharp remarks. Simmy was torn between gratitude to her mother for trying to behave appropriately and anxiety that she would say something disastrous. Quite why she was so concerned to hide baby Jerome from Dan Bunting was unclear, but it was a strong instinct.

'I'm not sure Dad's done the little one's bedtime drink,' she said carefully to Angie. 'He might be wanting it by now, don't you think?'

Angie looked at her watch, and raised an eyebrow. 'He had a good drink at four,' she said. Then she looked directly at Dan. 'Have you got children?' she asked.

'No, no,' he said quickly. 'That was never on the cards, thanks to some trouble Fran had as a girl. It's just us. We don't know one end of a child from the other, to our shame.' He laughed rather mirthlessly. 'It always looks to be awfully hard work.'

'Oh, it is,' Angie agreed cheerfully. 'I can't imagine how people manage without grandparents standing by.'

'You did,' Simmy pointed out.

'It was easier then, for some reason,' said Angie. 'But maybe you're right. I'll get that little man a drink and run up with it.'

'Thanks, Mum,' said Simmy. With any luck she'd have a bottle all ready and waiting for when the baby woke up, as he surely would before long.

'So,' said Christopher heavily. 'Have we answered all your questions? Your car's going to be all iced up at this rate.'

Dan shuffled on the chair but did not stand up. 'I don't know,' he said. 'I've lost the thread.'

'*Was* there a thread?' Christopher teased. 'Or did you just want to check that we weren't harbouring Diellza – or something?'

Simmy winced. That was definitely too close to the reality for comfort. On the other hand, it could turn out to be rather clever, she realised. If Dan did actually suspect them of being actively involved in the disappearance of Diellza, this might flush him out. The man's motives could surely not be as simple as he claimed.

'I didn't think that. Of course I didn't. But I had to be sure. She's out there somewhere, in this freezing weather. Where did she go? She must have had a plan of some sort, a person she thought she could go to.' He looked at Simmy. 'She was talking to you, I saw her. She obviously liked you. I didn't know if you'd invited her, or something. Perhaps she thought a Christmas here would be nicer than with us. But that's ridiculous, because she would have *said* something. We never did anything to scare her, or make her feel unwelcome. We can't believe she'd just go off without a word, at a moment's notice. It's so . . .'

'Rude,' said Simmy. 'Ungrateful. But don't you think it must be to do with her husband being killed – probably by some sort of criminal gang? She could have found out about that and run away because she thought they'd be after her next. Isn't that what the police are bound to think, rather than that she'd killed him herself? They've got to be worried about her.'

'Probably,' he said slowly, frowning. 'It seems very far-fetched, though – criminal gangs out in the freezing fells. Don't you think?'

Simmy remembered Celia saying *It's a lot more domestic than that*, when she had suggested some nefarious Albanian connection. How did Celia know, she wondered now. And where *was* she? 'A bit too dramatic,' she agreed. 'Although . . .'

Christopher finished her sentence for her. 'It's already pretty dramatic, isn't it? A man murdered and left in a beck, hardly any distance from where his wife was holed up. And if I've got the timings right, it's quite possible that she is the one who did it. Isn't that the most obvious explanation?'

Not if she was in the middle of giving birth, thought Simmy, wondering whether Christopher was deliberately creating a smokescreen, or if he'd forgotten that detail.

'She did have a phone,' Dan said. 'But I never saw her use it, and nobody ever called her. There might have been texts, I suppose. The police asked about all that, obviously.' He clenched his jaw. 'We've *got* to find her, before . . .' he stopped for a few seconds, 'before something happens to her.'

'Okay,' said Christopher. 'So she fixed up something for herself, probably during Saturday, and then went off quietly without the bother of explaining herself to you. Maybe she met a car down the hill from you – by the shop, let's say. Very ungrateful, as Simmy says, but perhaps that's the way they do things in Albania. Lots of cultures are a bit low on gratitude, by our standards. They take it for granted that it goes without saying. I bet she thanked you when you first took her in, didn't she?'

'In a way,' Dan acknowledged. 'I probably told her no thanks were necessary.'

Simmy wished Christopher would stop talking, so the man would have no option but to get up and leave. While the conversation was still going, he was sure to stay, and Jerome might well make his presence felt at any moment, which felt as if it would be seriously bad news. She did her best to silently convey the wish.

It worked to some extent. 'Well, you really should get back,' Christopher urged. 'You must have things to do – it's Christmas tomorrow, don't forget.'

Dan sighed. 'You mean *you* have things to do. You've got a houseful. We've just got us – we don't make too much of it, to be honest. Friday's party was as festive as we're ever going to get.'

When he got no response to this, he finally heaved himself

141

out of his chair. Simmy treated him to a smile, giving him a good inspection. He was a fairly heavyset man, which was obvious as he stood next to the much more slender Christopher. He had opened his coat but not taken it off, and now he made much of zipping it up again. 'I hope the car starts,' he said. 'It wasn't too keen when I came here.'

Christopher bit back the ready offer to help if necessary, having received a look from Simmy.

'Well . . .' said Dan. 'Thanks for the wine. Sorry to disturb you.'

'No problem,' said Christopher heartily. 'You're obviously worried. I expect it'll all turn out right in the end, one way or another. Once Christmas is over, we can all get back to normal.'

'Hardly,' said Dan, and finally took himself off.

Simmy slumped bonelessly onto the sofa when Dan had gone. 'What was all that about?' she wondered. 'Something must have been extremely important for him to come out in this weather.'

'Checking that Diellza wasn't here? That's the only thing I can think of.'

'But he didn't, did he? She could easily have been hiding away upstairs – which her baby actually was doing, ironically. Are we assuming he has no idea the baby exists?'

Christopher shrugged. 'Looks like it. And there's no doubt he very much does want to find the woman.'

'I can't help feeling that he really does trust us, oddly enough. He believed what we told him. He never even asked to use the loo so he could snoop around.'

'Maybe he's snooping around now, outside, peering

through the window to see if Diellza comes out of hiding.'

'Too cold for much of that. But we'd better not bring the baby down for a bit, just in case.'

Christopher came over to her and sat next to her on the sofa. 'Um . . .' he began, 'where do things stand now, feeding-wise? Have you given up any idea of doing it yourself? Angie's given him two bottles now. If I remember rightly, that's not going to do anything to boost your supply.'

Simmy rested her head on his shoulder. 'I don't know,' she sighed. 'I *want* to. If we were keeping him long-term, I would never have considered a bottle. And it's better for him my way. But I know it's not sensible. It feels a bit silly, like a game, or an experiment. I suppose my hormones just took over last night, and I went with it. He's so small and new, I just thought I knew best what he needed.'

'He certainly makes Robin look like a giant.'

'What a funny evening we're having. What time is it now?'

'Seven-fifteen. Everything's nice and quiet upstairs. I don't know about you, but after that sleepless night I can hardly keep my eyes open.'

'I had a little zizz this afternoon. I don't feel too bad. You can't go to bed yet. We haven't done the stocking.' She lifted her head. 'Oh damn! I was going to get Robin to hang it by the fire with a mince pie for Santa. He'll be almost asleep by now. How could I forget that?'

'There's always next year,' said Christopher. 'And he's still a bit young for all that, anyway, don't you think?'

'Dratted Dan Bunting. I still don't understand what made him get us involved when he's got all those people

143

right on his doorstep to talk to. I thought we'd be far enough away to stay out of it.'

'Except we got very deeply involved the moment we agreed to take the baby,' Christopher reminded her.

'Only by accident,' she argued. 'At that point we had no idea that Jerome was linked to the murder – there wasn't really anything to get involved *in*. We were just being good citizens in a domestic emergency.'

'Yeah. Right,' said Christopher tonelessly.

Another phone call from Ben saved her from any further dispute. 'I have information,' he began. 'Can you talk?'

'Oh yes. Nobody's here, if that's what you mean. You missed the visitors.'

'Okay. So – the man definitely died from a knife wound to the neck, but that's only one bad thing that happened to him. He must have been pushed down into the Glenridding Beck, where it's full of big rocks, all icy and slippery and a fair drop from the path. The body was actually in the beck. There was ice on him. Almost impossible to ascertain the time of death. It must have been done in darkness, or anyone in the houses there would have seen. There are a few hardly any distance away. Surely, they can't all be holiday lets?'

'No,' Simmy agreed uncertainly. 'And isn't there a pub up there as well?'

'It's called the Traveller's Rest – I googled it just now. The body was found above that, but not very far. The police are going to be busy questioning anyone who could have heard something.'

'Actually, Ben, I think we knew most of that already.'

'Did we? It's all come from google so far – I really

want to go and see it all for myself. And I've been talking to my friend Nancy again. She's not privy to the police investigation, of course, but she's heard bits of speculation. The killer made no attempt to hide the man's identity, for one thing.'

'They've been doing house-to-house enquiries all day yesterday and today, apparently. Stirring everyone up, making them suspicious of each other. We're nicely out of it down here – or we thought we were. We had a visit from Dan Bunting just now, who appears to want to drag us into it, for some reason. He's the one in Glenridding where Diellza was staying.'

'Did he see the baby? I haven't forgotten about the baby, you know.'

'No, he didn't have any idea it was here. I'm sure he's got no idea there even *is* a baby.'

'So what did he want?'

'Diellza. The police have found out she was staying with him and Fran, and obviously want to find her. He says he feels responsible.'

'And there's absolutely no news of her?'

'Seems not. That's why Dan came down here, or so he says. She was staying with him and disappeared without a word on Sunday – yesterday – and he says he's terribly worried about her, in this cold.'

'You sound as if you don't believe him.'

'Do I? That's not exactly it. He was definitely very worried about her. I just don't get why he fixed on us. He says he saw me talking to Diellza and thought she seemed to like me, and that maybe she came here for sanctuary. He didn't say sanctuary,' she added, knowing how literal Ben could be. 'But it was probably what he thought.'

'Which implies that she was scared of something – possibly him, or the police. Is there any chance she killed the husband, then? The police are going to think that, aren't they? So it would be sensible to run off and hide somewhere. Leaving the baby fits – it'd be far easier without him.'

'She would have to be very tough. As far as we can work out, she was in labour right through Saturday night, and maybe much of the day. The police don't know about the baby. Neither do the Buntings, unless they're lying. The only person who definitely knows is Celia and she's gone missing as well.'

'So she's with the Albanian,' said Ben with certainty.

'She might be,' Simmy agreed. 'They might even be huddled in Celia's house with the lights off, but that wouldn't work for long. There's a nosy neighbour, for a start.'

'Simmy,' he began slowly, 'do you think you might have been set up somehow? That the plan all along was to dump the baby on you?'

'I can't imagine how or why. They can't have known when he would be born, for one thing. Are you suggesting the Buntings knew all along she was pregnant?'

'It's hard to believe they didn't.'

'Dan says they don't know anything about babies. I'm fairly sure they have no idea at all that Jerome exists.'

'What about the wife? Mrs Bunting?'

'Good question. Actually, I'd be more interested in a woman called Aoife' – she spelt it out for him – 'who is no fool and doesn't strike me as being very nice.'

'Anyone else?'

146

'Just a pregnant person called Louise. It's her third. She's pushy. The thing is, Ben, I really don't *know* any of these people. Ever since we came here, it's all been Robin and the shop and getting the house straight. I don't feel part of the community at all. I'm hoping to change that once we get Christmas out of the way. But there could be a powerful Mafia gang operating in Patterdale and I'd have no idea.'

Ben laughed. 'I think it's some other outfit in Albania. But the dead man's from Manchester, not Tirana. Has he ever even been there?'

'How would I know? Isn't there a lot of crime there? Diellza did imply she was escaping from something, sort of. Celia said it was domestic not political, but she might be wrong.'

'Drugs,' said Ben. 'And a bit of political unrest here and there. I don't know much about it, to be honest.'

'Does anybody? I couldn't even have named the capital.'

'Diellza must be *somewhere*,' he pointed out. 'And she probably had the sense to get indoors, given the outside temperature. If the police don't know about the baby, they won't be too concerned about her physical welfare, I suppose. But they'll definitely be making an effort to find her. They really *should* have been told about the baby. Bonnie and I both said so from the start.'

'Don't start that again.'

'So does anybody else know that you've got the child of the dead man hidden in your attic?'

'Well, Moxon did see him,' said Simmy. 'I haven't got around to telling you what happened to poor Moxon, have I? It was a real drama, but then Dan Bunting showed up, and we had him to think about instead.'

'So tell me,' Ben urged her.

She gave a rapid summary, up to the moment when he registered the fact of a small infant on Angie's lap. 'He wasn't even sure it was real, from the look of him. His head was banged pretty hard, and he was scared about his lung. And his elbow hurt.'

'Will he think it's yours? When did you last see him?'

'Um . . . probably four or five months ago. I suppose that would work. He'd be very upset that we hadn't told him, though.'

'If you haven't seen him since the Borrowdale business, that's six months ago, so it would certainly work.'

'That feels so awful – letting him believe a lie like that.'

'So tell him. Tell the people in Penrith. What have you got to be scared of? Nobody's going to come now and snatch the baby away, are they? It's Christmas Eve.'

'They might want to come and look at him and ask a hundred questions. I don't know what it's safe to tell them. I'd be getting Celia into trouble, for a start, as well as the Buntings. And besides, they won't want to get into a whole new area of investigation just hours before Christmas, as you said yourself.'

'They will if it helps to find the killer. Christmas doesn't matter to them when there's a murder to deal with. I was talking about social services, who I suspect aren't so keen to work all hours.'

'How would it help? Apart from removing Diellza from the list of suspects?'

'That would be pretty big. But they'd still want to find her, on the assumption that she probably knows who killed her man and why.'

148

'I'm not going to, Ben. Not until Wednesday, and then I might. We're all going to bed very early, and have a lovely family Christmas, with all the usual nonsense. I owe it to Robin.'

'He won't remember a single thing about it. He's not even two yet.'

'All right, then I owe it to myself. It's a time for bolstering relationships, catching up and having fun. We're going to do all that. My dad's in his mid-seventies, remember.'

'So what? You think this might be his last Christmas?'

'Something like that,' she said, feeling hollow at the very idea.

'Where is he? Can he hear you?'

'No. They're upstairs, both of them, with the children. They've been ages, come to think of it. I'd better go and see what's to do. Have a lovely day tomorrow, you and Bonnie and everybody. I don't want any phone calls before Wednesday, okay? That's an order.'

'Understood. And Merry Christmas to you too.'

Simmy went upstairs to find her father quietly reading to Robin, as the child dozed off in his cot. The room was chilly and she went to find another blanket. 'We still haven't got the heating working properly up here,' she whispered. 'Come down and sit by the fire,' Russell nodded and closed the book.

In the spare bedroom, Angie was stretched out on one of the twin beds with little Jerome snuggled into the crook of her arm. 'Is he asleep?' Simmy asked, still whispering.

'Not really. He had another half a bottle and seems to

149

be just drifting now. He really is very sweet, isn't he?'

Simmy felt a pang of irrational jealousy. Her mother had monopolised the baby all afternoon, becoming increasingly attached to him, by all appearances. 'We can put him to bed, then. I got the carrycot all nice for him, and he slept in it last night.'

'It's not very warm up here. Can you plug something in somewhere? Which room is he going to be in?'

'Ours,' said Simmy firmly. 'I'll get the fan heater out. Or maybe I'll have him in bed with me.'

Angie gave her a look. 'I thought the baby police had banned you from doing that, along with fifty other perfectly obvious and harmless things.'

'And you told me to ignore all that and do whatever worked. Robin didn't really like it. He got too hot. And Christopher always edged away until he was almost falling out. But it's the best way to keep this one warm – and he's so *new*. He must want the contact.'

'When Robin was this age, you'd only just come out of hospital. I don't imagine he got much contact for the first couple of days.'

'Right.' Simmy sighed. 'We do everything wrong in this culture, don't we?'

'As I've always said,' Angie agreed. 'But I have to admit that most kids turn out more or less all right, in spite of it all.'

'Although we'd never know how much better they might have been, would we?'

'I dare say we romanticise the practices of other societies. They might be more cheerful, but their health isn't much to boast about, is it?'

'If he wakes in the night I'm going to put him to the breast,' Simmy asserted. 'If it works, it'll save going down and trying to make up a bottle and disturbing Cornelia.'

'We can leave a bottle – or even two – in the fridge. You'd just have to warm it up for about five seconds in the microwave.'

'I don't want to,' said Simmy, stubbornly.

'Your milk probably isn't as good for him as formula, you know,' said Angie, slowly sitting up and laying the baby down on the bed. 'It might seem miraculous that you can produce it so readily, but it's unlikely to be very nutritious. I'm no expert, but logic suggests that what's right for a toddler is not the same as a newborn needs. When did you last feed Robin?'

'He was just over a year, and we were down to about two minutes once a day. Must have been April, I suppose. And there was a day when he was poorly and nothing else would pacify him. That was in May, I think.'

'Well, I can see it's a natural instinct. Believe it or not, I've felt a few flickers myself, cuddling him all day. One way and another, I think we can pride ourselves on giving him a perfectly satisfactory start in life, whatever happens next.'

'Moxon saw him, remember. Ben thinks he'll think it's mine. That hadn't occurred to me. But it's obvious, really.'

'And by far the best outcome, at least for another day or two.'

'It's eight o'clock, Mum. Come down and have some port and lemon. And help me with Robin's stocking. And we're roasting some chestnuts. It's Christmas Eve.'

'So it is. Let's leave this little man as he is for a bit.'

151

'He needs to be wrapped up better. Have you changed his nappy?'

Angie folded one side of the duvet over the little body, and pushed her daughter out of the room. 'He's perfectly fine,' she said. 'Sleeping like a little angel, as your father used to say.'

Chapter Thirteen

Much of the evening was spent talking about Detective Inspector Moxon, retelling stories from past episodes where he and Simmy had somehow managed to solve murders. 'He was good in Bowness,' Russell said, with a glance at Christopher. 'Poor old Kit.' The murder victim had been Christopher's father, which made the subject rather sensitive.

'And in Askham,' said Simmy. That was another time when things had come uncomfortably close to home, especially for Bonnie Lawson. 'And Threlkeld, in a way.'

'He was *hopeless* in Threlkeld,' Angie corrected her. 'Ben and Bonnie did all the work for him.'

'Coniston, Hawkshead, Staveley,' Christopher listed them on his fingers. 'At least he was always there, doing what detectives do, to the best of his ability. I hate to think of him spending Christmas Day in hospital. That's all wrong.'

Simmy sniffed, suddenly overcome with emotion at the thought. 'They might not keep him in,' she said optimistically.

'What's the treatment for a cracked occiput, I wonder?' said Russell.

'We need Ben to google it,' said Simmy.

'We do not,' argued Christopher. 'I can do that.' He fetched their laptop from the small room under the stairs and fired it up. 'How do you spell it?' he asked Russell. Half a minute later, he raised his eyebrows at his father-in-law and informed him that the word was actually 'occipital' and it was rare for it to fracture. 'I never knew any of this,' he said, having browsed the topic, feeling his own skull bones as he read about their construction. 'Looks to me as if Mr Moxon's going to be fine. Except for the lung and elbow, obviously.'

'Russell always thinks he's an expert in medical matters,' said Angie. 'But he mostly gets it wrong.'

'I might get the details a bit squiffy, but I do know the basics,' said Russell with dignity. 'Those ambulancemen listened to me, didn't they?'

'They didn't have much choice,' muttered Angie. 'So what happens when the man gets home and starts to wonder how come he saw a baby here?'

'We already decided he's going to think it's mine,' Simmy reminded her.

'Even then, he's going to want to get the story, isn't he? Boy or girl, date of birth, name. He'll probably want to be godfather. If he isn't already?'

'You know he isn't,' snapped Simmy. 'Besides, after tomorrow, we'll go to the police of our own accord and tell them about Jerome. It can't make any difference to the murder investigation.'

'You keep saying that,' Angie accused her, 'and I keep thinking it probably isn't true. It seems to me that the fact of the baby might well be the key to the whole thing.'

Simmy was increasingly conflicted where the baby was concerned. Not only was she questioning her instinctive wish to feed him herself, but she was starting to dread parting with him. His presence filled the house, even when he was silently sleeping. 'He can't possibly be,' she insisted. 'That would be like something in a fairy tale.'

'The much-awaited prince, heir to a kingdom,' said Russell. 'We'll have King Herod after him before we know it.'

They all laughed uneasily at the obvious reference. 'It's all in the timing,' said Christopher. 'I mean—'

'We know what you mean,' said Angie. 'We're getting ourselves all confused between fiction and reality. It's a sign of the times, I suppose. What's the word they use – *fluid*. That just about says it all. Nothing's concrete or definite any more.'

'Stop sounding like a grumpy old woman,' said Simmy. 'It seems to me that much of what your generation got up to in the eighties has laid the ground for how things are now.'

'You're probably right,' Angie nodded. 'We reap what we sow, or something.'

'More port, please,' said Russell. 'If there's any left.'

Five minutes later, Jerome came awake and made the whole house aware of the fact. 'They can probably hear him at Lily's house,' said Christopher. 'And everywhere in between.'

It was true that the frosty evening was so still and silent that any sound would carry a long way. But the doors and windows were all double-glazed and firmly closed. 'No they can't,' said Simmy.

There was a degree of bustle as Angie and Simmy both rushed to prepare sustenance for the infant. 'We haven't got one of those sterilising tanks,' Simmy realised. 'And only one bottle. Can we reuse the milk he didn't finish? I'm pretty sure you're not supposed to.'

'Of course we can,' said the rule-breaking Angie. 'It was only a few hours ago. Mix up some fresh in a jug, and I'll give him this for now. Then we'll wash out the bottle and refill it. I never did hold with all that sterilising. It's not healthy.'

Russell had gone to fetch the baby, while Christopher settled Robin, who had been rudely awakened. Simmy felt superfluous, and at the same time the rightful mother substitute. It was to her that Celia had handed the baby, trusting that she could keep him safe. Her mother had taken over just a bit too enthusiastically, she felt now. It was, as Christopher had said, all in the timing. Literally any other day of the year would have meant everything would have been different. Jerome would have been handed to the social services and left to his fate. Simmy could not persuade herself that that would have been a good thing. Didn't every woman secretly wish for a baby to be left on her doorstep?

She was still trying to feel concern for Diellza, out there somewhere for a second freezing night. Was she dead too, under a crag on the fellside, frozen stiff, overcome by fear or guilt or just plain misery? Would her ample size protect her to some extent? Women took longer to die of cold than men, didn't they? Did they have cold winters in Albania? She suspected not. Shamefully Simmy found herself still not caring very much what happened to the woman. She had said she was relinquishing her child permanently, and that somehow rendered her irrelevant. And yet . . . she had only just given birth, possibly entirely unexpectedly, and her thought processes could not be remotely reliable. Given time, she might well return to claim her baby. The brief madness and panic would be dealt with, and she would find a home, an income and a settled life as a widow with a little boy.

Unless, of course, she did turn out to be responsible for her husband's murder. She could have arranged for someone else to do it, even if in no state to do it herself. Everything she'd said on Friday could be untrue; she could have been manipulating the Buntings and Celia Parker and everyone else who met her. But the baby was real. The baby was loud and hungry and entirely three-dimensional. But – the thought struck Simmy out of the blue – they had no proof that he was Diellza's. Some of the meagre evidence pointed to him being hers, but there were definite questions. Was it really possible for a pregnancy and labour to be so totally concealed?

But if he wasn't Diellza's, then whose was he?

'Colic,' said Russell confidently, after an hour of Jerome's persistent wailing. He had transformed into a tiny bundle of pain or rage or both, drawing up his knees and twisting his face into a howling mask of fury. He turned his face from Simmy's breast and closed his mouth against the bottle.

They were gathered in the kitchen, with the door shut, in the hope that Robin would not be woken again. The fire in the living room was enjoyed only by Cornelia, who found the infant decidedly objectionable while it made such a noise and kept her distance accordingly. It was not nearly as warm in the kitchen.

'He's sure to wear himself out soon,' said Christopher optimistically. 'We never had this with Robin, did we?'

Simmy barely heard the question. She was walking round and round the kitchen table, jiggling the baby, while knowing that was quite the wrong thing to do. Between them they had tried everything else. 'We're all so stressed, we're just making it worse,' she moaned.

'Colic,' said Russell again. Everyone ignored him.

Is this some cosmic message to tell me that I really don't want to keep him? wondered Simmy to herself. Life before Jerome looked so peaceful in retrospect. He was just an alien scrap of life, foisted onto her, and in her vulnerable hormonal state she had gladly accepted him. She should have slammed the door in Celia's face and focused on a lovely family Christmas.

'If it wasn't for disturbing Robin, I'd just shut him in our bedroom and let him cry himself to sleep,' she fumed. 'Or we could all go to bed and leave him down here.'

'If it wasn't so cold we could put him out like a dog,' said Christopher. 'Or take him for a drive in the car. We did that once or twice with Robin, I remember. But after Moxon's experience I don't intend to go out on these roads.'

'They're really not icy,' said Russell. 'Or only in very small patches.'

'Look on the bright side,' said Angie, with an expression

that was far from bright. 'After all this, he's sure to sleep well in the night.'

'He'll be starving hungry by midnight,' said Simmy.

'Let me try the bottle again. He associates it with me now. It worked so well earlier on.' Simmy almost threw the child at her mother, where she was sitting with the bottle at her elbow. Angie pulled him close to her, bending her face down to his, staring hard. 'Now listen, you,' she said loudly. 'We've had enough of this. Just have your supper and stop making such a fuss.'

The effect was not dramatic, but the baby did pause in his wails at the firm voice, and opened his eyes. 'There!' said Angie and pushed the rubber teat forcibly into his slack mouth. She shook it so that some drops of milk fell onto his tongue, and he swallowed. Everyone in the room held their breath.

Simmy fought down a mix of negative feelings and tried to focus on the practical. 'I should be doing something about food, shouldn't I? Making stuffing, was it?'

Her father put an arm around her shoulders. 'All that can wait. It's only us. We'll all muck in tomorrow morning. I bags the sprouts and parsnips. The main priority now is to get some sleep, if you ask me.'

'We can't go yet. We'll all be up at five if we do that.'

'He's taking it, look,' whispered Angie. 'At last.'

'Nothing lasts forever,' said Russell.

The night was a lot less disturbed than they had feared. Jerome had a feed at 2 a.m., administered by Simmy from the bottle, and both dropped off again soon afterwards. The morning summons at ten to six seemed blessedly

159

generous. Christopher took Robin down soon afterwards to find his Christmas stocking hanging by the log burner, and then helped him to empty it onto the big bed, with Simmy, Jerome and Cornelia all witnessing the excitement.

Outside, it was still pitch-dark, but Christopher observed that it had felt slightly less cold when he'd let the dog out for a quick pee.

The morning passed in the customary welter of wrapping paper and mince pies and hurried trips to the kitchen to check on everything. Carols blared out from the audio system and a bottle of Prosecco was quickly emptied. Robin hurtled from one adult to another, clutching a succession of new toys. Christopher's siblings had all sent him a present, which bulked up the pile under the tree substantially. His present to Simmy, successfully kept secret until now, was a beautiful early Victorian writing slope that could be used to store papers or jewellery or any other small thing. He had treated it with wax, rubbing away enough dirt to disclose the inlaid pattern on the top and sides. 'It's more decorative than usual,' he said modestly. 'I bagged it months ago. It's got a lock to keep Robin out, and a hidden drawer, as well.'

Simmy had given him a hefty book about German porcelain that he had asked for, and a big warm jumper made of pure wool. 'I didn't knit it myself,' she admitted.

Jerome was largely ignored. He lay in a little nest in one corner of the sofa, with Cornelia next to him. Russell and Simmy occupied the remainder of it, with Robin climbing onto them now and then. 'Look how careful she's being!' said Russell, watching the dog curling herself around the baby.

'She's like that with Robin as well,' said Simmy. 'It's

very sweet.' She was feeling less stressed after the relatively peaceful night, but somewhere inside she had gone numb, knowing the relaxed atmosphere couldn't last, but not allowing herself to worry about it.

Shortly before eleven, Simmy's phone rang, and Bonnie gushed exuberant thanks for the wonderful top. 'It's *perfect*,' she trilled. 'The nicest thing I've ever had from anybody. I'm wearing it now. And the money! That's far too much.'

Simmy had opened the book that Bonnie had given her, to find a lavish hardback version of *Alice's Adventures in Wonderland* and the looking-glass sequel. 'We love the book,' she told Bonnie. 'It'll be an heirloom.'

'I knew *Alice Through the Looking-Glass* off by heart when I was about eight,' Bonnie boasted. 'It was my most precious possession for years. I give a copy to every kid I know, even though Ben says it's very old-fashioned, and has been for fifty years or more.'

'Sounds as if you're having a good time,' said Simmy, on the basis of nothing more than girlish laughter in the background, which could only be coming from Ben's sisters.

'Yes, it's nice. Such a lot of us. Wilf's here, with a girlfriend nobody knew about. He forgot to tell his mum he was bringing her, which didn't go down too well.' Wilf was Ben's older brother. Bonnie's voice had gone quiet as she conveyed this news. 'She's called Chloe. Why does everybody's girlfriend seem to have that name?'

Simmy did a rapid calculation. 'Nine of you, right?'

'I know. It's bedlam. They wanted Corinne to come as well, but she's gone off with her friend Mavis. They're having a slap-up dinner at the Belfield, would you believe?

Just as well, really. We'll have to have two tables for the dinner as it is. Oh – Ben wants a word. Is that okay?'

'If he's quick,' said Simmy, forgetting her edict of the previous evening.

'Have you still got that baby?' Ben asked without preamble.

'And thank you for the present,' she prompted him. She had given him a recent novel based on computer gaming, which she thought might enlarge his horizons.

'Yes, thanks. I'd heard of it. Something to think about when there's a moment. I don't read fiction, as a rule.'

'Well, you should. And yes, the baby is still here. My mother's taken him over, more or less.'

'And how's Detective Moxon?'

'No idea.'

'So there's no news?'

'Not a flicker. There won't be tomorrow either, probably.'

'I wouldn't rely on it,' said Ben. 'Sorry I never got you a present.'

'I assumed the book was from you and Bonnie jointly.'

'Oh – yes, that's right. Hope you like it.'

Simmy refrained from accusing him of having no idea what his girlfriend had given her in his name. Christopher would be just as bad if she let him. 'Have a lovely day, Ben. See you soon,' she said, and finished the call with a sense of getting away quite lightly.

'One of the best things about Christmas Day is that you don't get annoying phone calls from people you barely know,' said Angie, observing her daughter's demeanour.

'Does that happen a lot?' asked Christopher.

'More all the time. There's been a veritable epidemic of

it lately. People can't afford to send cards any more, so they phone up instead.'

'It's your own fault,' said Russell. 'You gave everybody our new number.'

Angie conceded this point. 'I just thought it was the usual thing to do. I can't keep up with all this new stuff, and I never did like emails, except for business. People so often get the wrong idea.'

'It gives the illusion of genuine communication,' said Russell sententiously.

'And it facilitates ever-increasing levels of fraud, so you don't even know for sure that it's from who it says it is,' Angie added. 'I don't know where it'll all end.'

'Not with a bang but a whimper,' said Russell.

Christmas lunch was accomplished with minimal disruption from Jerome. Robin rejected the meat completely, but attacked roast potatoes and stuffing with relish. There was not enough gravy and the sprouts were too soft. Crackers were pulled and paper hats worn throughout. It proceeded along the normal groove with little conscious thought or need for decisions. The word *festive* occurred to Simmy with a degree of irony. What a pale shadow of the great climax this was meant to be, after all those weeks of shopping and planning and worrying. Everywhere festooned with flashing coloured lights, millions of innocent trees cut down, not just to be placed in the corner of a living room but also turned into garish wrapping paper. Too much of everything, in short.

'Penny for them,' invited Russell, observing her expression.

163

'Oh, just the usual feeling of anticlimax,' she confessed. 'Wondering what it's all for.'

'How can you ask, after everything I've told you since you were Robin's age? Humankind needs a midwinter festival, even now. Look out there' – he pointed at the window and the frosty garden – 'how would you have felt, back at the beginning of December, if there'd been nothing to look forward to but three dark cold months? I grant you that it's utter nonsense for the Southern Hemisphere to try to create the same rituals in the height of summer, but for us Northerners it's essential. Biologically we need to fill up on carbohydrates to get us through the hungry times ahead. It gives us hope, and something to distract us.' He took a long swig of the good red wine that Christopher had provided. 'So there,' he concluded.

'Well said,' Christopher applauded. 'Seems as if we needed reminding.'

'I did, anyway,' Simmy admitted. 'You're right – December would be unbearable without all this.'

'All pretty obvious, if you ask me,' said Angie.

Nobody had room for much pudding, but it was issued anyway. After a pause for digestion, there was coffee, and a general focus on Robin and his new toys, before he fell asleep on the hearthrug. Simmy gave the baby a bottle and a new nappy. 'We've only got six nappies left,' she discovered. 'That'll hardly last through tomorrow.'

'You didn't tell me how many to get,' Angie defended.

'We can use Robin's big ones if we have to, I suppose.' She was standing by the fire with the infant in her arms. 'Look how wide awake he is! He's ever so alert.'

'Nice drug-free birth,' Angie nodded. 'All his needs

attended to. Now he's trying to work out where he is and what's going on.'

'Him and us both,' said Christopher. 'And I know my duty. Time to collect some more logs.'

'You've got company,' Russell suddenly observed. 'In the garden, look.'

Everyone turned to the window at the back of the big room, which overlooked the garden. 'It's Lily,' said Simmy. 'What on earth is she doing?'

Christopher rapped on the window, and the girl looked up. She put a hand to her mouth in an exaggerated display of embarrassment, and then pointed at the log shed. 'Sorry!' she mouthed.

Without thinking, Simmy went to the window, still holding Jerome. She beckoned Lily towards her and shouted, 'What are you doing?'

Lily waved a hand at the back door, and disappeared briefly from sight. 'I'll let her in,' said Christopher. Cornelia was ahead of him, sensing the presence of her best friend.

Seconds later the girl was in the living room, stamping her feet and trying to explain. 'We've totally run out of wood,' she said. 'My dad forgot to order any more, and we've used every single log. I remember you said we could always share yours if we needed to, so I thought I'd quietly sneak over and take a few, without bothering you.' She appealed to Christopher, with big eyes. 'I suppose that makes me a thief, technically.'

'But you can't carry more than about six,' he pointed out. 'How long's that going to last?'

'Nicholette's gone down to the beck to see if she can find some bits of dead tree. After that wind last week, there's sure to be some lying about. Mum says we'll have to burn the old table with a wobbly leg. I think she was joking.'

There was a brief silence, broken by a gurgle from the baby.

'Is that a *baby*?' asked Lily, and suddenly the atmosphere changed.

'Yes,' said Simmy. 'Go and help her find some logs,' she told Christopher, in a vain hope of averting further curiosity.

'Whose is it? Have you got more visitors?' Lily looked around the room, and up the stairs.

'He's just here for a couple of days. His mother's not well.'

'Can I see? Oh, isn't he *gorgeous*. I *love* babies. He looks ever so new. How old is he?' She frowned. 'And whose is he?' she asked again.

'Go and get the wood,' Simmy ordered in a cold voice. 'Stop asking questions.'

It was entirely counterproductive. Lily was a bright girl, with an uncanny knack of getting to the heart of things. Life so far had struck her as perfectly straightforward if you left out needless fuss and pretence. 'People don't just plonk babies on other people, do they? Especially not at Christmas. You're not a foster mother, are you? Nobody in your family's just had a baby, have they?' She knew the basic facts of the Henderson siblings, mainly from chatting with Robin, who had great fondness for his younger cousins, offspring of Christopher's sisters. He knew their names and favourite games. 'Robin would have said.'

'None of your business, my girl,' Angie interrupted firmly. 'It's nothing for you to be concerned about.'

Which Lily interpreted in just the opposite way. She narrowed her eyes. 'Has it got something to do with that dead man in Glenridding? Nicholette's been following it for days now. She's obsessed. Criminal law,' she added with a little nod.

'Of course it hasn't. Don't be ridiculous,' said Christopher. 'Now come and get the wood before I decide we haven't any to spare. There's going to be a great run on it by Thursday at this rate, and we'll all be fighting for supplies.'

'We've got masses,' said Simmy tiredly. 'Sorry, Lily. I'll catch up with you at the end of the week and explain it all. For now, it's all a bit too recent.' She wanted very much to add *And don't tell anybody*, but knew this would also be counterproductive.

'How in the world did she make that leap?' wondered Russell when Lily had gone. 'It was uncanny.'

'Good question,' said Simmy glumly.

'Two unexplained events in close proximity, I presume,' said Angie. 'It's natural for a brain to make a connection like hers did.'

'They'll have been talking about the murder obsessively at her house,' said Simmy slowly. 'With that sister there. Did Lily say "criminal law"?'

'She did,' said Russell.

'She's going to tell them about the baby, isn't she? Even if I'd asked her not to, she would. How could she not?'

'Does it matter?' asked Angie, looking as if she thought it very likely did.

'It might. The sister might decide something fishy's going on and phone the police.'

Russell was eager to supply reassurance. 'And then what? What would they do on Christmas Day? They can't say the baby's in danger, or there were any suspicious circumstances. They've got no idea there even *is* a baby, remember?'

'Unless Celia tells them, or they find Diellza.'

'And then there's your friend Detective Moxon,' said Angie. 'He's going to be lying there thinking about it all, and possibly even suspecting that it isn't your baby after all.'

'Stop it,' begged Simmy.

Christopher came in at that point and started to empty the willow basket they kept fireside logs in. 'I'm helping Lily carry logs,' he said briefly. 'Won't be long.'

'Don't—' Simmy began.

'Don't what?'

'I was going to say don't tell Lily not to say anything. Because that would just make everything worse.'

'I know. She hasn't asked any more about it. I kept her busy out there and made her feel bad for sneaking round without asking us first.' He disappeared again with the empty basket.

'A secret is not a secret if even one person's told about it,' quoted Russell thoughtfully. 'And now how many people know about this baby?'

'Only Bonnie and Ben, and Moxon, sort of. Anyway, it was never meant to be a secret exactly,' said Simmy. 'Just a kind of holding operation.' She frowned. 'That sounds ridiculous, doesn't it? Like a game. As if he's a *thing*, rather than a person.'

'None of it has made the slightest sense from the

start,' said Angie. 'The only conclusion I can draw is that you've been comprehensively lied to by everybody involved.'

Simmy moaned gently. 'Even if you're right, we can't *do* anything, can we? Not more than we've been doing.'

'We've kept him alive,' said Russell. 'Which is no small thing. They say babies are tough, but if this one's as new as we've been told, it can't be taken for granted that he'd survive. Although I suppose all those foundlings left on doorsteps in Victorian times made it, by and large. I wonder what they were fed on.'

'Mm,' said Simmy. 'Poor little things.'

'You know – I'm starting to wonder just what really is going on,' said Angie. 'Under all the urgent stuff about keeping him safe. Now you've got me wondering if he really is that Albanian woman's child, or could that be a smokescreen of some sort? What evidence do we have for *any* of it?'

'Don't start, Mum,' Simmy begged. 'You're sounding like Ben. All we know for sure is that he exists. And a woman called Celia Parker brought him here.'

'We know a man was killed and that the wife of that man was at the house of the couple that had a party on Friday,' added Russell. 'Funny that, come to think of it. There being a party, I mean, just when a murder was happening and a child was being born. If we're looking for smokescreens, that's a bobby dazzler.'

Simmy tried again. 'I actually don't want to think about it today. Or tomorrow, if possible. I just want to have Christmas.'

'We've had most of it,' Angie pointed out. 'Presents

opened, food consumed. It's all anticlimax from here on. Depressing, really.'

'Nonsense, woman,' her husband chastised her. 'We've got a whole evening of games, mindless television, plans for the new year. And let me remind you that this is meant to be the *first* day of Christmas, not the last. Twelve more days to go. Or eleven now, I suppose.' Russell rubbed his hands, and then got up to throw another log into the stove. 'Where's Christopher got to?' he asked.

Chapter Fourteen

Christopher had been gone about twenty minutes. 'They'll have asked him in for sherry or something,' Simmy sighed. The thought made her uneasy, as if letting her husband out of her sight admitted the possibility of intrusive curiosity – or worse – from outsiders. She wanted to gather her little family around her and lock the doors. 'I wish Lily hadn't seen Jerome.'

'If you ask me, it's DI Moxon you should be worrying about,' said Angie. 'If he was part of the murder investigation yesterday, he'll have to make a report, from his sickbed if necessary, and you're highly likely to feature in it.'

'He won't have to mention the baby, though. Why would he?' Simmy groaned softly. 'We've said all this already. Can't we talk about something else?'

But nobody could think of anything, other than waking Robin from his little nest on the sheepskin hearthrug and giving him a drink. His new toys were strewn around the room, and Simmy fetched a cardboard box from the kitchen to put them all in. Jerome also woke and began to make little bleats, as if working up for a full-scale wail. Angie took him, laying him on her lap and bending over him to pull faces. 'They can only focus for a few inches at first,' she said. 'The distance from breast to face, presumably.' She was making exaggerated expressions, and suddenly cried, 'Look! He's imitating me. Isn't that clever!'

'They do that,' said Simmy. 'It's terribly sweet.'

Then Christopher came back, bringing gusts of cold air and stamping his feet. 'You were a long time,' said Simmy.

'The sister came in while I was there, with an armful of dead sticks. She said she'd met a man and his dog and they started talking about the murder. He lives in Patterdale, apparently, and they're talking of nothing else up there. Nicholette wants to go tomorrow and find out for herself what's what.'

'How does she think she can do that?' said Russell. 'Nobody's going to tell *her* anything, are they?'

'Just morbid curiosity,' said Angie. 'Like gawpers on the motorway. Although I always think that's natural human feeling, actually. I suppose it applies to murder as well. People are bound to feel nervous and want to get as much information as they can.'

'Except there won't *be* any information,' said Russell again.

'Aoife said the same thing about people on the motorway,' said Simmy. 'It's starting to sound like a cliché.'

'Well, pardon *me*,' said Angie, in mock umbrage.

'There might be more information than we think,'

172

Christopher said. 'If everyone gathers at the pub and talks about what questions the police have been asking, they might well construct a pretty good picture. Now they know who the dead man was, there'll be all sorts of scope for speculation.'

'But nobody's going to know there's a baby,' Simmy insisted, trying to convince herself. 'Especially if Celia's gone off somewhere.'

'You're safe for another day,' Russell assured her. 'After that, it's all going to change.'

Simmy pulled Robin to her, in an effort to console herself for the inevitable separation from Jerome. 'Let's have a look at this book,' she said, picking up the lavishly illustrated *Alice* volume. 'There's a rabbit – see that?'

'Rabbit,' said Robin seriously. 'Big rabbit.'

The day ended at ten, with Robin fast asleep and the baby being kept awake in the faint hope of a relatively peaceful night. 'He's really tired,' said Angie optimistically.

'Aren't we all?' said Christopher. 'Is there a rota for the night feeds?'

His wife and mother-in-law both looked at him with the same expression. 'Why?' said Angie. 'Are you offering?'

'I will if you want,' he said.

'But we all know you'd make a mess of it, so that gets you out of it,' said Russell. 'Every man in the land knows how to work that particular trick.'

'And women are catching on to it, at last,' said Angie, achieving the last word.

* * *

173

Boxing Day dawned with a cloudier sky and a slightly higher temperature. Christopher opened the curtains and searched the sky for any signs of a sunrise. It was half past seven. Robin was singing loudly in his cot, and Jerome was deeply asleep in his own little basket beside the bed.

'Turkey curry, turkey soup, turkey risotto,' muttered Christopher. 'Not necessarily in that order. Your father can do the soup.' Russell had made a point of boiling up the giblets the previous evening, warning everyone not to throw anything away.

'He will,' said Simmy. 'As always. You forgot turkey sandwiches, with cold stuffing and pickle.'

'I hate cold stuffing,' said Christopher.

Things then began to happen in a steady stream that lasted all morning. Shortly before eight, Ben Harkness phoned Simmy on her mobile. After very brief remarks about Christmas, he dived into an impassioned account of why it was vital for him and Bonnie to come up to Hartsop that morning, and for them all to go to Glenridding to see for themselves the layout, with a view to forming theories about the murder. 'We've wasted so much time already,' he moaned. 'And it's traditional to go for long country walks on Boxing Day.'

'Not with a four-day-old baby in sub-zero temperatures,' Simmy protested.

'Leave him with your mum. She won't mind, will she?'

Simmy was reminded of a similar expedition in Borrowdale, some months previously, where five people and a dog had spread themselves across a small road in search of clues to a murder. It had been thoroughly unproductive, if she remembered rightly. 'It's a silly idea,' she insisted. 'There's no reason for us to go barging in at all.'

'Speak for yourself,' he huffed. 'At least let us come and we can brainstorm for a bit. I'm missing loads of details that you probably know. That party on Friday – I bet the murderer was there. We can go through everybody and see what comes up.'

Simmy knew she couldn't stop them, and acknowledged that she didn't really want to. There were no plans for the day, and Russell for one was very likely to propose a long walk at some point, despite the cold. And she knew Bonnie would be dying to see the baby. New babies were a vanishingly rare occurrence in the life of Bonnie Lawson. Or anybody's life, she supposed, these days. 'All right,' she said. 'But don't come before ten.'

Russell had already been out with the dog, walking her down to the main road and back, ostensibly to check the driving conditions. The original plan had been for him and Angie to return home in the late afternoon, and nothing had been said to change it. Whatever was decided about Jerome's future, the Straws did not intend to be there for the next step, as far as Simmy could tell. Angie had thrown herself into his care and would miss the little body in her arms, as much as Simmy would. Robin would probably find himself excessively cuddled as a result.

The kitchen was still showing much of the ravages of the previous day, with glasses still unwashed, the ingredients for Russell's soup sitting around in pans and dishes, bins overflowing. The fridge was bursting with salad, Christmas pudding, cheese and more. 'We won't need to buy food for a fortnight,' said Christopher.

'Ben and Bonnie will probably want lunch. That'll help,' said Simmy.

'The road looks perfectly all right,' Russell reported.

At nine o'clock Simmy got a text. *'Hope all's ok? Sorry about Sunday. I'm away for a while now. It's up to you what happens next. Celia.'*

She read it aloud to the three people in the kitchen. 'Why bother to send that? It doesn't say anything,' she complained. 'Just making the same point, that she washes her hands of the whole thing. Well, she can just stew. I'm not going to answer it.'

'Irresponsible,' nodded Russell. 'That's if I'm right in thinking she's the one who left the baby here.'

Simmy was trying to think. 'It's as if she wants us to know she's alive – or is that too dramatic? Why not say where she is, at least? You know what? I'm glad Ben and Bonnie are coming, because we can't go on like this, can we? Everything's so up in the air and weird. What about the way Dan Bunting came here on Monday? That was weird in itself. Was he playing some horrible game with us? Did he know about the baby and came looking for him?'

Christopher was also clearly trying to think. 'I believed him when he said he was looking for Diellza and they were all worried about her. He showed no sign of suspecting we had a baby here, which makes me believe he has no idea a baby even exists. If he did, he made a pretty poor job of checking it out.'

'Or he would just assume that the baby and Diellza were

together somewhere, if he did know about it,' said Simmy. 'And that we could hardly hide them both, without some sort of sign – a bag or a coat or something.'

'What on earth would give him the idea they were here in the first place?' wondered Russell.

'Good question. I don't actually think he did have that idea. He was more worried about our association with the police,' said Christopher. 'He seemed to think we'd tell him anything we'd gleaned from cosy chats with Moxon – something like that.'

'Poor Moxon was on his way to hospital at the time,' Simmy remembered. 'Speaking of which, we should see if we can find out how he is. What an awful Christmas it must have been for him and his wife.'

'Everybody lies,' said Angie in a hollow voice. 'Haven't we learnt that by now? We know nothing about motives, or connections or past history of any of these people. If you ask me, it's a mug's game trying to work it out like this.'

'It's what we do,' said Simmy helplessly. 'There's no stopping Ben and Bonnie – and somehow they usually arrive at a conclusion sooner or later.'

The next event of the morning was a knock on the door at nine-forty. 'If that's Ben, I'll be cross,' said Simmy, going to answer it. 'I told him not before ten.'

It was not Ben, but the woman with the Irish name – Aoife. Simmy first reaction was to slam the door in her face, but she restrained herself. 'What are you doing here?' she said instead, not caring if she sounded ungracious. *Where was the baby?* she asked herself. Had Angie brought him downstairs after breakfast? For a moment, she could not remember. All she could do was hope, because her instinct was still to keep him hidden.

'Can I come in? I gather Dan came over on Monday. I thought you might be interested to know what's been happening.'

'Couldn't you have phoned? Who else is going to descend on us with no warning?' She sighed inhospitably, but there was no way of stopping the woman entering the house, short of physical violence. 'We've only just finished breakfast.'

'It's a Boxing Day tradition where I grew up. Everyone goes out and visits their neighbours in the morning,' Aoife chirped. 'Admiring each other's presents, and helping to finish up the leftovers. That sort of thing.'

'Hm,' said Simmy, and stood aside. 'We've got friends coming in a minute. They want to go for a walk as well.' She laid special emphasis on the word *friends*. This sudden onslaught of Patterdale society was not proving greatly to her liking. She could hear her mother saying *Everybody lies*, and braced herself for a conversation in which she would be forced to remain sceptical and cautious. Christopher appeared and offered coffee, which was accepted.

'So what *has* been happening, then?' Simmy asked the visitor. 'Did they find Diellza?'

Aoife pulled a face. 'What do you think? The main theory is that she sneaked up the fell late on Friday, and slaughtered her husband, then did a bunk sometime on Sunday.'

Simmy opted for discretion and something almost sneaky. 'Really? So what about Saturday? Why hang about all that day, when his body had already been found? And how long have you known he was Diellza's husband?'

The woman's eyes widened in an expression of triumph. 'You *have* been keeping up, haven't you. I knew you would. Once we worked out who you were – which took us a stupidly long time for some reason – we guessed you wouldn't be able to stay out of it.'

Christopher came back with a mug of instant coffee. 'Who's "we"?' he asked.

'Me and Louise, mostly. She's got a thing about true crime and follows local stories. She grew up right here and knows practically everybody. We both went to school in Penrith, though I'm a bit older than her. She keeps up with half her class, after ten years or more. And Nicholette's here for a few days – she was at that school as well. Her parents live almost next door to you, I gather.'

'Must be nice to all meet up again, then.' Simmy had not yet begun to take any interest in the availability of secondary education, but was suddenly struck with the prospect of her child travelling the fifteen miles or more on a school bus twice a day for years and years. She made a silent resolution to move house before that day arrived. 'Haven't they all gone to Leeds or Liverpool and places like that since leaving school?'

Aoife nodded. 'Most of them, yes. But she still keeps in touch. Very sociable person, is Louise.'

'I noticed,' said Simmy with minimal enthusiasm.

'I'm meeting her in a bit, as it happens. She thinks long walks might bring the baby on a bit early, so we're having a little hike round Brothers Water. You can come, if you like.'

'I can't. I told you – we've got people coming. Although

179

they might be up for a walk, I suppose.'

'Bring them too, then,' said Aoife airily. 'The more the merrier. There's quite a bunch of us. Have you met Nicholette Harris? She grew up right here in Hartsop.'

'And went to school with you and Louise,' Simmy nodded, to show she was keeping up.

'Right. She's done very well for herself, apparently. I've rather lost touch with her, but as she's here for Christmas this year we'll have time to catch up.'

'We know her sister Lily,' said Simmy.

'Much younger than Nicholette, and every bit as bright, or so I hear. Anyway, Louise suggested I come and fetch you. We're meeting in the car park at eleven, so you've got time to think about it. The Buntings might be there as well. It's Boxing Day,' she finished, as if that explained everything.

It was almost ten o'clock, and Simmy found herself wondering whether it might be helpful for Ben and Bonnie to meet this woman, being sure to want to participate in the proposed walk, if most of the characters from Friday's party were going to be there. She noticed there'd been no mention of Celia Parker – nor any direct reference to the police investigations. 'Will your husband be coming?' she asked.

'Nigel? Well, he might, I suppose. He hasn't been well, but now Christmas is over, he seems to be reviving a bit. It might do him good.' The implication was that she had not given him a thought until that moment.

'And will Louise bring her kids?' Simmy asked. 'It'll be slow going if I take Robin.'

'Oh, no. Strictly adults only. And dogs, if you like. The

dads are going to have to babysit.' She threw Christopher a smile. 'If that's okay?'

As if on cue, Jerome chose that moment to announce his presence. An unmistakeable wail was heard from upstairs. Robin, who had been quietly piling up bricks behind the sofa, emerged with a knowing look. 'Baby cry,' he said.

There was a short silence before Aoife frowningly asked, 'You haven't got another one, have you?'

'It's a visitor,' said Simmy hurriedly. 'All a bit short notice. My mum's up there with him, having a wonderful time. It's a sort of relative,' she lied, instantly wondering if that had been a great mistake.

'Your mum?'

'And dad. Sorry I didn't call them down to meet you. I think they're packing up to go home. It's all box and cox today. Chaos.' She was prattling, and forced herself to stop, looking to Christopher for rescue. He said nothing.

'Right,' said Aoife slowly. 'What a surprise. You never said anything on Sunday.'

Sunday seemed a long time ago to Simmy. She could barely remember anything that had taken place at the pub. 'Didn't I?' was the best she could manage. Then she glimpsed Ben's little car, drawing up in the street outside, and turned to Christopher. 'There they are! They'll never find anywhere to park, will they?'

He went to the door and opened it. 'Looks as if there's a space outside the Reeves'. I think they might be away. Hey, Ben!' he shouted, waving at the parking space. He turned back to Simmy. 'His exhaust sounds terrible. He shouldn't be driving with it like that.'

The diversion was providential. Aoife had no choice but

181

to drain her coffee and prepare to go. There were no more cries from upstairs. Cornelia and Robin began to swirl around at the realisation of beloved visitors. 'Ben!' Robin shrilled. 'Ben, Ben, Ben!'

'And Bonnie,' Simmy added, hoping to keep the excitement going. Cornelia obligingly barked.

Russell appeared at the top of the stairs. 'What's happening?' he asked, rubbing the top of his head as if he'd only just woken up. Simmy suspected that he was trying to help by pretending to have been disturbed. The logic escaped her for the moment. It took her nearly half a minute to grasp that her mobile was ringing, where she had left it on the cluttered mantelpiece.

When she managed to get to it, the screen informed her that the caller was Detective Inspector Moxon.

Chapter Fifteen

'I wanted to thank you for your help on Monday,' he began before bursting out, 'Was that a real baby, or was I hallucinating?'

'Real,' Simmy confirmed, knowing she could never lie to him. 'You're going to be cross with us.'

'Not yours, then?'

'No. But how *are* you? Are you at home now?'

'Don't change the subject. Whose baby is it? Have you still got it?'

'I can't talk about it now. We've got a houseful of people. You sound all right. Did they fix your lung and your elbow?'

'Mrs Henderson, may I remind you that you are speaking to a senior police officer, who requires you to answer his questions?' His tone was a lot lighter than his words and made little impact.

'Remind me all you like. I reserve the right to silence,

as Ben might say. Ben's here, actually, among others. Just tell me you're all right, and we can talk properly later. There's nothing that won't wait a while longer,' she added with confidence.

'All right, then,' he conceded far too easily. 'Yes, I am at home. The hospital was half empty, not surprisingly, and patched me up very nicely. I stayed in one night and then they took me home, almost as good as new. Although my face is grotesque, and my poor car is probably fatally injured. And there has been disappointingly little progress in the murder investigation. I'm hoping you can be of some assistance, seeing as how you live so close by.'

'Phone me again this afternoon,' she told him. 'I imagine you've got a few days off, haven't you? What with a bruised face and no car. Although Christopher seemed to think it wasn't too badly damaged.'

'Three o'clock,' he promised, ignoring all other remarks. 'And say hello to Ben – and everybody. Including that baby.'

By the time she'd ended the call, Ben and Bonnie had taken their coats off and Aoife was just leaving. Christopher had somehow conveyed to the youngsters that they should do nothing to detain her. 'We might see you later,' she heard him say firmly.

'Moxon says hello,' she told Ben.

'Where is it?' demanded Bonnie, the moment the front door was closed. 'Have you still got it?'

'I assume you mean baby Jerome,' Simmy smiled. 'He's been upstairs all morning with my mum. She's taken him over, pretty much.'

'Have you told the police about him yet?' asked Ben.

'Come in properly, and we can have coffee and catch up.' Simmy observed that Bonnie was wearing the sky blue Christmas present. 'Is that warm enough?' she worried. 'It wasn't meant for a day like this.'

'It's not so cold today,' said Bonnie. 'And I love it so much I'm going to wear it every day for a year. It is warm, anyway – real alpaca!'

It looked every bit as good on her as Simmy had hoped. The soft wool clung to her, emphasising her slender shape and making her look both fragile and irresistibly cuddly. 'You look like a fawn,' said Simmy. 'Or maybe a koala.' Bonnie giggled and bent over Cornelia, who was extremely fond of her.

'Ignore her,' said Christopher. 'She's gone all to mush since the baby got dumped on us.'

'Can we all sit down and get the whole thing straight, do you think?' asked Ben.

'All of us?' echoed Christopher. 'That's six people, not counting Robin.'

'Or the baby,' said Bonnie. 'Did you say he's called Jerome? Whose idea was that?'

'His mother's,' said Simmy briefly.

'Yes, everybody, if they're willing,' Ben was saying officiously. 'Your kitchen table's big enough, isn't it?'

The house was a converted barn, which meant all the rooms were big, including the kitchen. Angie and Russell came downstairs, Angie holding the baby, who was asleep. 'Put him on the sofa,' said Simmy.

'He'll wake up if I put him down.'

'So what? Bonnie can deal with him if he does. She's been dying to meet him.'

185

They quite quickly got themselves arranged around the table, once Bonnie had devoted a few minutes to worshipping the baby, who miraculously remained asleep. Ben produced his laptop as well as an A4 writing pad and pen. Russell found the whole business very entertaining. 'I didn't know we were holding a tribunal,' he joked. 'By what right, may I ask, is this happening?'

Simmy patted his hand. 'You know the routine by now, surely. This is what Ben always does. He can't help himself.'

Ben laid the pad in front of himself and took up the pen. 'I'm making a list of questions,' he announced, writing as he spoke. 'First – who does the baby belong to? Second – how does he connect to the murder? Third – what does the woman who brought him here know about the murder? What's her name?' He looked at Simmy.

'Celia Parker,' she supplied, and started to say more.

Ben held up his pen. 'No, don't say anything else for now. Question Four – how many people know the baby is here?'

'What does that have to do with the murder?' asked Russell, who was paying so much attention that it was obvious he was being ironic. He leant forward, his gaze intent on Ben. 'I don't follow that logic.'

'It should soon become clear,' Ben assured him.

'All right. Please proceed, then.'

'Question Five – where are we with the police investigation? How involved have any of you been?'

Bonnie interrupted at this point. 'I think that's enough to start with, Ben. Can we go back to the top and fill in some answers?'

Ben nodded. 'I was going to anyway. Answering what we've got here might inform further questions. I'm sure there are things I've missed. Let's start with the baby's parents.'

'His mother is an Albanian woman called Diellza. She is married to the dead man, Alexander McSomething,' said Simmy.

'McGuire,' said Bonnie. 'I told you that.'

'I know, but since then I forgot.'

'Are we absolutely sure he was her husband?' asked Ben. 'Could we be conflating two different men?'

'Seems not,' said Christopher. 'We've had quite a few visitors, and they tell us the police are searching for Diellza as the dead man's wife. Looks as if they think she did him in.'

Again, Ben raised the pen as a signal to say no more. 'We'll come to that. So, the child is McGuire's, we presume. And its mother abandoned it hours after giving birth?'

'I'm losing sight of the logic again,' Russell muttered.

The conversation continued in a similar vein, throwing half-baked theories around and interrupting each other, for another thirty minutes, after which Ben had covered two and a half sheets of notepaper, and consulted his laptop a few times. He had copied down the results of some instant googling. 'Well, we now know significantly more about the murder victim and some residents of Glenridding,' he said, and went on to summarise progress thus far. 'Alexander McGuire was a lecturer at Manchester University, his main subject being the Soviet era. That included studying outlying states such as Romania,

Bulgaria and Albania, with some interest in Yugoslavia. He had a PhD. Met his wife while travelling, brought her here and married her, when she must have been early twenties and he about sixty.'

Simmy was lost in admiration. 'We didn't know any of that,' she marvelled.

'There's more. A woman by the name of Celia Parker was one of his prize-winning students, two years ago. She wrote an essay about relations between Albania and Yugoslavia over the past five centuries.'

'My God!' This time it was Christopher who expressed amazement. 'That puts a whole new light on things.'

'Better not speculate yet,' Ben cautioned. 'I didn't find anything much on the Buntings or Aoife – mainly because we don't know her surname.'

Simmy was holding her head in her hands. 'You're telling me Celia knew the McGuire man? I can't believe it. She teaches psychology. How does that fit? Where does she work now? Can you find that?'

Ben shook his head. 'She seems to have ended her connection with Manchester once she got the doctorate, and not popped up anywhere else that I can see. I didn't find anything about psychology, but I wasn't really looking.'

'She must have known Diellza before she came to the Buntings – that's obvious, don't you think? And all that stuff about Dan rescuing her, as if she was an illegal migrant, must be absolute lies.'

'Is that what they said? In so many words?' asked Ben.

'Well, no. She could just as easily have been an abused wife. I still don't know what Dan's job is exactly. Some sort of social work. He was providing sanctuary over Christmas, because she had nowhere else to go. But I got a feeling she was a bit scared of him. Had to ask his permission before meeting me again.'

'Really?' It was Bonnie chipping in. 'Do you think she could have been their *slave*?'

'Not really. It might just have been a way of being polite – checking her movements with him first.'

'And then running off without a word,' said Christopher.

'So, any of them might have had reason to kill McGuire,' Ben summarised. He pointed to the list of names he had written down. Simmy pulled it across the table for a look. 'I can't see why Fran or Aoife or Louise might have wanted to,' she said.

'There were loads of others at the party, but we didn't catch their names,' said Christopher. 'Those on the list are just the ones we spoke to, and Simmy met again on Sunday.'

'And they all know each other, and at least one of them knew the murdered man,' said Ben. Everyone nodded.

'We're really getting somewhere now,' said Bonnie with a little bounce. 'Except I still can't believe Diellza didn't know she was pregnant. And we haven't asked *why* she dumped the baby.'

Angie spoke, almost for the first time. 'Don't forget her husband had been killed by the time she ran away, so she was probably terrified that the killer would come for her next.'

'Which assumes that she *knew* he'd been killed,' said Ben thoughtfully. 'Or does it?'

'It was on the news by the middle of Saturday. She must

have had a phone that could get the news. She spent all that day locked in her room, not speaking to the Buntings, apparently,' said Simmy.

Bonnie was still looking sceptical. 'So, we're meant to believe they never had any idea that she'd got a baby? That seems even more incredible. Babies cry.'

'As Robin will tell you,' said Simmy. Her small boy had been contentedly pottering in and out, climbing onto Russell's lap at one point, and then quickly getting down again. The sleeping infant held no interest for him.

'We don't know exactly when he was born,' said Simmy. 'She might have been in labour all day Saturday and not had him till late that night.'

'But why keep it secret from the Buntings? Why not ask them to call a doctor?' It was Christopher repeating questions that had already come up.

'Paperwork,' said Russell. 'There are all sorts of laws that kick in.'

'Right,' nodded Ben. 'It's even illegal to do it without a medical attendant, as far as I know.'

'That's no answer,' Bonnie insisted. 'There has to be more to it than that.'

'She was scared – obviously,' said Angie. 'So as soon as she could get herself together, she bundled herself and the baby up and got away while the Buntings were both out. Plus, I'd say the baby came early, judging by the size of him. That would be scary in itself.'

Simmy grabbed this idea. 'You mean – even if there were plans, they were thrown because it was sooner than expected?'

Angie nodded, but Ben shook his head and nibbled the end of the pencil. 'It's all wrong,' he concluded. 'We still can't get the connection between the murder and the baby, except that the victim is the kid's father. Probably. That raises a whole lot of ideas, none of them with any evidence whatsoever.'

'At least we know there *is* a baby,' said Bonnie. 'Nobody's told the police about him, have they?'

'Moxon saw him here on Monday,' said Simmy, who had failed to report this fact up to now.

Ben looked up. 'Did he? What did he say?'

'He thought it was mine. I'll have to tell him the truth this afternoon. But I still can't see how it'll affect the murder enquiries, other than to give Diellza a pretty good alibi.'

'Which is bound to be absolutely crucial,' shouted Ben, throwing down the pencil and pushing the pad away. 'All this is going to be just so much rubbish when they find out the truth.'

'Calm down,' said Simmy. 'You were saying all this days ago. We decided to shelve it for Christmas, and we did. Moxon's been in hospital. The police will have been concentrating on Mr McGuire's background, and Albanian connections, and looking for Diellza. Nothing we could tell them would affect that. And they're bound to have worked out for themselves that Celia Parker knew the dead man. They'll be searching for her. And they'll think she's with Diellza somewhere. When I tell Moxon that Celia brought Jerome here, that'll just confirm what they think already.'

Ben was mulish. 'I still think we've wasted all morning

191

on completely the wrong questions. Why didn't one of you stop me?'

'Tell you what,' said Simmy, standing up. 'It's almost eleven. We can go down to Brothers Water and meet some of the people on that list.' A thin cry came from the living room. 'The baby's awake. Bonnie – do you want to go and get him? We've got a bottle in the fridge – you can feed him if you like.'

'Don't get too attached,' said Angie with a sigh. 'It's all too easily done.'

It didn't take long for a small party of three (plus dog) to assemble with a view to walking down to Brothers Water. Simmy, Ben and Russell donned coats, hats, scarves and gloves, causing Robin to assume that he would be included. 'No, kiddo – you're staying with me. I want to see all your new toys,' said Bonnie. Christopher said he had to thank all his siblings for the predictable things they had given him, and anyway they didn't want too many, did they.

Angie made no excuses. Cold country walks were not her thing, and she gladly took on the role of matriarch, supervising 'the children' – including Bonnie is this group, by implication.

Simmy tried to hurry them towards the main road, and the designated car park. 'They said eleven,' she worried. 'We'll be late.'

Ben laughed. 'In my experience, this sort of arrangement always takes a lot longer than you think. People stand around arguing and changing their footwear and waiting to see if Miss Bloggins is going to turn up. We used to do this a lot, you know, before my mother got so lame.'

Russell joined in. 'That's exactly right. Walking groups can be dreadfully annoying like that.'

It turned out just as they'd predicted. As they approached the Cow Bridge car park, Simmy could see Aoife standing on a bridge, waving impatiently at two people sitting in a car. 'That's her,' she told the others. 'Trying to organise everybody. Doesn't look as if the husband came, though.'

'Where's the pregnant one?' wondered Ben.

'Over there, look,' said Russell, ducking his chin at a woman standing a short distance away, staring over the bridge at the beck running slowly between them and the woodland to the west.

'It goes down to Ullswater,' said Russell, as he went to stand close to Louise. Simmy joined them, gazing about her.

'It's the one that runs through the fields where I walk the dog,' she said. 'I hardly ever come this way. Isn't it lovely?' She looked at the domineering fells on every side. 'I still don't know all their names. That's obviously High Hartsop Dodd?' She pointed across the road. 'Funny how different it all looks from here. I thought I knew exactly what Brothers Water was like – you can see it close up from the road. I've passed it a hundred times, and yet I've never actually stood here and looked at it properly.'

'High Hartsop Dodd,' repeated her father with a laugh. 'You must admit the names tend to be somewhat unimaginative.'

'For a start, I didn't know what this path was like,'

Simmy went on. 'It's obviously well used.' In the distance there was a couple with two dogs. The woods rose up on the right, the moss-covered trees the only colour in the drab grey-brown landscape. On their left, the water was on a lower level. Cornelia ran down the bank beyond the bridge in pursuit of a duck.

'You'd expect there to be ice around the edges,' Simmy said. 'Isn't there some story of two boys falling through when they walked across it when it was completely frozen over?'

Russell patted her approvingly. 'Fancy you remembering that,' he applauded. 'That's why it's called Brothers Water. It happened sometime in the late eighteenth century. Colder times, so they say.'

Louise had kept on walking, not looking back, but conveying impatience all too starkly. She had shown little interest in Ben and Russell had only managed to introduce himself briefly and extol the wonders of the landscape before she started outpacing him.

'Hey – that's enough yakking,' said Ben in a low voice behind Simmy and Russell now. 'Remember why we're here. Introduce me to the people.'

'Wait for them to catch up, then.'

Aoife had gone up to the car, which turned out to contain both the Buntings. The three realised they were holding things up, and hurried to the bridge, having evidently arrived in the correct footwear.

'Hi!' Simmy chirped. 'We decided to take you up on your suggestion. You've been quick, getting home and out again. This is my friend Ben, and my dad. Nobody else wanted to come.'

Aoife smiled distractedly. 'That includes my husband as well. He says he's sure to get a chill after spending so long in an overheated bedroom. And Louise says she's only going as far as Hartsop Hall and back again. I was hoping we'd go all the way round and back along the road. I think the inn's open – I thought we could have a quick snack there. But Fran says she's with Louise, and anyway she's not feeling very well.'

'Oh?' The couple were at the small gate onto the path, which Russell was politely holding open for them.

'I'm all right,' said Fran. 'Too much Christmas indulgence, that's all.' Her husband threw her a sceptical look, as if to say *When did you ever eat too much?*

'Well, for heaven's sake let's get going,' snapped Aoife. 'Louise is impatient to start off. She says she's only got an hour.'

'It would be nice to do the circle,' said Russell mildly. 'I do like a circular walk, and this is a classic. I did it back in 2002, if I remember rightly. Doesn't seem to have changed.'

'It's not looking its best,' said Dan Bunting, who was wearing a large sheepskin coat, and giving Simmy some very complicated looks. 'Your other half not coming, then?'

Simmy shook her head. 'He's writing his thank yous to his brothers and sisters before he goes back to work.'

Aoife laughed. 'Thank yous? What – in a proper letter?'

'Emails, actually. But it's only polite, isn't it. They gave him some nice things.'

'Lucky him. I just got some bubble bath from a cousin, and a few cards. Nigel didn't feel up to going shopping.'

She sighed and then shrugged.

'Families,' said Russell. 'They come in so many guises, don't they.' Nobody knew what he meant, and nothing was said in response.

Simmy found herself missing Christopher. He had met these people and could better keep conversation going than either Russell or Ben could. She found herself in a fog of confusion as to who had heard Jerome crying. She knew she had lied to Aoife that morning, and that Dan Bunting had gone away from his Christmas Eve visit none the wiser. That seemed to cover it, because she didn't think Aoife could have had time to say anything to Louise or the Buntings. And now that Moxon was soon to be told the whole story, it no longer seemed to matter anyway. The baby would have to be given up in another day or so, and the whole unhappy business left to the rightful authorities. These thoughts only made her miss her husband even more.

The walkers were pairing up. Simmy could see that she would be landed with Louise by default if she did not take action to avoid that. Of the whole group, Louise was the one she thought least likely to be interesting, despite her apparent interest in 'true crime', whatever that might be. That meant, of course, that she ought not to be consigned to Ben, either. With a sense of throwing him under a bus, she sidled up to Russell and walked him over to the pregnant woman, who was showing signs of increasing impatience. 'This is my dad,' Simmy told Louise. 'He's been here before, ages ago. I imagine you come here quite a lot?'

'Hardly.' The woman sniffed. 'It's a red letter day when I get out of the house long enough to come down here. The car park's always full, for a start. And now everybody's faffing that I need to get back by lunchtime.'

'Let's go, then,' said Russell gallantly. 'If we're in front, we're more likely to spot the red squirrels and interesting birds. I saw a siskin at the weekend, you know. That doesn't happen very often. They come into the garden when it's cold. We keep a feeding station going. You wouldn't believe the price of peanuts these days.' He prattled cheerily, as the pair set off along the path. The small lake soon came into better view, and he did his best to engage Louise in conversation about it. Simmy could hear snatches of his discourse, and wished he would leave the woman some space for her own comments. He appeared to have forgotten all about the fact of a murder and the potential involvement of the people they were walking with.

Simmy joined Fran Bunting, as pairs automatically formed. Aoife was with Ben, leaving Dan Bunting following close behind on his own. It took Simmy a moment to realise that her companion was very red about the eyes. 'How was Christmas?' she asked carefully.

'Horrible, if you must know. We had the police hassling us for most of Monday, scaring us about poor Diellza and obviously thinking we'd failed somehow. Or worse. I mean – it's so unfair. We're as worried about her as anybody – more so, probably. We only had her best interests at heart, giving her somewhere to stay, including her in that party and so forth. And then she just goes off without a word, as if she was *escaping* from us. That's what they think. When the truth is, we miss her, and can't think of anything else. I didn't want to come on this stupid walk – what if she comes back and we're not there? Dan feels even worse than I do, with her being his protégée, much more than mine.'

'That's not very likely, is it? That she'll come back, I mean?'

'I don't know. Aoife keeps saying she must be dead, out in this awful cold. But she wouldn't go off unless she knew somewhere to go, would she? And where the hell is Celia? She never said she'd be away for Christmas. Dan thinks she and Diellza are together somewhere. Celia knows most of the farmers around here – she's even got some land the other side of Ullswater. She'd know where there was an empty barn or something.'

'Did you say all that to the police?'

'Not really. They didn't seem interested in Celia – or no more than anyone else. They've questioned everybody in the whole damned village. Stirring up any number of wasps' nests in the process. It's ridiculous. None of them had ever even seen Diellza until Friday, and then she went off to her room halfway through. She only talked to you and Celia, as far as I could see.'

'But they obviously want to find her because it's her husband that's been murdered,' said Simmy, trying to sound ingenuous. 'They must have delayed announcing who he was, until they were sure his next of kin knew he was dead.'

'And then they did it anyway.'

'I suppose they couldn't wait indefinitely. And the way she went off must have looked suspicious.'

'We told them over and over that it couldn't have been her who killed him.'

'How can you be so sure? Wasn't it done during the night? Not long after your party, probably? How do you know she didn't creep out when you were busy with all the people and do it?'

'We'd have heard her coming back. She was in her room,' Fran insisted.

'But how can you be sure? What if she went out in the small hours when you were asleep?'

'Stop it,' begged Fran. 'You sound like that police detective. There's a huge difference between what might work in theory and what can really happen with real people. You saw Diellza, how big and clumsy she was. She could never do anything quietly. The people in the next house to us have a neurotic collie that barks if a mouse sneezes. If anybody had gone out in the middle of the night, it would have let us all know about it.' She was speaking more loudly with every sentence, perfectly audible to everyone else in the group. Dan, walking behind Ben and Aoife, must have heard her. 'She didn't kill her husband,' Fran finished, on a quieter note. 'The idea is ridiculous.'

'Hey, babes, calm down,' came Dan's voice. He had moved up to just behind Fran's shoulder. 'Don't get started again.' He met Simmy's eyes with an apologetic smile. 'It's all been very upsetting. I told your husband on Monday, didn't I – how worried we are about poor Diellza. We've hardly slept for thinking about her.' He put an arm round his wife. 'I did hope this walk would be a good distraction. Oh, and you forgot, sweetie, that next door are away. The bloody dog's in kennels.'

Simmy heard this as a not-very-subtle way of suggesting

that Diellza could indeed have slipped out in the dead of night without raising any alarm. But it still made very little sense to suppose that her husband was up on the fell just waiting to be murdered. Unless he had texted his wife and instructed her to go out and meet him, without anyone knowing.

'Sounds as if you had a rather miserable Christmas,' Simmy sympathised. Fran's red eyes could perhaps have come more from lack of sleep than prolonged weeping, but she was not convinced. And if it had been weeping, that struck her as somewhat excessive. Anxiety didn't normally make a person cry. 'Had you got terribly attached to Diellza?' she went on to ask.

'Well, yes, I suppose we had,' Dan agreed. 'I can't pretend I knew her at all well before she came to stay, but she was always very sweet and friendly. It was a pleasure to be able to help her. We thought everything was working out really nicely – until Sunday.'

'Did you ever meet her husband?'

Dan and Fran both shook their heads. Dan spoke as if for them both. 'She hardly mentioned him, actually, and we didn't like to pry.'

'She couldn't possibly have had any reason to kill him,' Fran interjected with some force.

'But what was he doing out there in the first place?' Simmy asked, before choosing to voice some of her recent thoughts. 'Did he know she was staying with you? Surely, he must have been looking for her? Maybe he wanted to speak to her without you knowing about it, for some reason.'

'Oh God, you sound just like the police,' moaned Fran.

'They went over and over all that about twenty times.'

'What's got you lot so serious?' came Aoife's voice a few yards ahead. 'And can you walk a bit faster? You've practically stopped.'

Simmy looked back, catching Ben's eye. It was clear that he had heard most of what had been said. 'Sorry,' she said. 'We're talking about Diellza, as you probably heard.'

'Well don't,' said Aoife with a quick smile to soften the words. 'We're here to enjoy the views, and get some good fresh air. Look at those two, steaming ahead.' She nodded at Russell and Louise, who should have been the slow ones, on the grounds of age and pregnancy respectively, but who were setting a good pace. 'We'll meet them coming back, at this rate.'

It suited Simmy well enough to quicken her steps and gain some space for thought. The baby had not been mentioned at all, which suggested that the Buntings had no suspicion that such a being existed. Aoife, however, knew that it did. At any moment she was likely to say something about it, unless she feared the reaction from Dan and Fran. Would they mock any suggestion that Diellza had been pregnant? Would the idea never even occur to them? And what about Celia Parker?

All that she had gleaned so far was that there was a strong emotional connection between the Buntings and the Albanian. Strong enough to evoke tears and ruin Christmas. With a surge of impatience, born of a complicated need to know where she stood regarding Jerome and her own future, she chose to further rock an already unsteady boat.

'You probably met DI Moxon on Monday,' she said to Dan. 'I think he was doing some of the local questioning. He's an old friend of ours. Did you know he had an accident, on his way home? He turned up on our doorstep with a huge bump on his head, cracked ribs and a painful elbow. We had to call an ambulance for him.'

'Poor man,' said Dan with minimal feeling.

'While he was there, he saw the baby we've been minding ever since Sunday night.' As soon as she spoke, she knew it was a colossal mistake. It was as if she had stepped into quicksand, with nothing to hold onto. What was she thinking? How was she going to extricate herself? 'Ben?' she appealed, adding a silent *Help!*

'Sweet little chap,' said Ben easily. 'Ever so good, he is. You know my girlfriend Bonnie – grew up with a foster mother – well, no you couldn't possibly know that. But she did, and she understands all about family problems and the way somebody sometimes has to step in at short notice. There's quite a network down in Windermere, which Simmy knows all about.' The meaningless burbling had the desired effect, or so Simmy hoped.

'Is that why Bonnie didn't come on the walk? Because she's minding a baby? Is it hers or something?' asked Fran.

'That's right,' Ben grinned sheepishly. 'I mean, no it's not actually *hers*, but there's a connection. All very complicated. But he really is a little cutey. Much nicer than my sisters when they were babies – though I don't really remember much about that.'

Aoife had pushed herself between Dan and Ben, listening closely. 'I heard a baby at your house,' she said. 'I was going to tell Fran about it, but haven't had a chance.'

'Why me?' said Fran, staring at Simmy with an unnervingly hard gaze.

'Well, why not?' demanded Aoife. 'You and Louise, and Celia if she ever comes back. I mean – it's a nice story, isn't it?'

'I don't think we've really heard the story, such as it is,' said Dan slowly. 'How old is this baby? What does it have to do with your friend the detective? I don't get the connection.'

'Nor me,' said Ben with a cheeky look at Simmy. 'If you ask me, there isn't one. Simmy never was very good at logical thinking. She just strung the two events together because they're both interesting.'

Simmy forced a laugh. 'That's right. They both make good stories, that's all, like Aoife says. Tomorrow, I need to find out how poor Moxon is getting on.'

'And the baby?' asked Dan Bunting.

'Oh, well, that's all in hand. He's a month old. We've only got him for a few days, until his family get sorted out. Christmas, you see . . .' she finished vaguely.

But Dan had not finished. 'But I was right there, at your house, and there was no sign of a baby. I thought at the time you and your mother were talking in some sort of code – and I was right, wasn't I? You were deliberately hiding it from me, the fact of a baby.'

'No, not at all. He was asleep upstairs with my little boy. My mother was enjoying fussing over them both. There wasn't anything at all underhand about it.'

'Well, I think there was,' said Dan Bunting flatly.

'For myself, I find the fact of a murder within a few

yards of your house a lot more interesting,' said Ben rather loudly. 'It's why I'm here, to be honest. Bonnie and I have been involved in quite a few investigations in the past year or two, and the police find us useful, believe it or not. I'm thinking we need to go and look at the place where the man was killed. We'll come up after lunch. You can show us, if you like.'

'It's half a mile from our house, to be exact. And there's no way we'll show you. Why on earth would we?'

Ben shrugged. 'I just thought . . . well, it doesn't matter. There's bound to be police tape and stuff to show us the spot.'

The walk proceeded with an air of huffiness from Dan and amusement from Ben. Fran showed no signs of cheering up, despite some efforts from Aoife to raise her spirits. Simmy realised she knew almost nothing about Aoife, except that there was an unhappy husband and no children, and she lived closer to the site of the murder than almost anyone else.

'Was it some sort of gang, do you think – who killed Diellza's husband?' she asked, into a prolonged silence. 'To do with drugs or something.'

'That's what we've all been assuming,' said Aoife briskly. 'But it does raise a lot of awkward questions. I mean – why here? If he was trying to find his wife, would sinister gang members follow him up onto the fells? It seems very unlikely.'

Ben snorted. 'It's a bonkers idea. People involved in pushing drugs don't come out to places like this, do they? And who says the McGuire man was involved in anything like that, anyway? From what I can gather, he was a more or less harmless university lecturer. Whatever that is,' he laughed.

Dan Bunting gave Aoife a little push. 'Ben's right. We haven't all been assuming it was a gang, not at all. That's just because of the Albanian connection. Stereotyping. I spend my life trying to get away from that sort of thinking.'

'Then what?' persisted Simmy. The whole conversation was making her more and more uncomfortable. It was quite wrong to discuss the murder without reference to the baby, and yet to disclose his parentage still felt impossibly dangerous. She badly wanted somebody to suggest a credible perpetrator with a motive entirely unconnected to Jerome, while knowing that was not going to happen.

'We're all completely stumped,' sighed Dan. 'The only scenario that fits the facts, that we can see, is that somehow Diellza must have done it.'

Fran turned an angry face to him. 'No!' she snapped. 'I keep telling you, there's no way it was her. And what about Celia? Why doesn't anyone suspect her? Where is she? If you ask me, she knows something, and is scared the police will get it out of her.'

'Okay,' her husband tried to soothe her before addressing Simmy. 'Do you think we could talk about something else? You can see how painful it is to go over and over it like this. We've said the same things a thousand times.' Simmy observed that his vicarish persona was being rather battered, but had not disappeared entirely.

Russell and Louise had slowed down, waiting for the others to catch up. It was evident that their conversation had been considerably more peaceful and harmonious than that of the others. Russell waved an admiring arm at the surrounding scenery, with an ecstatic expression. 'How classic is this!' he exclaimed. 'You've got everything right here. Ancient trees covered in moss, woodlands, fells and water. Not a man-made artefact in sight.'

'Not even any stone walls,' said Simmy. 'But there's a house or two that I can see.'

'I'm talking about this side of the road,' he said, irritably. 'Don't spoil it.'

'He's right, though,' said Louise, who looked healthy and cheerful, her cheeks red and her hair escaping from the woolly hat. 'It is lovely and your dad's brilliant at pointing out the details I never would have noticed otherwise. We haven't seen a squirrel, though. Too many dogs about, I suppose.' They had passed three or four dog walkers on the path.

'Nor a siskin,' added Russell. 'But the fish have been jumping. I always like to see them do that.' He looked from face to face. 'You lot look horribly serious. I hope you haven't been talking about murder.'

'Of course we have,' said Ben.

Chapter Sixteen

'There's never as much turkey left over as you think,' grumbled Christopher. 'I've used almost all of it in the curry.'

'We are rather a greedy lot, I suppose,' said Simmy. 'We can have soup this evening, when they've all gone.'

'There's hardly any bread left.'

'Rubbish – there's at least two loaves of brown sliced in the freezer.'

'Well, I couldn't see it.'

Simmy shrugged eloquently.

After lunch, Angie and Russell started half-heartedly to gather up their belongings and prepare to return to Threlkeld. 'We don't have to go until three or even a bit after,' said Russell. 'I'd hate to miss anything. Can we stay till then?'

'Course you can,' laughed Simmy. 'Stay all week if you want.'

'We need to check that everything's all right with the house,' said Angie. 'There might be burst pipes.' Yet again, she had the baby, this time slung over her shoulder, where he seemed blissfully comfortable.

By two o'clock they were all gathered once again around the kitchen table. Ben returned to his businesslike self and tried to extract all meaningful observations from Simmy concerning the morning's interactions. 'I'm afraid I won't be of any use to you,' said Russell. 'That Louise had almost nothing to say for herself. I tried any number of times to get her onto the topic of crime, but she kept going off on stories about her schooldays and how her mother was a terrible cook.'

'All I could hear was you going on about the drowned brothers and the wonders of the Lakeland landscape,' Simmy teased him. 'I don't think she could get a word in.'

'You're quite wrong,' he said huffily. 'You were so far behind us most of the time, you couldn't possibly have heard us.'

'You're right,' she conceded, and turned to Ben. 'All I know about her is that she went to school with Aoife and Nicholette Harris. Which doesn't seem in the least bit significant.'

'Unless they formed some kind of secret society,' said Russell. 'Dedicated to righting wrongs and catching criminals.'

'Like us,' said Bonnie with a laugh. 'Maybe we've got competition.'

'I doubt it,' said Ben, although he did begin to look thoughtful.

'The others were almost *too* forthcoming,' said Simmy.

'Luckily you heard it all as well. I'd never be able to remember everything.'

Ben chewed his pen and said, 'None of it felt very constructive. And what about you splurging about the baby like that! What on earth came over you?'

Christopher and Bonnie both stared at Simmy. 'You didn't!' Bonnie's indignation was almost comical. 'How could you?'

'I think I thought it would be a sort of test – to see how they reacted.'

'And?'

'Well – they didn't much. Dan was more interested than Fran, and asked some fairly sharp questions. I said the baby was a month old, to throw him off the scent. Then I backed off and Ben came to the rescue. We told outright lies.' She sighed. 'The whole thing was a fiasco. I lost my nerve.'

'I didn't see how Aoife took it,' said Ben. 'She's the one I find most interesting. I couldn't work her out.'

'She already knew there was a baby. The walk was her idea. She's buddies with Fran, and she's got a husband,' Simmy summarised, with an air of self-reproach. 'I'm sure there's a lot more I should know about them. I'm being a rubbish detective.'

'We still don't think enough about that poor woman giving up her baby,' said Angie. 'And do we really believe she kept it quiet all through Saturday night and half of Sunday, right there in the house with that couple? It isn't credible, surely? Haven't we been naive to think that's what happened?'

'We don't know exactly when the baby was born,' Simmy reminded her mother. 'I was talking to Fran this morning, and I honestly think she had no idea what was going on. I floated the theory that Diellza killed her husband sometime on Friday night, after the party, and she said it was impossible. Although Dan corrected her about the dog next door. She said it would have barked, but he reminded her it was in kennels over Christmas.'

'What else did she say?' asked Ben. 'I didn't hear all of it.'

'She'd been crying,' Simmy remembered. 'About Diellza, apparently. Worrying about her, and whether she was all right.'

'Does worry make people cry?' asked Bonnie.

'Sometimes, I suppose,' said Simmy, uncertainly. 'Although I did wonder about that myself.'

'If it's their child or husband – somebody they can't live without, perhaps,' said Ben. 'But not so much in this case, surely. Unless she felt guilty, or that she'd lost somebody really important to her.'

'She didn't show much sign of being especially attached to Diellza at the party, did she?' said Christopher.

'Dan was a lot more so,' Simmy agreed. 'I got the impression that he rather foisted Diellza onto Fran, and she had to make the best of it.'

'And where's the Celia woman?' asked Bonnie suddenly. She was studying Ben's pages of notes, tracing connections with a finger, and pencilling little asterisks here and there, 'Do we think she knew all along there was going to be a baby? Can we believe what she told Simmy on Sunday?'

'Everybody lies,' said Bonnie, not unlike the way Robin kept saying 'Baby cry'.

'She might even have written that note herself, come to

that,' sighed Christopher. 'If we go down that route, there's no firm ground anywhere. You have to feel sorry for the police, don't you?'

'Oh, that reminds me,' said Simmy, looking at the kitchen clock. 'Moxon's going to phone again at three. What am I going to say to him? We're sure to be in real trouble for hiding the baby. He'll never trust us again. Especially since the thing in Borrowdale. He'll think we've got into the habit of concealing evidence.'

'A bit late to worry about that now,' said Christopher.

'I told you to go to the police, on Monday,' said Bonnie.

'They're sure to say it's hampered their investigations,' said Ben.

'It got worse when he actually *saw* Jerome,' Simmy agonised. 'I let him believe he was mine.'

'He wasn't in any state to do anything about it at that point. He still might not be,' Christopher tried to reassure her.

It didn't work. 'He'll be tainted by association with us, in the eyes of the police. He'll never get promotion. They'll give him the rubbish jobs. And it'll be all our fault.'

'He can take it,' said Angie with a laugh. 'If you ask me, it's more than outweighed by the kudos of having you three as his pals. Everybody knows you've been instrumental in solving any number of murders, one way and another. He's got to take the rough with the smooth. I think he probably understands that.'

If the detective had been able to hear all this, surely he would be mollified, thought Simmy. The affection they all held for him was indisputable, even if it was mixed with a sliver of condescension in one or two of the group. 'We

211

have to tell him absolutely everything we've discovered,' she announced.

'Might be a long phone call, then,' said Russell. 'We should probably go before that gets started. Our bags are by the door. I'll load the car.'

Nobody tried to stop him. Despite the clear sky, darkness would fall in little over an hour. The driving would have to be slow and cautious. Neither of the Straws enjoyed driving very much. Simmy recognised a shared anxiety in herself and both her parents. 'Call us as soon as you get there,' she ordered.

'Your phone's going to be engaged,' said Russell.

'Moxon's bound to use my mobile. You can use the landline.'

'We would, anyway,' said Angie, who had begun to realise that landlines might be destined for extinction and raised loud complaints as a result.

Then they were gone, and the house felt marginally less full. But with Bonnie and Ben and the baby, and Robin throwing a rare tantrum for no reason, it was far from peaceful. 'Anyone for cake?' asked Simmy, desperately.

'We've only just had lunch,' Christopher pointed out. 'I'm going out for more logs.' He looked at the young couple. 'How long are you two staying?'

'Don't know,' shrugged Ben. 'We should be here when Moxo calls. Pity we can't do a Zoom, with all of us.'

Simmy laughed. 'I'd be surprised if he even knew what that was.'

'Don't be daft,' said Ben. 'Nobody's that much of a dinosaur.'

* * *

The call came promptly at three, but lasted a far shorter time than anticipated. 'We can't do this over the phone,' Moxon said at the start. 'Not if we're going to do it properly. But we can at least clear up the mystery of that baby.'

'The thing is,' said Simmy, 'once we start doing that, a whole lot more stuff is going to follow, and I might not know where to stop.'

He laughed. 'Don't worry. I'll tell you when.'

Something about the sound of his breathing reminded her of his very recent physical injuries. 'First – how are you? Does it hurt?'

'Only when I breathe,' he said. As a joke it fell very flat. 'I'm so glad to be home. It's safer here,' he added ominously.

'Pardon?' Unbidden images of Albanian drug dealers wielding huge knives came into her head.

'They were short-staffed. Nobody came when you pressed the buzzer. They accidentally deleted my X-rays. My wife's much more attentive.'

'Oh dear.'

'Yes. It's all rather terrifying, although I expect it's better than it looks. I mean – you don't hear much about droves of dying hospital patients, do you?'

'You need to be able to trust them, though.'

'That's the thing,' he agreed. After a short pause, he went on, 'So – the baby.'

'He's the child of an Albanian woman called Diellza. It was her husband that got murdered, so it's probably his child as well. She gave birth sometime on Saturday, and dumped him on a woman called Celia Parker, who lives in Glenridding, on Sunday. She brought him here, because I've got the equipment he needs. Or most of it. Diellza's gone missing. So has Celia. They might be together somewhere. The Buntings seem not to have had any idea she was pregnant, or has had the baby, even though she was in their house. We're not sure whether or not to believe them. And there's a woman called Aoife. And another one called Louise.' She paused for breath. 'That's it, basically.'

Ben caught her eye, as he smilingly held up a thumb of approval. Down the line, Moxon was spluttering.

'Sorry – was that very garbled?' she asked.

'It's very . . . *significant*,' he managed. 'You've known all this since – what? Sunday? Really?'

'I know. We're very sorry. We didn't know the dead man was Diellza's husband then. And it was Christmas, and Celia said . . . something about danger and everything going wrong. I don't remember now, but it persuaded us to keep him. It never even occurred to us that you might need to know about him for the investigation. I mean – how could his existence make any difference?' She could hear her own self-deception, loud and clear. 'It does mean Diellza couldn't really have done the murder. She was in labour when it happened. Or so we think.'

'It changes everything,' said Moxon heavily. 'You did this before,' he remembered. 'I thought I could rely on you not to do it again.'

'It's not that simple,' she defended. 'We were scared you'd take him into care, poor little thing. He's been fine here. My mother's been brilliant with him.' Only then did she recall that Angie would never see Jerome again, and might suffer as a result. 'She'll miss him.'

'Ah – so what were you intending to do with him, once Christmas is over?'

'I'm doing it now. Telling you. You must know the procedure.'

'That'll be the procedure for dealing with a newborn baby left with a strange family, will it? If I'm forced to quote the rule book, I'd say it involves hospital checks, social services, appeals for information through various media outlets. For a start.'

'That's what we thought.'

'But in this case, the infant appears to be the offspring of a murder victim, which rather complicates things.'

Simmy said nothing as she tried to assess the level of his wrath. With cautious optimism, she thought it was fairly low. 'It was Christmas,' she repeated. 'That made a difference.'

'Sunday wasn't Christmas. Not even Christmas Eve,' he told her. 'And not everything closes down or ceases to function over the festive days, anyway.'

'Doesn't it?' she said weakly.

His breathing was becoming louder with every passing minute. 'You don't sound very well,' she observed. 'Do you think we should leave it for another day or two? Honestly, we can't see any way that the existence of the baby affects your murder investigations. You were looking for Diellza anyway, weren't you? And there's sure to be all sorts of background stuff we don't know about, to do with the dead man. Lots of leads to follow up. We can't see why anybody around here would want to kill him.'

'Stop it,' he said. 'You don't know what you're talking about.'

These were strong words, coming from the affable detective. Simmy winced. 'I expect you're right,' she said meekly. 'We were hoping you might fill us in on that side of things.'

'I would if I felt well enough. I promised Sue I wouldn't be more than five minutes talking to you. She's waving at me to point out that it's been rather more than that. So, I have to go. You've given me rather a lot to think about.'

'Sorry,' she said, again catching Ben's eye. 'But we can't just leave it there, can we?'

'Come down here and see me tomorrow, then,' he said, making it sound like an order. 'Ten o'clock.'

'All right,' she said. 'But I need your exact address. I don't remember which house it is.'

He gave it to her with a small sigh.

Ben and Bonnie departed shortly before four o'clock, after Bonnie had enjoyed a prolonged cuddle with Jerome. 'I don't expect I'll see you again,' she told him. 'I might never see another baby as young as you.' She looked up at Simmy. 'He really is incredibly sweet and so *tiny*.'

'Nature's way of ensuring he gets properly cared for,' said Christopher.

'Right,' said Bonnie with naked scepticism. 'That worked well, didn't it? Did his mother never even look at him?'

'She'll be back for him any time now, I bet you,' said Ben. He seemed as surprised as the rest of them at his own words. 'We didn't properly consider that, did we?' he went on. 'And it's really the most obvious outcome. She's just parked him while everything gets sorted out.'

'Could be,' said Christopher. 'But the note she left sounded pretty definite. Nothing about it being a temporary arrangement.'

'We can't be sure it was her who wrote it,' Ben reminded them.

'It might have been Celia,' said Simmy. 'Or anybody.'

'Diellza might be dead,' said Bonnie, holding the baby even closer as she crooned over him, 'Poor little orphan.'

Simmy had Robin on her lap, helping him explore a bright plastic puzzle box that his Auntie Lynn had given him. 'I had one of those when I was his age,' said Ben. 'Apparently I was a child prodigy, fitting all the bits in years ahead of the average.'

'And see where that got you,' said Christopher. 'Working for a country auctioneer for a pittance.'

'It suits my skill set very nicely, actually,' said Ben stiffly.

'Like fitting lots of antiques onto a narrow shelf before the viewing day,' said Simmy, guiding her son's hand towards the square hole. 'Wonderfully useful.'

'We're going,' said Bonnie, holding the baby out for someone else to take. Christopher was the only candidate, accepting him awkwardly. 'Don't forget to tell us everything that happens tomorrow with Moxo. We're opening the shop on Saturday – right?'

'I suppose we ought to,' said Simmy with minimal enthusiasm. 'We'll have to check the stock and order new stuff, and see everything's okay. There will have been seven days closed. That's a lot. I hope Verity goes in and does some watering.'

'She's been already,' said Bonnie. 'I got a text to say the cold had done awful things to the poinsettias.'

'Why didn't she tell me? Why you?'

Bonnie shrugged. 'She thinks I'm on the spot and might go and have a look. You know what she's like about taking responsibility.'

'Nobody wants poinsettias after Christmas, anyway,' said Simmy. 'We shouldn't even have any left.'

'So Saturday, then? Will you be there?'

'I will,' Simmy promised.

Chapter Seventeen

'It's still Boxing Day,' said Christopher at six o'clock, with a kind of wonder in his voice. 'I have to keep reminding myself. It feels as if the whole Christmas thing is over and done with for another year.'

Simmy smiled, sharing the feeling. 'We've got all those lovely new presents to play with. And more days off work.'

'And a murder to amuse us.'

'Don't! We're liable to be in trouble about that. Although I expect they'll forgive us – they usually do.'

'Murder isn't very Christmassy, is it? It's a disjunction, if that's a word. They don't fit together at all.'

'Except that Jerome made a sort of bridge between them. I hadn't thought of that until now. He's a lynchpin.' The baby was lying on the sofa again, waving his hands gently and squinting at the ceiling. 'It's really not like having your own, is it? None of that blind panic and sense of everything being impossible to organise.'

'It is a bit the same, the way I see it,' Christopher disputed mildly. 'Unpredictability, for one thing. No chance of a full night's sleep. We were well past all that with Robin.'

'Maybe.' She briefly tried to capture the essence of how she was feeling. 'I really shouldn't have tried to breastfeed him. That was pretty silly of me. I just followed an animal instinct. It was interesting, though. It taught me something.'

'It was probably very good for him. Made him feel secure. He's very relaxed now, anyway.'

'What's going to happen next? Poor little thing – whatever it is, he's going to have to adjust to another person. It's got to be harmful. He'll grow up autistic or schizophrenic or something.'

Christopher snorted. 'Babies are tougher than that. Most of the human race throughout history have had to cope with being passed around – wet nurses, grandmothers, minders, nannies. It's more or less the norm. Nearly everybody copes with it perfectly well.'

'They don't cope with being in care, though. Those terrible Romanian places. And apparently they're almost as bad in Ukraine. And it's worse for boys.'

'His mother's highly likely to reclaim him, I think. Ben was right about that. She's scared because of the murder, but when that's all sorted, she'll come back for him.'

'They won't let her if she did the murder,' said Simmy darkly.

'Even then, I think they'd give her a few months before taking him away. Besides, we don't think she did it, do we?'

'I can't see how,' Simmy said, trying to convince herself.

A new thought struck her. 'I've got to go to Moxon's house tomorrow. Should I take Jerome as well? Where did we put that car seat? Robin's got the bigger size one now.'

'I dare say you can pad that one out so it fits.'

Simmy gave him a look. 'Actually, you're going to be here with Robin, aren't you? So I could just leave the baby with you. You can do a bottle as well as I can. That's much better than taking him out in the cold.'

'It's going to be better tomorrow, they say. Barely freezing at all once the sun comes up. And Moxon's going to want to see him, isn't he?'

'I can't think why. A baby's a baby.'

'They'll want to DNA test him. And check his health and all that.'

'Not at Moxon's house, though.' Her heart clenched at the prospect ahead of them. Not merely parting with the baby, but letting him get sucked into a system where procedures would frighten him, strangers would talk over him in loud voices, bottles be rammed into his mouth with no proper care. The images grew darker as she entertained them. 'Nobody's going to love him, are they?' she whispered. 'Even his mother might never love him.' She stared up at Christopher, who was standing beside the sofa. 'Don't you think we should just keep him? Where in the world would be better for him than here?'

Christopher went very still, assessing the effect of anything he might say. He was aware that men – husbands – always rejected suggestions of increasing the family. Dogs, cats, hamsters and even additional offspring – the initial reaction was almost always resistance. Something about responsibility and taking a hostage to fortune. 'I don't know,' was all he managed. 'It would be a big step.'

'If we were his foster parents, the state would pay us. Then we could adopt him later. And even if we had another of our own, that would be all right, wouldn't it?'

'His mother's probably coming back for him,' said Christopher doggedly. 'Don't get ahead of yourself.'

'And Celia?' The pink-haired woman floated in front of Simmy's mind's eye for the first time in several hours. 'She didn't tell us anywhere near the whole true story, did she?'

'Don't ask me. I'm no good at distinguishing truth from lies, never have been. I simply assume everything's true until proved otherwise.'

'You do, and it's one of your greatest virtues,' she told him sweetly.

He changed the subject. 'Robin had a good Christmas, didn't he? In spite of everything.'

'He had a *lovely* Christmas. Pity he won't remember any of it.' Silently, she added *And if we keep Jerome, Robin's never going to remember a time without him.*

'It's gone very quiet, just us. He must find it quite boring after all the excitement.'

'He's exhausted. I just hope the baby is as well. I could sleep for ten hours if they'd let me. Even Robin wouldn't stay quiet for that long.'

'It's not bedtime yet,' protested Christopher. 'We haven't had any supper.'

It was just past six. 'Oh, *food*,' Simmy groaned. 'Let's have scrambled eggs with bits of turkey and ham in it. And I could fry up the rest of the roast potatoes. I did far too many.'

'And I'm opening that bottle of white that your parents brought. It is still Christmas, after all.'

'There are many more days of Christmas still to go, according to my father. We've turned it all upside down these days.'

'As far as I'm concerned, it's all over and done with for another year.'

'Spoilsport,' she accused. Somewhere on the kitchen table her mobile was whirring, trying to tell her a text had been received. She found it under a tea towel and had a look.

'How's it going with the baby? Hope he didn't ruin Christmas? What will you do next? Celia.'

'The barefaced cheek of the woman!' Christopher exploded when she showed him. 'Irresponsible. Dishonest. Cowardly.' He ran out of epithets, but his reaction was unambiguous.

'Infuriating,' Simmy agreed mildly. 'We've been exploited, let's face it. But we went into it more or less willingly. What shall I say to her?'

'Nothing. As you said before, let her stew. If she's with Diellza, they'll be going mad wondering how the baby is.'

'Asking us what we'll do next, as if the whole thing's our problem and nobody else's.' Simmy was warming up slowly, anger just starting to erupt. 'I could tell her she's out of order and we're going to the police.'

'She'll have worked that out for herself. What other choice do we have? Is she more worried about that, or the state of the poor little thing? For all she knows, we've fed him the wrong mix and practically killed him. Or let the

223

dog savage him. Or put him out in the cold because we couldn't stand the crying.'

Simmy flinched. If she'd been Diellza, all those thoughts would very much have filled her head. 'Celia has no reason to care about him,' she said. 'She's not his mother.'

'But she's right in the middle of it all, isn't she? She could very well be the killer, remember. She knew the McGuire chap, probably had an affair with him or something. Didn't Bonnie suggest that at one point? Let's hope the police have cottoned on to her. Make sure you ask Moxon about that tomorrow.'

'All that brainstorming,' sighed Simmy. 'I lost track of it, to be honest. I should have made Ben leave me his notes, so I can remember what to tell Moxon.'

'Ben lives about half a mile from him. Let him do it himself.'

'He probably will,' she nodded. But the list of possible disasters that could befall little Jerome was nagging at her. 'I think I'll have to reply to Celia this time,' she concluded. 'Just a few words.'

'Up to you,' said Christopher. 'But don't be too nice.'

Simmy composed a brief text. '*All still alive. Seeing the police tomorrow.*' She showed it to Christopher, who nodded in satisfaction.

'That'll give her something to worry about,' he said.

The night was fractured into three-hour sections, Jerome punctuating it with apologetic demands for food. 'He's only five days old,' Simmy reminded herself and Christopher. 'It's only to be expected.'

'In a sane society, he'd be cuddled up in bed with us, and

could latch himself onto a teat with no fuss.' She could hear the quotation marks – and rightly ignored the comment as irrelevant, not to mention inconsistent. Christopher had never been happy to have a baby in the bed at night. First thing in the morning was a whole different matter.

'Sleep is overrated, anyway, according to my mother,' she said ten minutes later. 'And at least Jerome gets on with it. He's really very businesslike.'

'He'll be prime minster in no time,' murmured Christopher.

Which led Simmy to lie awake for fifteen minutes contemplating Jerome's future. The Christmas associations were impossible to avoid. Even Bonnie had voiced them aloud. Did this child have some glorious destiny, which she, Persimmon Henderson, had been selected to protect from deviation? She had never asked herself the same questions concerning her own child. All she required for him was health – mental and physical – and contentment. A facility for perceiving beauty, perhaps. A wholesome sense of belonging to a society. With Jerome, the possibilities seemed far wider and grander.

In the morning, she had forgotten all about these midnight fantasies. She had to get herself down to Windermere for an interview with DI Moxon that might turn out to be uncomfortably formal. Before she could leave, however, she had to ensure that her menfolk would survive her absence. Preparing a bottle for a very small baby was not something Christopher had ever done before. 'Was Robin ever this tiny?' he asked, more than once.

'Possibly not, because he was eight pounds at birth, and

Jerome doesn't seem anywhere near that much. But it's very subjective. He's bound to look minute compared to a strapping great toddler.' She took the baby and weighed him in her hands. 'Light as a feather,' she agreed. 'He might have been premature, of course. We never thought of that.' A flash of panic went through her at the idea that she had unwittingly succoured a thirty-six-week infant, which might normally have found itself in a hospital incubator. It only served to make Jerome even more special. Jesus might well have been premature as well, brought on by that long journey on the back of a donkey.

Christopher remained unaware of these thoughts, focused as he was on the hazardous task of mixing formula and getting it into the child. 'If you feed him now, he might not want any more till you get back,' he said optimistically. 'You won't be more than three hours, will you?'

'We can try,' said Simmy tolerantly. 'But he's not really due any more until about eleven.'

'Due? That sounds like a routine already.'

'I know it does, but he has been pretty regular every three hours or so. Hadn't you noticed?'

'Subliminally,' said Christopher with a sigh.

'It'll be fine. He'll probably be gone by the weekend. You'll probably have more trouble with Robin, actually. He's not in a very good mood today.'

'Not to mention the dog, cooped up all day.'

'We can all go for a walk this afternoon. Jerome can go in the sling, if I can find it.' Tired of the need for reassurances, she got away at nine-forty. 'Might be a bit late,' she muttered. 'See you when I see you.' And she was gone.

* * *

Moxon met her on the doorstep, looking grey and crumpled, his arm in a sling and his eye still swollen and discoloured. 'You really shouldn't be doing this,' she told him. 'Why hasn't your wife stopped you?'

'She's laid down a few rules. We have strictly one hour and not a minute more.'

'That'll please Christopher. He thinks being left with two small boys and a dog is well out of order.'

He gave no sign of registering the presence of the second 'small boy' but ushered her in and asked, 'Did you have a good Christmas?'

She laughed. 'We did, actually. Probably a lot better than yours. Does it hurt?'

'Don't ask. You'll just get a silly answer.'

'Like "only when I breathe"?'

'Precisely.'

Mrs Moxon was audibly in the kitchen, but did not make an appearance at first. 'Can we get you some coffee?' the detective offered.

'Only if you're having some. I think we just need to get on, don't we?'

'Yes, ma'am.' His mock compliance told her that her attitude was just slightly too heavy. She had never spent more than a very few minutes in his house and was less comfortable than expected to be placed in one of his armchairs as if a welcome guest.

'Sorry,' she said. 'This is all a bit awkward, don't you think?'

'Unusual, certainly. So let's get down to business. I'll just tell Sue she can stand down if you don't want a drink.'

He went to the doorway and called, 'No coffee, thanks, love.'

Five seconds later, a woman made an appearance, gazing at Simmy in open curiosity. They had never met before. 'You're Simmy Henderson, then,' she said.

She was the same height as Simmy, which was taller than average, in her mid-fifties at least. She had pale skin, a long face and rather thin hair. *She looks like a Quaker* came the idiotic unbidden thought. Something in the kindly expression and the calm self-confidence made her seem timelessly benign and patient. The presence of a younger woman towards whom her husband harboured open affection was clearly no threat to her. Simmy waited in vain for her to say, 'I've heard a lot about you.'

'I'm glad to meet you at last,' said Simmy. 'You must think I'm an awful nuisance.'

'I don't think that. Nolan's had good reason to be grateful to you, many a time. I know you have a little boy and a husband and coming here now can't have been especially convenient. So no – you're not a nuisance. After all, you gave him some vital help on Monday, didn't you? He might have died of hypothermia without your sanctuary.'

'We didn't do much. It was just luck that it happened near our house.'

'Well, I'll leave you to get on with it. He's still not well, as you can see. I'll trust you not to make him any worse.'

'I'll do my best,' said Simmy, throwing a worried look at Moxon.

'Let's get on with it, then,' he said, when his wife had closed the door on them. 'Although I don't exactly know where to start.' He had a folder in front of him, with a scanty collection of papers in it. 'I've printed these off this morning. Just the basics. I've left a lot of space for your contribution. I'll read it to you.'

'Okay.'

'Name of the deceased, Alexander McGuire. Sixty-two. Working at Manchester University as tutor and lecturer in Balkan Studies for the past twelve years. Married to Diellza Alija, Albanian national, nearly two years ago. Nothing of concern in her status, as far as we can see. Cause of death, stab wound to the neck. Time of death between late on Friday 21st December and 6 a.m. on the 22nd. Body found in the Glenridding Beck by walkers staying at an Airbnb close by.'

Simmy's attention was fixed on a single fact. 'Sixty-two?'

'That's right. He was married before, thirty-five years ago. That wife died after many years of marriage. No children.'

'That makes him more than thirty years older than Diellza. Doesn't that suggest it was to give her the right to come here? A marriage of convenience?'

Moxon shrugged. 'Possibly. But they lived together for two years, close to the university campus, appearing quite normal to colleagues and neighbours.'

'That's not what she told me.'

His head came up sharply. 'Explain,' he ordered.

'Well, I can't remember exactly, but she said she'd had to stay with the Buntings because . . . well, I don't know why, but she was obviously in trouble. I assumed she was trying to hide from him. Dan rescued her.'

'This is where everything gets extremely murky. We questioned as many of his colleagues as we could find, looking for people who knew them both, and got a somewhat hazy picture. Nobody had seen either of them for at least a week. She was never at all sociable, anyway, but they all knew her by sight. One or two mentioned her size. The fact of her being Albanian didn't go down too well with some, apparently.'

'Nobody noticed she was pregnant?' Simmy spoke carelessly, forgetting how little she had yet told the detective.

'What?'

'I told you – it's her baby. Born on Saturday, we think.'

He clutched his face, trying to use both hands, in spite of the sling protecting his injured elbow. 'I'm still trying to process it all.' His voice was cracked. 'I was rather hoping you'd got it wrong.'

She watched him anxiously, hoping the effort to follow the story wasn't harming him. 'Sorry,' she said. 'It doesn't seem such a big thing to me now, after so many days to get used to it. We know we should have told the police on Sunday, but it was Christmas.' Even that excuse was feeling tired and stale. 'That was the major consideration at the time. We didn't think the social services or police would be able to find anywhere for him – not as good as us. We had all the stuff already, more or less. He is very tiny,' she concluded, with a soft smile. She almost told him about the breastfeeding, but bit it back. It still felt mildly transgressive. 'We think he must have been rather premature.'

'She gave him to you, then?'

'No, she left him with Celia Parker, or so we think.'

'Explain,' he said again, with a look of apprehension. 'Slowly.'

She did her best to describe the events of the past

Sunday, briefly including the lunch at the Patterdale pub, and the later visit from Celia. 'Oh, and I brought the note that Diellza left with the baby.' She produced it from her bag.

'But what about the Bunting couple?' He looked dazed, but had managed to write down several lines of notes while Simmy was speaking. 'How could they not know she was pregnant? How could they fail to notice a baby in their house?'

'That's exactly what we've been wondering.'

'They've been lying,' he said with certainty. 'It's obvious.'

'But why would they? We think it might be true. Diellza's really very big. A pregnancy could be hidden quite easily, under winter clothes. And they probably never even considered it as a possibility. I mean – I saw her just before she gave birth, and I never suspected a thing. And he's a very small baby,' she said again.

Moxon shook his head. 'It's incredible.'

'But true,' Simmy added with a smile. 'And you do hear of it happening. Women living in a family, seeing them every day and managing to conceal their pregnancy. We think it's even possible that Diellza herself didn't know. The baby could have come as a massive shock to her, so all she could think of doing was giving him to someone she thought could cope.'

Moxon fingered the note. 'This reads as if she very much knew what she was doing.'

'She'd had a day to think about it. If the baby was born during Saturday, maybe quite late at night, she could have left him at Celia's while we were at the pub. One of her neighbours phoned her while we were at the pub and said

231

he'd heard funny noises. That must have been the baby, presumably.'

'Keeping him hidden from the Buntings for all that time? Wouldn't they have heard crying? Didn't she come out of her room at all?'

'It wasn't really very long, and mostly night-time. Dan was out on Sunday, anyway. She must have used the bathroom, I suppose. Maybe she had a radio playing loudly, or something. And somehow hidden the bloody sheets and the placenta. It's probably all bundled up under the bed.'

Moxon shook his head. 'We searched her room. Nothing unusual, except the window was wide open.'

'To get rid of the smell,' said Simmy. 'Childbirth is quite a smelly business.' Her mind's nose recalled the aroma of amniotic fluid. 'There's nothing quite like it.'

He winced. 'I'll take your word for that.'

'So, she gathered everything up and dumped it outside somewhere when she went down to Celia's. I bet the mattress is wet, and I bet your search people never checked it.'

'Why would they? Nobody had the least idea there was a baby in the picture.'

'We can't see that it would have made very much difference,' Simmy insisted. 'Except that it gives Diellza a pretty good alibi.'

He shook his head. 'It raises a whole lot of new issues. Questions. Lines of enquiry.'

'You can do a DNA test to see if he's McGuire's son.'

He looked at her with a mixture of reproach and weariness. 'And so much more. You withheld a crucial element from the investigation. You perverted the course of justice. You must surely see that you're liable to be in a whole lot of trouble.'

'I don't really see why,' she countered defiantly. 'We gave Jerome a safe warm refuge on a very cold Christmas. He disturbed our sleep and needed a lot of care and attention. Some people might think we were rather heroic.'

'You might be right, but I doubt it.'

'Well, let's leave that for now. What else do you want to know?'

'We don't have any record of a Celia Parker,' he said, referring back to his notes with an effort, acknowledging that time was short and much more had to be discussed. 'Where is she?'

'Ah – good question. She's gone off somewhere. We think she might well be with Diellza. She knew Alexander McGuire, by the way. We thought you might have worked that out. And we're not at all sure about a woman called Aoife something. She lives up at the top of Glenridding, quite near the beck. You're bound to have questioned her already. There's something about her – she's bossy and seems to know everybody. She's very pally with Fran Bunting. And she's got a depressed husband who never goes out. He might be more important than we think. We don't know anything about him.'

'Did the Parker woman tell you she knew McGuire?'

'No. Ben found it on the computer. She was his student a few years ago.'

He threw himself back on the sofa, causing his ribs and lungs to protest sharply. 'Aarghh,' he groaned.

'Careful.'

He took a few careful breaths and looked at the clock on the mantelpiece. 'Fifteen more minutes. What else haven't you told me?'

'I can't think of anything. Of course, there are lots of people who were at the party on Friday who might be involved. I didn't talk to them all, nowhere near. We're three miles from Glenridding. We hardly know anybody there. It was a surprise to be asked to the do. We assumed it was because people know Christopher, at least by reputation, as the auctioneer, you know.'

'Not to mention his wife who solves murders. Surely, they'd be aware of that as well?'

'Maybe Aoife was. And she might have talked to Fran about me. There was a bit of an undercurrent at the pub on Sunday, now I think about it.' She frowned. 'I hate to think I was the victim of some sort of conspiracy. I get all confused every time I try to work out how it might have gone. Surely, if someone there was planning to kill McGuire that very night, it would be pretty silly to invite me and Christopher up there?'

Moxon took another cautious breath. 'I'm not as good as you at speculating over conspiracies – at least, as young Ben Harkness has a habit of doing – but I can imagine one or two scenarios. Perhaps someone was aware of the intention to commit murder, and hoped to avert it by inviting you in. Or using you as a kind of smokescreen, or double bluff. If you see what I mean.'

She chewed her lip gently, and then shook her head. 'That's giving us far too much power. We've never yet managed to avert anything, have we?' She gave it more thought. 'And that would mean it had to be one of the

Buntings. Although – I suppose Aoife or even Celia could have put the idea in their heads. And we haven't mentioned Louise yet. She's pregnant. We saw them yesterday, you know. Did I mention that?'

'Who, exactly?'

'Everyone except Celia. The Buntings and Aoife and Louise. We walked along the edge of Brothers Water for a bit.'

Moxon waved this aside. 'Enough,' he said. 'I have to decide what to do now.' He looked at her severely. 'You don't seem very worried or guilty. I suppose you're assuming that I can get you out of trouble – and you shouldn't. At the very least I'll be forbidden from ever including you in an investigation again.'

'I don't think I'd mind that,' she smiled. 'And I am sorry we withheld information, but I think we've got a pretty good excuse, as I said already. We're helping now, aren't we? You can ask local hospitals if Diellza's been in – although I never believe that rubbish about new mothers possibly needing medical attention. They only say it to try and catch them.'

'No, they don't,' he said, suddenly angry. 'All kinds of things can go wrong.'

She shrugged his annoyance away. 'So what else?'

'Evidence,' he said, as if checking an invisible list. 'There is virtually no hard evidence to be had. The murder weapon appears to have been a short blade, very sharp. The neck was more slashed than stabbed, across the carotid artery. All too easily done, if you know where it is.'

She flinched. 'Yuk! Lots of blood, then.'

'Indeed. Although he was lying with his top half in the beck, so it was all washed away. He was exsanguinated, as they say, and half frozen when he was found. The cold water would have slowed the bleeding, so there's a suggestion that he wasn't able to move of his own accord – not enough to get out of the water. He might have been held down, possibly, although that would mean the killer having to get down a steep-sided bank and up again. He's more likely to have assumed nobody could survive losing so much blood and landing in freezing cold water – bashing himself on rocks as he fell, for good measure.'

'Poor man.'

Moxon kept on with his description, as if once started he didn't like to stop. 'There were two people staying very nearby, and they found him. There was blood on the pathway which alerted them.'

'Funny time to be there. Terribly cold, as well.'

'We've been very thorough in checking their background.'

'Not Albanian, then? Or jealous colleagues from the university?'

Moxon shook his head. 'Two men in their forties from Norfolk. Businessmen with very little free time, decided to spend Christmas up here, as some sort of extreme physical test. Both very fit from regular visits to a gym, both divorced. Members of a club. Finding a dead man was seen as an annoying interruption of their plans. One of them had to be given treatment for shock.' He sighed. 'Never seen a dead body before, apparently.'

'Right,' said Simmy. 'And they didn't hear any screams or anything?'

'Not a thing. Indications suggest the killing happened some hours earlier, like one or two in the morning.'

'But what was McGuire *doing* there? Was he chased all

across the freezing fells in pitch-dark by some determined killer?'

'It wasn't pitch-dark. There was a moon, almost full. Surely you noticed that when you left that party?'

'Not really. We went as fast as we could back to the car. It was too cold to stand around stargazing.'

'Well, it was crisp and bright. Easy to see your way.'

'He was more likely chased up there from the village, then. Why didn't he bang on someone's door for rescue? Or hide behind a wheelie bin?'

Moxon just looked at her and she abandoned her unhelpful brainstorming. 'Sorry,' she said.

The door opened and Mrs Moxon stood there like a headmistress. 'Time's up,' she said. 'Sorry, but that was the deal.'

'That's all right,' said Simmy, getting up from the comfortable chair. 'I think I've got myself in enough trouble for one morning. It was lovely to meet you.'

Moxon put out a hand, and for a second she thought he wanted her to shake it. Instead, it connected with her arm. 'Thanks for coming,' he said. 'And thanks for what you did for me on Monday. I'll have to pass all this on to Penrith, and they might well be in touch. They'll want to see the baby.'

'They'll take him away, I know,' she said. 'We never thought we'd be able to keep him after today. Although . . .'

'These things can move very slowly at times,' said Moxon. 'You might find yourselves fostering him for quite a while.'

Suddenly full of powerful mixed emotions, Simmy said nothing. Leaving him in the sitting room, the two women went to the front door. 'He's really not well,' said Sue Moxon. 'I think he'll be back in bed for much of the afternoon.'

'I made him cross,' Simmy admitted. 'I hope that won't hurt him.'

'I'm sure he'll be all right,' Sue reassured her. 'Just rather drained. He really is horribly bruised.'

'Well . . .' There did not seem to be anything more to say.

'He'll be in touch.'

'Oh yes,' said Simmy.

Chapter Eighteen

Back in Hartsop, Christopher was both relieved to see her and proud that he'd coped. 'Jerome missed you,' he said, with a soppy smile. 'How was poor old Moxon?'

'Struggling rather, although he did his best to hide it. We had to keep it strictly to an hour. There's lots I never managed to tell him. I thought of about six things on the drive home.' She was careful not to comment on Jerome's soaking nappy or the streaks of Marmite down Robin's chin. 'And I stopped in Troutbeck for more formula and nappies. Most of the shops were open.'

Christopher was sitting back on the sofa like a farmer after a hard day carting bales. 'So, are we in trouble about the baby?'

'Pretty much. He tried to scare me, but I think we'll escape jail. We've broken the rules too many times and got away with it for him to be very convincing.'

'Embarrassing for the poor chap, though. He must

spend his life defending us – or you, anyway. Did he say when we'd have to hand him over – Jerome, I mean?'

'He's got no idea. I very much doubt if such a situation has ever happened to him before. He did say he thought it might not be very soon.'

'Because . . .' he started to form a slow sentence, 'I'm wondering how we'd manage, with you having to go to the shop at least one day a week. He is terribly young, after all. Your mother would have him, probably, but . . . well, you know what I'm trying to say.'

The surge of irritation took Simmy by surprise. 'This is all my problem, then, is it?' she flashed at him. 'As usual.'

He gave her a weary look. 'For heaven's sake, don't come over all feminist on me. Face facts, Sim. For a start, my business earns at least four times as much as yours does. It's a lot closer geographically, and its future very much rests on my shoulders. Yours is miles away, and you've got a nice team of capable females who can run it without you if they have to. But if you're going to keep it going, you have to devote a lot of time and attention to it. Nothing stands still. You'll always have to be looking for new outlets, new lines, new ways of doing things. That's business.'

'New suppliers. New fashions. Yes, I know all that. You've seen me gearing up for Valentine's Day already. Bonnie's always full of ideas and if she'd just get driving, she could manage without me nearly all the time, and still keep up with all these changes you're talking about.'

'And you'd be happy about that?'

'Have you forgotten we've been trying for another baby since the summer? You never said anything about my divided loyalties, or whatever it is you're on about, until now.'

'We'd have had nine months to plan it,' he muttered sulkily.

The landline saved any further disagreements from escalating, with a call from Russell. 'What news?' he began, as soon as Simmy answered.

She gave him a brief summary of her meeting with Moxon. 'It seems we can keep the baby for a bit longer. There was a lot I never got round to telling him.'

'I've been going over something that girl Louise said yesterday. It stuck in my mind, and I was awake in the night thinking about it.'

'What was it?'

'She was talking about the Albanian woman, as we all were, and she told me about a few words she overheard at that party you went to. Actually, it was almost the only thing she said about anyone connected to the murder. Apparently, it had been niggling her, and she wondered if she ought to tell the police about it.'

'What *was* it, Dad?'

'She wanted to borrow some money from the one who dumped the baby on you. Celia – is that right? Louise called her "Madame Pink Hair". I didn't know who she meant, of course. But later on, your mother mentioned you saying she'd got pink hair. Celia, that is.' He paused and gave a little cough. 'Sorry, I'm not explaining it very well, am I? I didn't sleep much last night and it's catching up with me.'

'Louise heard Diellza asking Celia if she could borrow some money,' Simmy paraphrased. 'Got it. I think we've already come to the conclusion that those two knew each other pretty well. If Celia knew McGuire, then it's a fair guess she knew his wife as well. Although I'm not sure he was married when she was his student. They must have kept in touch since then.'

'So you don't think it's important, what Louise said?'

'It might be. It confirms what we're starting to think. I can tell Moxon, if I remember. Do you think Louise was seriously worried about it?'

'Probably not. She's told me, hasn't she? She might think it'll get back to the police through me and she needn't think any more about it. I keep thinking it can't be at all important, but on the other hand, it just might be.'

'You mean because you're my dad, and I'm famous for helping with police investigations, we'll pass it on?' She sighed. 'I really don't like the idea of that. It makes me feel like a pariah. Maybe it's why nobody seems to want to be my friend.'

'Too late to worry about that now,' he said heartlessly. 'You need to make a virtue of it. Some people would find it reassuring, I'd have thought.'

'I doubt that. They've probably all got some secret habit that breaks some law or other. They'll worry I'm going to shop them.'

'Cynic,' he accused.

'Realist,' she countered.

'Besides, that Aoife girl wants to be your friend. She was all over you yesterday.'

'No, Dad – she was just making sure she didn't miss anything I said.' The prospect of having Aoife as a friend struck her as decidedly unappealing. 'She really isn't very nice. The funny thing is, the only one I really felt friendly about was Celia. And she's probably top of the list of murder suspects.'

'Because she's gone missing?' Russell sounded uncertain, as if he was losing track. 'Is that right? Honestly, Sim, there are far too many women in this story. Barely a male person to be found.'

'Just Dan Bunting,' Simmy agreed. 'Who looks as if he's the one that started the whole thing off in the first place, taking Diellza home with him. We still have no idea why she needed sanctuary, when she had a house and a husband in Manchester. And presumably the husband knew perfectly well she was pregnant.'

'Which brings us back to sinister machinations involving Albanian gangs and illegal drugs. That's still my preferred explanation. They were going to kidnap his wife and child and blackmail him into selling drugs to his students. Makes perfect sense.'

'I don't think it does, Dad,' said Simmy with regret. 'Now I've got to go and have some lunch. Looks as if it might be ham sandwiches and reheated Christmas pud.'

'Lovely,' said Russell Straw with a chuckle.

The Hendersons were still finishing off their reheated Christmas pudding when a uniformed policewoman came to the door to take Jerome's DNA. She introduced herself as Sergeant Inskip, smiling meaningfully at Simmy. 'We have met before,' she said. 'You might not remember.'

'Have we? When?'

'A few years ago now, it must have been. I've lost a bit of weight since then and I think my hair might have been darker. Don't worry about it.'

'I won't,' said Simmy, still none the wiser. 'You haven't wasted much time, have you? DI Moxon must have reported in the minute I'd left this morning.'

'Right. You really set things arse over tit, as they say. Where's this baby, then?'

'Over here.' Jerome was in his usual nest on the sofa, with Cornelia providing warmth and protection. At the sight of the newcomer, she jumped off and stood to attention, tail slowly wagging.

'You let the dog do that?' The woman was clearly horrified.

'She's very careful with him.' *Haven't you read Peter Pan?* she wanted to ask. Nana had been one of her absolute favourite characters for years.

'He's so *tiny*.'

'I know. But he's quite robust. And very placid, considering.' She was resisting the urge to show any sign of apology for being in possession of the baby in the first place. Criticism of her substitute parenting was not to be tolerated. However careless she might be, she was an improvement on the child's natural mother.

'He must have totally disrupted your Christmas.'

'In a nice way.' Simmy looked to Christopher for backup. He was hovering in the kitchen doorway, chewing the last of his pudding. 'Isn't that right?'

'It's been . . . interesting,' he said non-committally. 'We had most of the essentials already, you see.'

'No need to get into that now,' said the sergeant, opening a medical pack. 'I always seem to get this job, but I've never done a baby before.'

'He won't like it,' Simmy worried.

'Sorry about that.'

The procedure was brief, but uncomfortable and very intrusive. The spatula was too big for the little mouth, and besides, he'd been woken up from a peaceful sleep. Cornelia and Robin were both deeply concerned at the resulting howls.

Simmy rocked him gently, walking round the room, holding him close, until he went quiet again. Sergeant Inskip did not appear to be in any hurry. 'I gather the normal rules about sharing information with the police don't apply to you,' she said. 'You're the talk of the station in Penrith.'

'Oh dear,' said Simmy insincerely. At some point during the past year, she had resigned herself to this sort of remark. In Windermere it had somehow been different, perhaps because she lived so close to the small police station, everything more cosy and personal. The Penrith people were more distant and much less known. Whatever they were saying about her was unlikely to have much basis in reality.

'So, what's happening with the investigation?' she asked.

'We've found Mrs McGuire's GP and questioned him.'

'Already?'

She nodded. 'Twelve-thirty today, or thereabouts. He was perfectly forthcoming – up to a point, anyway. Apparently, this little man wasn't due until the first week of February. Normal pregnancy, given the mother's weight issues. He last saw her in mid-November. She missed her two December appointments.'

'Don't pregnant women go to the hospital clinic for

their checks, not the GP?' asked Simmy. 'I did.'

'She was booked for a home birth. Against his advice, but he wasn't especially concerned. He's very old-school, should have retired ages ago. Said he'd delivered twenty babies in the nineteen-eighties, when there was a fad for having them at home.'

'Were you there?' asked Christopher. 'You seem to have gathered a lot of detail.'

Sergeant Inskip smiled. 'I'm personally interested. I'm having one of my own in June.'

'Congratulations,' said the Hendersons in unison.

'Thanks.'

'So Diellza did know she was pregnant,' said Simmy slowly. 'We've been thinking otherwise.'

'Of course she did. How could she possibly not?'

'But she didn't tell the Buntings and they didn't guess. Or so they say. They haven't once mentioned a baby, anyway.' She shook her head in confusion. 'It's all wrong, isn't it?'

The woman adopted a severe expression. 'You might say that. You concealing the baby's existence has very much impeded the investigation. We've had to start all over again, basically. But DI Moxon spoke up for you. After all, it was Christmas.'

'Thank you,' said Christopher. 'We knew we'd be in trouble, but it just seemed the best thing in the circumstances. It sounds as if you're catching up now, anyway.'

'We need to find Mrs McGuire more urgently than ever, as well as the Parker lady. I understand she's got pink hair?'

'She has – but she might have changed it, of course.'

Simmy looked at Inskip's own hair, which had apparently become lighter in recent years. 'Or be wearing a wig. The pink was pretty distinctive.'

'So he is premature,' said Christopher. 'Doesn't seem to be causing him any trouble.'

'Lucky. Mind you, dates can be very imprecise. I don't think she ever went for a scan, which is highly unusual. Practically unheard of, in fact.'

'Verging on the illegal, I shouldn't wonder,' said Simmy, channelling her parents, who never let authoritarian tendencies go unchallenged.

'He's small, though. I bet he wants to feed all the time.'

'You're very well informed,' said Simmy.

'My mother's a midwife,' said Inskip carelessly. 'I have every scrap of theory at my fingertips. It's the practice that's going to be the trouble.' She looked at Cornelia, who was back on the sofa, despite the absence of the baby. 'I mean – I'm sure the books say you shouldn't let a dog lie on a newborn baby.'

'She wasn't *on* him. She just cuddles up to keep him warm. It's instinct.'

'They told me you don't take much notice of rules,' sighed the officer. 'Anyone else would be under arrest by now.'

Simmy was preoccupied with thoughts of Diellza and her murdered husband. 'How soon do you get the DNA results?' she asked.

'A few days, maybe longer with the holidays. But I can tell you now, he's not McGuire's.'

'What? How?'

'Look at him! There's no way that's the son of a ginger-haired Scot. If I had to guess, I'd say his father was from somewhere east of Turkey. New babies always resemble their fathers, you know. It's nature's way of reassuring the man of his wife's fidelity.'

'Oh,' said Simmy, struggling to process this new turn of events. 'But you can't be sure. He looks more or less averagely European to me.'

'Dangerous ground, I admit. But McGuire was in his sixties, not in great health, and thought to be on pretty poor terms with his wife. If she'd gone off with some other bloke, it wouldn't be too surprising, would it? In fact, it would explain quite a lot.'

'Have you *seen* her?'

'Pictures. What's your point?'

'I'm not saying anything else. She was a pleasant enough person, I suppose. It's hard to think back to how she was last Friday, after everything that's happened.'

'You're judging her for abandoning her baby.'

'I expect I am,' said Simmy. 'Wouldn't anyone?'

'Including the baby, in years to come,' Inskip agreed. 'Unless she's dead, of course.'

Simmy hadn't allowed herself to consider that possibility, for fear of secretly and shamefully wishing it to be true. 'She's not dead,' she said. 'Someone would have found her if she was.'

'Huh,' said the police sergeant.

Jerome passed a restless afternoon, rejecting the bottle but crying piteously when it was removed. 'Colic, according to your father,' said Christopher.

'It's a catch-all for any unexplained crying,' Simmy

complained. 'I think he's just in a mood because we woke him up for the DNA test.'

'You forget how time-consuming they are, don't you? Hours wasted in trying to pacify them, or entertain them, or get food into them. You can't do anything else but give them your whole attention.'

Simmy looked at him in surprise. When had he ever devoted more than ten minutes to any of those activities when Robin was tiny? Presumably he was trying to reflect her experience back at her, with all due sympathy. 'That's true,' she said neutrally. 'All part of the package, as they say.'

'A deceptively small package, which expands like one of those Christmas stocking toys, until it's filled the entire house.'

'Like in *There's No Such Thing as a Dragon*. Maybe that's the real moral of that story.'

He went up to her, where she stood by the window rocking the baby. 'Sim – do we really want to take him on permanently? Two boys, close in age, rampaging round the place when we're in our fifties? Is that really us?'

'I don't know,' she confessed. 'I always liked to think of myself as a sort of earth mother, wearing floral prints and baking for a whole family of kids. I still like that picture of myself. The truth is, there's not really anything I'd rather be doing. The shop's all very well, and I love the whole business of flowers and learning more and more about them. But I do like babies. I like the whole physical business that comes with them. Skin on skin, and all that emotion.'

'Blimey! I hadn't expected all that.'

'Christmas. New Year. Time for reassessing and making plans. New life.'

'Not to mention our regular involvement in police investigations into violent deaths.'

'That doesn't fit with what I'm trying to say.'

'Well, it should. It's come to be part of our identity now, like it or not.'

She thought for a moment, before admitting, 'I do love Ben and Bonnie and their enthusiasm for all that. And I suppose we've all got quite good at it, without really meaning to.'

'Even me?' He cocked his head sideways.

She laughed. 'You do have your moments,' she assured him. 'And in your line of work, you can hardly avoid some of the seamier side of life.'

'Perish the thought!' he protested. 'I've told you before, stop bracketing me with *Lovejoy*. It's not like that at all.'

'All right. I'm just saying – with Ben working for you now, any shady practice is going to have to get past him. And I don't fancy its chances, do you?'

'We've got away from the question of babies,' he pointed out.

Jerome had gone quiet, unable to compete with the intensity of the conversation. 'I have a feeling that when it comes to babies, it's almost entirely out of our control,' said Simmy, with a small, satisfied smile.

He could find nothing to say to that, other than favouring his wife with an exaggeratedly worried frown that was mostly intended to convey a less-than-serious response. Christopher Henderson had always been known as someone who took life pretty lightly. Marriage and parenthood and running his own business had dented some of his frivolous outlook, but not dispelled it completely.

Neither of them was surprised when another knock came on their door at half past two. 'I bet it's Lily,' said Christopher.

'And I bet it's bloody Dan Bunting,' said Simmy, wondering at her own antipathy. It also flicked across her mind that her husband was noticeably quick to think of their young neighbour. Did Lily linger in his consciousness more than was appropriate?

Cornelia's bark was half-hearted, not enough to disturb Jerome who was fitfully dozing. Robin was still finding his new toys sufficiently absorbing that he ignored any outside distractions. Simmy went to the door. They were both wrong about the identity of the caller.

It was Corinne. 'Bonnie sent me to put you straight on a few things,' she announced without preamble. 'Seeing as how it's my area of expertise, as you might say.'

Simmy experienced a flood of relief, spiced with genuine joy. 'Sent by the angels,' she laughed. 'Although Bonnie might qualify as one, on a good day.'

Robin detected the presence of glad feelings and trotted over to the newcomer holding his puzzle box in both hands. 'Present,' he said, rightfully identifying the source of his mother's happiness.

'Hey, that's lovely!' Corinne gushed, taking the toy and shaking it. 'Full of all its pieces, at that.' She addressed Simmy. 'Why do all their favourite things involve so many small pieces of plastic? Well, you might not have got to that stage just yet. It'll come, believe me.' She bent down to Robin's height and said, 'Have you got a little baby to show me?'

Robin waved a vague arm towards the sofa and nodded.

'Come on, then, let's have a look,' she invited. Then, with a warm arm still around the toddler's shoulders, she crouched beside Jerome, gently pulling the blanket away from his face.

'Looks like a five-pounder to me,' she murmured. 'I had a whole string of them at one time. Little scraps of trouble, the lot of them.'

The Hendersons had barely moved since Simmy had opened the front door. They stood back as if witnessing a masterclass in some vital skill. Which they were, Simmy realised.

'Can I pick him up?' Not waiting for a reply, Corinne gathered the little bundle, and settled herself on the sofa, still including Robin. Jerome whimpered and Robin sighed, but did not utter his usual observation.

'Tea?' offered Christopher weakly.

'Lovely,' said Corinne. 'This is a brilliant sofa, by the way.' Somehow she found a hand to reach out and pat Cornelia on the head. 'Sorry, doggo – I forgot to say hello to you, didn't I? I bet you're good with the baby, aren't you?'

'She's amazing,' said Simmy. 'Treats him like a puppy, only gentler.'

'They mostly do,' said Corinne comfortably. 'But only if the people are relaxed about it. Which you obviously are.'

'I remembered what Bonnie told me about you and dogs and babies,' Simmy said, with a flicker of surprise. 'I must have taken it on board more than I realised. We never had a dog when I was small.'

Christopher was listening from the kitchen and came to the doorway. 'Plus, I had a bit of input,' he pointed out. 'I stayed in a village in Guatemala for a month or more, when I was travelling, and learnt a lot about how babies work. We do it very badly over here.'

'Tell me about it,' said Corinne.

'Mind you, you had to be wary of those dogs. You wouldn't want their fleas all over your little ones. They're not like the pampered things we have here.'

Tea was produced, which the women took as a signal to get down to something more serious. 'Bonnie's told me the whole story,' Corinne began. 'And I thought I might have something to say about it, out of my own experience, if you like. The thing is – quite a lot of women give up their babies when they're first born – or they try to. Especially if it's a bit prem and scarily small. They panic, and think they won't love it enough, that they're not worthy of the responsibility. Your lady sounds as if she's got herself in a right royal mess, and she wants to protect the baby from it all. Right?' Without waiting for a response, she went on, 'But nine times out of ten, they change their minds and settle down. All those tinies that came to me for fostering – nearly all of them went back to their mum within a couple of weeks. We had a brilliant team of social workers in those days, led by one really amazing woman. She kept everything calm, no judging, no firm decisions that would be hard to change. "Take it to Corinne for a few days," she'd say, and I'd lose another two or three nights' sleep, before the mum agreed to share the care, and before you knew it, everything was going on as it should. Not always, mind, but most of the time.'

'You're trying to warn me that we've only got Jerome for a little time? We knew that. I told Moxon about him this morning. A woman came and did his DNA just now. But – what if both his parents are dead? What happens then?'

'Why would his mother be dead? She's just staying out of sight somewhere in the warm. Chances are she's with the woman who brought the baby here. Stands to reason, if they've both gone missing – surely?'

'Maybe. Celia can't have been telling me the truth on Sunday. Not all of it, anyway. She made me think she'd got no idea where Diellza had gone. And the policewoman who came said Jerome can't be the son of the murdered man, anyway. His colouring's all wrong, she says.'

'Phooey to that. But if it's right, then he's still got *two* living parents, hasn't he?'

Simmy clutched her head in melodramatic despair. 'Don't make it even *more* complicated. My head can't take it. My mother and Bonnie both keep saying "Everybody lies" and it's true. The Buntings especially can't be trusted. And the other women we've met. They might all be in some awful conspiracy together. It does feel like that sometimes. We don't know whether they knew Diellza was pregnant. We thought at first that *she* didn't know, but now we're told she was having proper antenatal care from a GP and was booked for a home birth. But then she just walked out, a month ago probably, and ended up being rescued by Dan Bunting, for some reason.'

'Maybe *he's* the father,' said Corinne.

Simmy stared at her, and then at Jerome's little face.

'That would explain a lot,' she said. 'But Dan's face is nothing like that. He's got a small chin and a low brow. And quite pale skin.'

'You never can tell,' said Corinne with a smile.

'DS Inskip thinks you can. She's the one who did the DNA test. She's pregnant herself.'

Corinne merely shrugged.

'The main point we should be thinking about has to be the murder,' Simmy insisted. 'It might not have anything to do with Jerome at all . . .' She faltered, hearing for herself how unlikely that sounded.

Corinne snatched up the thread. 'Don't be daft. If I've got it right, he was here looking for his wife, probably wanting her home for Christmas. Bonnie says he was at some sort of bunkhouse above Glenridding. He must have thought she was staying there, probably because he'd tracked her phone. People do that these days, you know.'

Again Simmy just stared. 'Of course! That would explain it perfectly. But – Moxon never said anything like that. Do you think the police have worked it out as well?'

'As well as Bonnie, you mean? One would hope so.'

'Except Diellza had been at the Buntings for days already. Why didn't he come sooner? In daylight, before it got so cold?'

'Presumably he'd been phoning or texting her pleading with her, or even threatening, before he went to the hassle of actually coming here. And I'm not actually sure how it works – tracking someone if they don't want to be tracked. He might have had to get some help.'

Simmy sighed. 'Everything keeps coming back to guesses. It's all "might" and "maybe". His neck was slashed, you know. Can you imagine doing that to someone? Wouldn't you need a terribly sharp knife? And probably a lot of force? Would a woman do that?'

'You mean you think his wife did it?' Corinne gazed thoughtfully at the baby's face. 'She'd have to be in a right old state, wouldn't she?'

'At least she'd have been in a hurry,' said Christopher. 'If she was in early labour, she'd have wanted to scoot back into the warm where she could get on with it.'

'Heavily pregnant women in early labour don't *scoot*,' laughed Corinne. 'They can barely walk.'

'I wonder about Celia,' mused Simmy. 'If she was actually there with Diellza somehow for the birth. She's used to dealing with sheep and things. She can probably use a knife on warm flesh if she has to. She might even have cut the throats of a few ewes with some incurable condition.'

'She couldn't have been at the Buntings, though. They'd have seen or heard her.'

'Not necessarily. It's a big house. She might have hung about after the party and gone back in.'

Christopher shrugged. 'Far-fetched, if you ask me.'

Corinne drained her tepid tea and stood up. 'I won't stay,' she said. 'I've given you my bit of advice, for what it's worth. You're doing everything right with this little man. Don't let the social people bully you – that's important. They're a lot less sure of themselves than they used to be, and they're permanently short of people. Once you decide what you really want, just stand your ground and smile sweetly and you might be surprised at how easy it gets.'

'Thanks,' said Simmy, stuck on the words *once you*

decide what you really want. That was the part that did not feel easy at all.

'I'm surprised Ben and Bonnie didn't come with you.'

'Oh, but they did. Didn't I say? I left them up at Glenridding having a look round. I've got to collect them again in a few minutes.'

'Ah.' Simmy felt unfairly excluded, not for the first time. The freedom the youngsters had to roam around the fells and meres was sometimes a source of mild resentment. The fact of a small child needing to be taken into consideration could be sorely limiting at times. She found herself looking forward to the days when Robin would be in school all week and she would have those hours to herself. And yet . . . the same old dilemmas and debates swirled around her head once again, with all the associated frustration and guilt. It was society's fault, she decided. It was society that made life almost impossible for the parents of young children.

'Come with me, if you like,' Corinne invited. 'They can tell you if they've found anything, and Chris can mind the kids for a bit, I'm sure. Bring the dog. She looks a bit cooped up.'

'Right – I will.' And without even consulting her husband, she was into her coat and out of the door, with Cornelia exuberantly running ahead.

Chapter Nineteen

There was barely an hour of daylight left. 'You'd better not leave it too long before getting home,' she advised Corinne. 'The roads can't be very nice. I saw a few dodgy patches when I went down to see Moxon this morning. It'll be nasty in the dark.' She forbore to mention the ramshackle state of Corinne's car, which was always on the brink of losing a vital part, or running out of something.

Cornelia jumped happily onto the back seat, and they quickly covered the three miles northwards to Glenridding. There was very little traffic. 'I always think this is a funny time – the days between Christmas and New Year,' said Corinne. 'Nobody really knows what to do with themselves.'

'I've been dying to do this since Sunday,' Simmy admitted. 'I want to see if I can spot Aoife's house – she's a woman we've seen a few times lately. She knows everyone we've been talking about. There's something not right about her – although I can't imagine her slashing anybody's throat.'

'Sounds as if she's on the list, all the same,' said Corinne.

'Ben would probably agree with you.'

'They told me to drive as far as Rattlebeck Bridge, if we can find that. I've got a map somewhere.'

Simmy was embarrassed at her ignorance of an area so close to home. Whenever she examined the map for herself, with the vast expanse of uninhabited fells stretching in every direction but south, she felt intimidated. It was wild and frightening, right there. Even on a sunny summer day you could get hopelessly lost and overwhelmed if you set out inadequately prepared to reach Helvellyn or even the more modest Knott, hardly more than two miles from Hartsop.

Corinne drove confidently through the little settlement of Glenridding, turning off the main road and passing a row of terrace houses. Helvellyn looked as if they could almost touch it. 'Apparently we come to it up here somewhere.'

'Where did you drop them?'

'In the car park back there.'

'Cornelia thinks we're going for a walk.'

'She might get lucky. It depends whether we can find a place to park. The ground's nice and hard – there's bound to be somewhere.'

'We can phone Ben and see where they are,' Simmy said, reassuring herself. Within a minute they had left anything resembling civilisation and were in an empty land of rising fells scattered with bare winter trees. 'How far are they likely to have gone?'

'I don't think it's far. They were assuming they'd see police tape to mark the spot. The map shows the beck running all the way down from one of those pikes. But they'll still be around here somewhere. It's only an hour since I dropped them.'

'They'll have spoken to five people, found a vital piece of evidence and be on the phone to the police, I shouldn't wonder.'

Corinne laughed. 'This is it, look,' she said a few moments later. A bridge crossed the beck, close to an old white cottage, with a farm driveway going off to the left. The waterway beneath them was quite a low and narrow business at that particular spot. Judging by the generous stretch of the bridge, there had to be times when it rose significantly higher and spread a lot wider. Floods were a regular occurrence, with a spectacular one in 2015 still painfully vivid in local memories.

'We can leave the car over there and walk up to meet them,' Corinne decided. She pointed to a patch of gravel evidently intended as a parking spot. 'We won't even have to resort to leaving it in a gateway.'

Parking in gateways was normal behaviour in the cluttered Lake District. So long as enough space was left for vehicles to squeeze through, it generally went unprotested. Umpteen million cars came into the area every year and had to be parked somewhere. Without the cars the tourists wouldn't come and without the tourists the locals would starve. So ran the reluctant logic. So long as the wilderness areas survived, complaints remained muted. Russell Straw regularly voiced the general feeling, adding his own special beef about the excessive presence of sheep. To his mind, sheep were a pernicious blight on the landscape and should be reduced by about ninety per cent. 'It's never going to happen,' his wife repeatedly told him.

Cornelia ran ahead as the two women strolled along the narrow road, saying little. Simmy found herself scanning the landscape for any sign of Ben and Bonnie. There were stone walls and sudden bends that could conceal them, but the dog would find them if they were anywhere close by. It was still cold, but noticeably less so than in previous days. The brown of dead bracken coated much of the fellsides to their left and right. 'Good place for a murder,' said Corinne carelessly. 'Bonnie says he probably deserved it. She thinks he was an abusive husband and got what was coming to him.'

'I suppose we've all been tending to think something like that, but we've got nothing substantial to go on. He might have been an absolute pet, and she exploited him to get British citizenship.'

'It's the baby,' said Corinne. 'It'll be all about the baby.'

'I hope not, because that gets us into worse trouble with the police, for not telling them about him.'

'Better late than never.'

Clichés were seldom of much consolation, Simmy reflected.

'There they are!' Corinne pointed to the right. 'They've got somebody with them.'

A trio of figures were coming down a track that very soon deposited them on the road in front of Simmy and Corinne. They were less than half a mile from where they'd left Corinne's car. Cornelia joyfully pranced around them all. 'That's Aoife,' Simmy muttered, shortly before they were all united in the little roadway.

'She's been showing us how everything fits together. We

went up there to get a better view of it all,' said Bonnie, once perfunctory introductions had been made. 'Look, it's right here – just past the farm. Come and see.'

The group processed a short way along the track, where there was a sudden drop between the path and the beck. A strip of police tape had been strung between two temporary fenceposts, preventing anyone from getting close to the edge. 'This must be where they found the blood. And down there was the body,' said Ben. He went beyond the tape and pointed down the slope. Following his gaze, Simmy examined the scene with interest. Perhaps twenty feet below them, the beck trickled unspectacularly over an accumulation of rocks and stones of various sizes. She remembered Moxon's graphic account of what must have happened. A brief struggle on the path, a violent slash across the throat, resulting in an instant gush of arterial blood, and an easy push over the edge. The bleeding body would roll down onto the icy slippery stones and come to rest in the shallow freezing water. She stepped back, saying nothing. The others made no attempt to follow Simmy's lead. Aoife had actually moved a few yards away, distancing herself from them all.

Bonnie approached Simmy. 'It makes it all so real, doesn't it?' she said.

'Poor man,' Simmy sighed.

'He probably didn't know much about it. He might even have been knocked out on the stones. He was pretty bruised.'

'It's really not far out of the village, is it? The Buntings' house is just over there.' She indicated a group of buildings clearly visible, between themselves and the car park.

'I know. We'd been thinking it was a lot further up the track than this.'

'I wonder what happened to the knife. It must have been terribly sharp.'

'Chucked it down there, probably. It's probably at the bottom of Ullswater by now.'

Ben had joined them. 'They haven't found it, anyway,' he confirmed. 'According to Nancy, that is.'

Bonnie shivered. 'We should go. Has Corinne been useful?' she asked Simmy.

'Very. And I want to get back, as well. It'll be dark soon.'

'Not for a while yet,' said Ben. 'And it's never as dark as you think, when you're out in it. We're fine for half an hour at least.'

Simmy felt a strong resistance to discussing anything further in the presence of Aoife. 'Well, I need to get back,' she persisted. 'Christopher's already been left in charge once today.' She had bitten back the words *of the children* just in time. Whilst the existence of little Jerome could surely not be much of a secret any more, she was still wary of mentioning him. Just what Aoife thought she knew was still unclear, given that she had heard Jerome on Boxing Day. There was so much as yet unexplained – especially where Aoife and the Buntings were concerned.

'Come on, then,' said Corinne, leading the way back to the car. 'Sorry, doggie – it wasn't much of a walk.'

Cornelia gave her a long-suffering look and followed them all back the way they'd come.

'Where's your house, exactly?' Simmy asked Aoife. There were very few buildings visible.

263

'Just above the caravan park. You have to go through it to get to us.'

'Doesn't that get awkward in the summer?' asked Corinne.

'Not at all,' said the woman, with the brisk, almost snappy, tone that Simmy had come to expect from her. *Had Ben and Bonnie shared anything with her that they shouldn't,* Simmy wondered. They were mostly quite discreet, but there were nuances that they could hardly be aware of. Ever since the Friday evening party, Aoife had lingered in Simmy's mind with an aura of disquiet. Who *was* she, with an invisible husband and a funny name? There was something witchy about her, living high above everyone else, watching them from her upper windows and making manipulative plans.

Don't be daft, she told herself. There was nothing to support her unease except vague impressions and too much imagination.

'The police are going to be back tomorrow,' Aoife said now. 'They'll be hunting for the murder weapon and checking everyone's movements all over again.'

'Really?' said Simmy. 'Are you sure about that?'

'Why? Do you know better?'

'Not at all. But I'd have thought they'd be giving more time to the background stuff. Connections and motives and timelines – all that stuff.'

Ben laughed. 'Get you!' he said.

Simmy looked at him, detecting a flash of warning in his eyes. He was trying to divert her, she realised. Perhaps he had picked up some of the same causes for concern in Aoife as she had herself. He had met her twice now, and might well be forming a few conclusions.

Once they were all in the car, Cornelia firmly on Bonnie's lap in the back, there seemed to be an awful lot to say.

'She's a case, isn't she,' said Bonnie. 'The minute she spotted us she was dashing up the track to catch us. Wouldn't stop talking, all about Diellza and the pregnant one . . .'

'Louise,' Ben supplied.

'What did she say about them?' Simmy asked.

'How everyone was totally thrown by the murder, and Christmas, and Fran Bunting on the verge of a breakdown. It was classic smokescreen stuff,' Bonnie summarised smugly. 'A whole lot of hot air saying nothing at all important.'

Corinne was taking the road slowly, listening to the chatter, and peering out at the fells, which were rapidly disappearing as they dropped down to the settlements of Glenridding and Patterdale. Ullswater could be glimpsed now and then as it stretched away to the north and east of them. 'I still haven't seen the new bridge,' she said idly. Nobody heard her, and she tried again. 'The one that was washed away in the flood. You know,' she went on.

'That's was *years* ago,' said Ben, finally attending to her. 'They've had the new one for ages now.'

'I know. But I never come up here, do I? It's all rather lovely, I must say.'

'Nicer than Windermere?' teased Simmy.

'Different.'

'I think the whole thing hinges on Celia Parker,' said Ben, out of the blue. 'It keeps coming back to her, whichever way you look at it. Plus, it was very obvious that this Aoife woman never once mentioned her. I kept waiting for her name to come up, and it never did.'

'And you think that's suspicious?' Simmy asked.

'Don't you? After all, Celia was right in the heart of everything, until she suddenly vanished. And the thing is – the police didn't know to set up a hunt for her, because they didn't know about the baby. They still might not be properly in the picture where she's concerned.'

'They probably aren't,' said Simmy, with a lump of remorse in her chest. 'Although I did say a bit about her to Moxon this morning.'

'She'll be with Diellza,' said Bonnie confidently. 'And it looks to me as if they killed the husband between them. It would work a lot better if there were two of them.'

'Do you think Aoife knows? Is she trying to protect them for some reason?' Simmy tried to think. 'I got the impression that Aoife doesn't like Celia very much.'

'All these women!' Corinne complained. 'Women, babies, jealousy, making plots together, all with history and crushes on each other's husbands. All the usual stuff, when you come to think about it.'

'There speaks a wise woman,' said Ben. 'I want to write some of this down, but it's too dark to see.'

'Dictate it onto your phone, then,' said Corinne, as if that was almost too obvious to be worth uttering.

There was a stunned silence, before Bonnie snorted. 'You know what – he never even thought of that,' she said.

Ben and Bonnie would have stayed all evening in Hartsop, but Corinne pulled rank as driver and vetoed any such plan. 'I want to be back by six,' she said firmly. 'You should have come in your own car if you weren't happy with that. I did tell you,' she reminded Bonnie.

'And I told you Ben's car has a hole in the exhaust, and can't be fixed till next week,' said the girl.

'We really appreciate you bringing us,' Ben assured Corinne hurriedly. 'We've got half an hour or so, anyway.'

Except that there was virtually no possibility of a coherent discussion in the Hartsop house, with Jerome apparently victim to more colic and Robin uncontrollably bouncing around the living room in some sort of sympathy. Christopher was a very disgruntled childminder. Even after Corinne's expert efforts, there was little semblance of calm. Ben urged Simmy into the kitchen for a very quick debriefing. 'We had another look at the actual scene of the crime,' he told her. 'It's quite a trek from the Bunting house, if it's in the middle of Glenridding. I forgot to ask you to point it out. It's impossible to imagine a woman in labour getting herself up there and back in the night, without some help. More than that, we could only come up with one explanation of why it happened there, anyway – and that's the theory that McGuire was being chased, and he was running back up to the bunkhouse where they think he was staying. And that's another reason why it was highly unlikely to have been Diellza.'

'What about a secret assignation with someone?'

'Unlikely, but possible. Who, though?'

'Celia Parker comes to mind,' said Simmy, trying not to hear the continuing howls from the next room.

'Of course,' Ben nodded. 'Anyone else?'

Simmy shook her head. 'We don't know enough about these people, even now. And we have to remember that it was Christmas. That makes such a huge difference.'

'Does it?'

'Yes, Ben. Normal life is put on hold for two days. Everyone's distracted, and obligated to relatives, and worrying about food, and trying to remember who gave who which present. There's no public transport – and this year the weather was desperately cold. You have to factor all that in.'

He did not look convinced. 'I suppose it explains why the Buntings threw that party,' he conceded. 'Everything started with that, didn't it?'

She gave this some thought. 'Only for us – me and Christopher. For everyone else it might just have been one more thing in a whole heap of things. They probably do it automatically every year. Or take it in turns or something.'

'You haven't integrated very well, have you?' He cocked his head at her. 'How long have you been here now?'

'Almost two years,' she admitted. 'But we have been rather busy. I've decided to make much more effort from here on.'

'If they accept you after you've fingered one of their favourites as a murderer.'

'If they're all in it together, the village will be decimated.' She laughed uncertainly. 'That won't happen, will it?'

'It might yet turn out to have been an angry Albanian,' he said. 'Diellza might have had a jealous lover, who's the father of her child.'

'It could well be,' she said, thinking that might be the least bad outcome.

'Anyway, we're not much further forward, in spite of coming up here. If I can borrow my mother's car, we'll be back tomorrow. She'll take a bit of persuading, though. Zoe's learning on it, and she's already moaning about that.'

'Don't give me that look. There's no way I'm coming down to fetch you – and take you back again. I've got enough to worry about here.'

'I never said a thing,' he grinned.

Corinne was at the door, summoning her passengers, and within two more minutes they were gone.

Christopher's mood was better than it might have been, given his trying day. 'Why do people have kids?' he wondered. 'Think how free we'd be without them.'

'Hush!' Simmy was genuinely afraid that fate would hear him. 'You love it, really, being a dad.'

'Do I?' He looked at Robin, who was grubby and dishevelled from his prolonged tantrum in sympathy with Jerome. 'He really lost it, you know. I thought he was going to bring the tree down on himself at one point. Lucky you had Cornelia – she would have been terrified.'

'He probably needed the exercise. He hasn't been out for days now.'

'I'll bear that in mind for next time, and just throw him out into the garden, then.'

'Good idea.'

'It was the baby's fault, anyway. Wouldn't stop bawling, the little brat.'

'They do that.' Simmy herself was feeling weary but knew better than to refer to it. Compared to her husband and son, she had certainly enjoyed a more interesting day.

'So, bags I not be the one to get supper,' said Christopher decisively.

'Fair enough. I'm going to do baked potatoes with sauce

out of a jar and some final shreds of turkey mixed in. It's mainly cold stuffing now, I expect. That'll do nicely.'

'It will if it's sausage meat.'

'It's not. It's tasteless old sage and onion.'

'Oh well. And don't forget to feed the baby. Corrine had a go, but he wouldn't take it. There's half a bottle still in the fridge.'

'Are we allowed to use that? Isn't there some rule about starting fresh every time?'

'Pooh to that,' said Christopher, much has Angie had done.

By seven o'clock, both small boys were upstairs asleep. 'It won't last,' said Christopher. 'I'm tempted to go to bed myself and snatch some sleep while I can.'

'We've had that conversation,' said Simmy. 'Stay down here and we'll find a film to watch.'

But then the landline rang, and Simmy's mother was saying something that well and truly woke them up again.

Chapter Twenty

'I'm sure I've just seen your missing Albanian and her friend,' said Angie excitedly.

'What? Where?'

'In Keswick. Your father and I went for a drink there, and some chips, with a couple we know. We were leaving to come home, when two women walked past us. One was really big, and looked as if she wasn't altogether well. The other one was older, with a woolly hat pulled right down over her hair. I wouldn't have given them a thought, until the big one said something about a baby, in a foreign accent. I nudged your father, and he got the message and we followed them a little way. They got into a car that was parked quite close to ours, and we got the registration number.'

'Why didn't you follow the car?'

'Russell wanted to, but I wouldn't let him. They're probably holed up in some remote barn on the fells, and I

271

wasn't going to risk that on a cold night like this. We're too old for that sort of thing.'

'Have you phoned the police?'

'Of course not. That's for you to do. I'm just reporting a sighting. Now we know they're still in the area, and we've got the car number. What more do you want?'

'You're right. Thanks, Mum. It's amazing good luck. Quite a coincidence, too.'

'They weren't trying very hard to stay hidden. The police have been asking the public to watch out for Diellza.'

'Not Celia, though. People seeing them together wouldn't make the connection.'

'Probably,' said Angie, with an audible shrug.

'Assuming it really was them.' Suddenly Simmy was unsure. 'We're rather jumping to conclusions.'

'They'll soon check whether it's Celia's car, won't they? That'll settle it.'

'You're right.'

Seven o'clock on a December evening could feel like the middle of the night, and that combined with the exhausting day they'd all had tempted Simmy to postpone everything until next morning. 'But I can't, can I?' she wailed to Christopher. 'If they found out, we'd be in even bigger trouble.'

'Phone Penrith, not Moxon,' he advised.

'That's another thing. It's so much easier to talk to him, but I know I can't when he's probably in bed with painkillers making him woozy. It's a much bigger deal trying to explain to some strange constable at the police station.'

'Just do it,' sighed Christopher.

But still she dithered. What exactly was she going to say? How much would the person she spoke to already know or understand? Should she disclose that the information came from her mother? 'I suppose they are looking for Diellza,' she muttered. 'They've probably got loads of people calling in to say they've seen a fat foreign woman.'

'Yes,' said Christopher impatiently. 'But try not to use the word "fat".'

'I wasn't going to. Have they been putting pictures of her on the internet, do you think? Or the telly?'

'Not that I've seen. In America they'd just say they're looking for a woman five feet eight in height and several hundred pounds in weight. People would get the message right away.'

'The thing is,' Simmy tried again, 'they won't be looking for Celia. Or they won't have been until today. If Moxon reports everything I told him, then they might be, I suppose. And on top of all that, we're not even completely sure it was them anyway.'

Christopher made a visible effort. 'What's your problem, Sim? It's not going to make any difference to how long they let us keep the baby, if that's what's bothering you. And if Diellza did kill her husband, she's not going to be in any position to have him back, is she?'

It helped to have things spelt out like that, and she pushed up against him on the sofa in a grateful cuddle. 'Sorry,' she said. 'I'm being all irrational.'

'I get it – I think. And I'm not trying to push you. It's fine by me if you want to leave it till the morning. We can even pretend Angie phoned then, if we want to cover ourselves.

And why didn't *she* call them – the police, I mean?'

'I'll phone Ben first,' Simmy decided. 'He'll put some iron in my spine, or whatever it is.'

But before she could do that, somebody was at the door. 'Not again,' she groaned. 'Who is it this time?' Her mind spent a millisecond listing the candidates, which included Sergeant Inskip and Dan Bunting, because they had already shown up uninvited and might do so again.

Christopher opened the door, revealing the Harris sisters, Lily and Nicholette. 'Sorry,' said Lily. 'Is this a bad time?'

'Not at all,' said Christopher, rather more heartily than Simmy liked. 'It seems to be a time for spontaneous visits. Makes sense, I suppose, given the season.' He led them in, with Cornelia joyously welcoming Lily and Simmy getting up from the sofa. Scraps of forgotten information were filtering through her crowded mind. Nicholette had an interest in criminal law. Lily had seen the baby and asked a lot of searching questions. And there was probably reference to him in the latest police requests for assistance. Belatedly, she wished she and Christopher had looked at Facebook and the rest, to see what the latest reports were saying.

'Is that baby still here?' Lily began, going straight to the point.

Simmy nodded.

'It belongs to the wife of the murdered man, doesn't it?' The challenge was naked in Nicholette's voice. 'You've been hiding him from the police. When they gave out that the wife had recently given birth, we soon made the connection. Do you know where she is? Are you hiding her as well? How *involved* are you?'

'Hang on, Nico,' said Lily anxiously. 'Don't be so aggressive. These are my friends.'

'That's all very well, but they're also well known as having been closely associated with a lot of local murders over the years. They've got their own hotline to the police, and they can get away with behaviour that wouldn't be tolerated in anybody else.' She paused for breath, before continuing, 'I've been hearing all about it from Aoife.'

There's a detail I forgot, thought Simmy ruefully. 'You are being rather aggressive, you know,' she said mildly. 'Sit down and have a drink. There might be some ginger wine left.'

'No, thanks. We really want to know about this baby. Aoife says she supposes it was Celia Parker who brought it here for Diellza, who hasn't got a car and couldn't possibly have got down here on her own. She's never liked Ms Parker, anyway. Has all sorts of suspicions about her. She thinks she must have known Diellza better than she let on.'

Simmy refrained from airing her knowledge that Celia and the McGuires had indeed known each other for some time. Clearly a lot of information had been concealed from Aoife as well. 'We don't know any of them,' she said innocently. 'We met them all for the first time last Friday.'

'Well, you haven't wasted any time in catching up, have you? Out yesterday with the Buntings and Louise and Aoife, and that clever detective boy going along, ferreting it all out. And again this afternoon, apparently. They're all talking about him, in the village.'

'Nico,' said Lily again. 'Ask her about the baby. That's the most important thing.'

Nicholette spread her hands in an expression of agreement. 'Well?' she said.

'It's not a secret,' said Simmy. 'You're right that Celia brought him here on Sunday, saying she'd found him on her doorstep when she got back from the pub, with a note attached, and decided to bring him here because she knew we'd got Robin and would make a better job of looking after him than she would. We've kept him alive since then,' she finished defiantly.

'And you believed all that rubbish? How would a newborn – probably quite premature as well – survive outside in a temperature of minus four, which it was on Sunday? Nobody leaves babies on doorsteps. It was obviously all planned in advance. They sized you up on Friday and chose you as the patsies who'd be left literally holding the baby.'

Simmy felt both defensive and oddly relieved. Here was a woman who did not mince her words, had no fear of causing offence, and probably knew what she was talking about. 'You think so, do you?' she said weakly. 'We have been wondering—'

Christopher interrupted her. 'Why have you come here? What do you actually want from us?' He looked at Lily. 'We haven't committed any crime, you know.'

Nicholette jumped in before her sister could reply. 'Of course not – that's not what I'm saying at all. Let's just say I'm a concerned citizen, who's walked into a very peculiar murder, which happens to connect to my line of work, and involves an old friend of mine. I know people around here. I want to be useful. And Lily assures me that you are law-abiding decent people, in spite of appearances to the contrary.'

Christopher and Simmy both laughed, to Lily's evident relief. But Nicholette was not amused. 'Listen to me,' she ordered. 'Aoife's told me about yesterday – hearing the baby and you saying it was a relative. She knew you were hiding something, but at that point she'd got no idea that Diellza had suddenly had a baby, like some sort of Christmas miracle. Now the police know about it and are asking people to watch out for Diellza more urgently than before.'

Lily intervened. 'I knew there was a baby, days ago.' She gave Simmy a reproachful look. 'You lied to me.'

'I did, and I'm really sorry. Celia told us it would be dangerous to tell anyone who he was, until after Christmas. We still don't know why.'

'Who else has heard him since he's been here?' asked Nicholette.

'Um – well, Detective Inspector Moxon, on Christmas Eve. I can't think of anyone else. Dan Bunting called in, looking for Diellza, but luckily Jerome stayed quiet while he was here. So unless Aoife's told them, they probably still don't know where he is. They might not even know he exists.'

'They know all right. The police were there this afternoon. Aoife saw their car.'

'Obviously,' said Christopher thoughtfully. 'And they're not likely to believe the story about the Buntings not knowing she was pregnant.'

'What story? Who said that?'

Christopher looked to Simmy for confirmation. 'Well, they can't have known, can they? They'd have said something from the start, if they had. It would have changed the way the police were thinking. That's why we're going to be in trouble, when they get round to us. They'll accuse us of perverting the course of justice.'

'And they'll take the baby away from you,' said Nicholette, with a close look at Simmy. 'How would you feel about that?'

'We knew we were only keeping him for a few days,' she said bravely.

'Who said his name was Jerome?' asked Lily.

'It was in the note Diellza left with him. She must have decided on it before he was born.'

'Maybe it's the name of his mystery father,' said Christopher.

'What? Isn't the dead man his father?' demanded Nicholette.

'We don't know for sure, but apparently he doesn't look anything like him.' Simmy felt suddenly impossibly weary with it all. 'They've done a DNA test – or are doing it. I suppose the results will take a while.'

Nicholette was clearly excited. 'Hey – if she was pregnant by another man, that would explain why she was hiding from the husband and sheltering with the Buntings. And why McGuire came looking for her, to give her what for. But that doesn't explain who killed him.' She subsided. 'What am I missing?'

Simmy abandoned all attempts at concealment. No further harm could come from anything she said, as far as she could see. 'We think Celia Parker knew them both

– Diellza and her husband. It's probably thanks to her that Diellza ended up with the Buntings. We think the most likely thing is that she's been protecting Diellza, and probably killed the husband before he could force her back to Manchester with him.'

'Hmm,' said Nicholette. 'First chasing him halfway up the fell and shoving him into the beck to bleed to death. She sounds positively Amazonian if she could manage all that.'

'Of course, there's no real evidence that any of our guesses are right,' said Christopher. As the only man in the room, he evidently felt he ought to keep a hold on any available threads of logic and practicality – although Nicholette was far from being a ditzy female.

'There's obviously been a lot of lying,' said Simmy.

Nicholette jumped on this. 'Oh? What, exactly?'

'I don't know – well, Celia for a start. You said it yourself. She must have known about the baby and planned to bring him here. Although it's weird to think that all the time we were at the pub, she must have been sizing me up and working out how to do it.' A memory struck her. 'And what about that phone call from her neighbour? The man who heard a funny noise at her house? She can't have manufactured that.'

'Can't she? Could you hear the voice?'

Simmy shook her head.

'So it might have been Diellza pretending, to strengthen the story they'd hatched together.'

The idea of something so deliberately devious and manipulative gave Simmy real pain. To be duped and treated as an innocent idiot was hurtful. She had liked Celia Parker. 'That's horrible,' she said.

'And unnecessary,' added Christopher. 'Why would we care about the details of where Celia found the baby?'

'Timing,' said Nicholette slowly. 'She'd need to be sure you believed she knew nothing about the baby during that pub lunch.'

'I can't take any more today,' Simmy burst out. 'It's just getting more and more confusing and complicated, and my head actually hurts with it all.' She put a hand to a spot over her left eye. 'Right here. It *hurts.*'

Nobody could argue with that, and the sisters took their leave, murmuring soothing apologies for being so intrusive. 'But you can see we feel anxious to get to the bottom of it all,' Nicholette threw back from the doorstep. 'We'll probably come back tomorrow.'

Christopher closed the door on them and went to his suffering wife. 'Is it really bad?' he asked.

'Just a stress headache, I suppose. I need a milky drink and a pill, and then I'm going to bed. I don't care how early it is.'

Christopher made no attempt to remind her that she had been going to phone the police, or Ben, or both. It could all wait until the morning.

Chapter Twenty-One

Friday was cold again, a degree or two lower than the previous day. Jerome had consumed two bottles of milk during the night, and Robin was listless. 'Oh God, he's sickening for something,' wailed Simmy. 'Somebody's given him a cold, or worse.'

'That explains yesterday, then,' said Christopher. 'He's not usually such a little beast as that.'

'I've a good mind to stay in bed all morning and let the world carry on without me.' She had both small boys snuggled under the duvet with her.

'Fine by me,' said Christopher easily. 'Although I seem to remember I told Fiona I'd go into the saleroom today. There's an auction next week. We need to be sure everything's been collected from the last one.'

'Ben's not going in as well, is he?'

'Not that I know of. Didn't he say his car's out of action? So he can't, can he?'

'If you go to work, I'll have to get up.'

'I needn't go until mid-morning.'

His very nonchalance was annoying. Jerome's destiny was a hopeless puzzle and Robin's apparent illness was worrying. 'I already don't like today,' said Simmy, angling for some sympathy.

'You sound about seven,' came the deeply disappointing response. 'I'll go and make some tea. Maybe that'll buck you up a bit.'

'I dreamt Moxon was so furious with us he was throwing things,' she remembered. 'It was awful. He brandished photos of Diellza and Celia in our faces and said we'd have to go to prison.'

'Nasty. So best phone him, then, and spill the beans, such as they are. Try not to make it sound too crucial.'

'How am I meant to do that?'

'Well, surely they already assume that Diellza's with Celia Parker? They'll have her car number already and be watching out for it. It's even possible someone else has reported seeing them in Keswick. You can say your mum wasn't really sure, but she took the number just in case. Say it was nine o'clock and you were just off to bed.'

'You can be alarmingly devious sometimes,' she told him. 'I'm not sure I like it.'

'I've been corrupted by the job. I used to be totally transparent.'

'And everybody lies,' she sighed.

'And we don't want to get into any more trouble with the police, do we?'

'They'll be round to collect Jerome, I shouldn't wonder.'

'And we're tempted to think they're welcome to him,' said Christopher, with a big, manufactured yawn. 'Then we can have our lives back.'

Simmy tried to protest, but just at that moment, it was a decidedly appealing prospect. But then she felt Jerome wriggle against her and remembered the sheer physical bliss that came from contact with a young baby. 'I'm not sure I want my life back,' she said.

'Took you a minute to think about it, though,' Christopher teased.

'Nothing's simple,' she said.

When he brought the tea, he also had her phone in his pocket. They had a firm rule about taking mobiles to bed with them, but there was a morning ritual of checking for overnight calls. Simmy took it carelessly and put it on the bedside cupboard. Robin was whimpering and rubbing his left ear. 'Something hurts, look,' she said. 'What's the matter, baby?'

There was no coherent answer, but he was clearly not happy. 'How's your head?' Christopher remembered to ask, perhaps prompted by his son showing a similar discomfort. 'Maybe you've got whatever it is, as well.'

'I'm fine,' she said, to her own slight surprise. 'Just tired, worried and confused. Physically everything's in good working order, I think.'

'Um . . . Sim. Didn't you get a text from Celia Parker on Wednesday? Have you told Moxon or anyone about that?'

She stared at him blankly. 'So I did. I had completely forgotten. Do you think I'm going mad? Or have I got early onset Alzheimer's?'

'Just the distractions of Christmas and all that, I should think. I forgot as well. After all, it didn't really say anything, did it?'

'That's it, I guess. All it did was tell us she's alive, which we never doubted anyway. And maybe a bit of provocation. Like poking a bear with a stick. Me being the bear.'

'Hmm,' said Christopher diplomatically. 'I'm guessing you never thought to tell Moxon about it.'

'You guess right. In my defence, it was all rather a rush. There was such a lot to tell him in a short time. It was silly, I suppose, going there instead of the Penrith police.'

'Easier, at least. And he did ask you. You'll be glad to have him between you and the proper cops, when it all comes to the crunch.'

'"Proper cops"?' she echoed. 'Don't let him hear you say that.'

'As if I would.'

'I feel a bit scared, actually. You talking about it coming to the crunch. I've gone all wimbly inside. It's not just that they'll take the baby away – we are going to be in trouble. My dream was right, although it's that superintendent or whatever he is I'm really frightened of. He already thinks you're in the habit of keeping back vital information, after last time.'

'I know. That's why I'm going to let you take the flak this time. It's your turn.'

Simmy waved this aside, still thinking about the text. 'You know – I don't like the idea that Celia's the killer,' she realised. 'She was nice to me at the party, and at the pub on Sunday. She might not have meant any harm by dumping the baby on us. It's a sort of compliment, in a way. And she might be rescuing Diellza from something terrible. Even if she did kill the man, it might have been from good motives. He might have been going to kill Diellza or steal Jerome . . . or something.' She tailed off, as the scenario began to lose focus. 'We keep coming back to that same theory, don't we? We're forgetting all the other people who might just as easily be the killer.'

'And as Ben keeps saying, we don't have nearly enough facts to form a proper picture.'

'Like what was Alexander McGuire really like? What sort of a marriage was it, with him so much older than her? How did they meet? I keep trying to remember what she said about him at the party. I thought she seemed afraid of him, but that could be wrong. At that point I thought she was a recent arrival here, under the eye of the immigration people and liable to be sent back to Albania. I got that totally wrong, didn't I?'

'Most of what we know came through Dan Bunting when he came here on Monday,' Christopher pointed out.

'And Fran, at the pub. But neither of them said much that was any real use. Basically, they seemed bemused at her disappearing like that. Fran was really upset on Wednesday.'

'Why would she be, though?' The quality of Christopher's attention was gratifying. 'You'd think she might be glad to wash her hands of the woman.'

'Not if the police were hassling them. When you think about it, the Buntings are just about the only real source of hard information. At least when it comes to Glenridding. People in Manchester will be providing all the background stuff. Fran probably feels guilty that they let it happen. If they knew about Jerome, they'd probably feel even worse.'

'Surely they do know about him by now.'

'Depends who they talk to, presumably. Although the police are sure to go back and cross-examine them about it. They won't believe the Buntings didn't know Diellza was pregnant, even if they managed to miss the fact of the birth.'

'It's all very Christmassy, isn't it?' Christopher mused. 'I still think there's an Albanian King Herod out there somewhere.'

'I hope not, because I'm the one he'll be coming for, if so. If you go to work, there's only Cornelia here to defend me.'

'He'll be staying clear while the police are crawling all over the place. And listen, Sim – if the social workers come for Jerome while I'm in Keswick, try not to get in a state, okay? For Robin's sake, if nothing else. Go and see your mum or something, to take your mind off it.' He squinted at her chest. 'And how are your boobs now?'

She laughed at the sudden change of subject. 'They're *there*, if you know what I mean. I'm leaking a bit, with Jerome cuddled up so close. But that's not so unusual. Two months ago I got all tingly just watching *Call the Midwife*. I think that probably goes on for years, once you've fed your own baby. It's quite nice in a mad sort of way.'

'We're all animals beneath the facade,' he said.

'I know. But I've calmed down since Sunday. I'll hand him over if they come for him without throwing a tantrum.

After a bit, it'll seem like a dream. A fairy tale that came real because it was Christmas.'

'Right,' said Christopher. 'So now I'm getting dressed, and I'll take the dog down to the Dodd, and bring more logs in, while you just lie there.'

'Lovely,' said Simmy.

She had plenty to occupy her thoughts. Robin was mildly feverish and should be given a big drink. Jerome would also want more milk soon. People focused on the murder investigation were going to intrude, making demands and accusations. It was cold outside, and there was another bank holiday looming. A week ago, things had been so different, she thought nostalgically. Although, perhaps less so than she assumed. They had been wanting another baby with increasing urgency, with an escalating sense of time running out. Without conscious intent they had avoided making any firm plans for the coming year. *I might be pregnant* had been the subtext to any thoughts about ambitious holidays, or even decisions about Simmy's shop.

So when a real live baby dropped out of the sky, it slotted all too easily into the household. Even Angie had understood that.

Outside it was barely light, despite a cloudless sky. Staying in bed really did seem the most sensible option for at least another hour. Christopher would be around for a while yet to field any importunate early visitors, before abandoning her. She dozed off, blissfully unconcerned about warnings against falling asleep with a small baby in bed with you. There were many such 'rules' that she and Christopher chose to ignore, largely thanks to Angie

Straw. And perhaps DI Moxon, in his own quiet way had added a similar influence. He might fuss and flap at the unorthodox methods used by Simmy, Ben and Bonnie to identify a murderer, but at heart he not only approved, but actually admired their failure to comply, at least sometimes. Christopher was an aberration in a family of relative conformists. 'Travel broadened my mind,' he would say. 'And it taught me to think for myself. It pains me to realise how unusual that is.'

It didn't always work like that, of course. A lot of the rules were sufficiently powerful that they simply had to be obeyed. The trouble mostly came from the greyer areas, where enforcers knew that the law was unreasonable, and yet found no option but to chastise those who broke it. Or the transgressor had made the wrong choice from motives that seemed sound at the time. Something in that area had happened a few months earlier in Borrowdale, when Christopher withheld important facts from the police. Now he and Simmy had done it again, probably with equally shaky justification.

But that was coming to an end, on this Friday, with Christmas fast receding. A week since the Buntings' party, and all those women making an appearance. At least six of them, counting Nicholette, which was a lot. Diellza, Aoife, Celia, Louise and Fran. A great gang of them with history and connections that Simmy was never going to unravel. Old loyalties and shared experiences would have a powerful influence on present behaviour. Except for Diellza, who had known none but Celia until a week or two ago. And no two of the women the same. Even Christopher had kept them all clear in his mind. Each one was distinctive in her own way. Husbands, offspring, careers – all that formed shadowy backgrounds to the vividness of their actual presence.

And Lily. She'd forgotten clever little Lily, who might yet provide keys to the mystery.

Christopher left shortly before ten, and Simmy got dressed. The fire was blazing, much to Cornelia's satisfaction. Robin nibbled at a piece of toast without enthusiasm. Jerome was in his usual nest, propped up so he could see the room and evidently in a good mood. It belatedly occurred to Simmy that he might catch whatever bug her own child might be spreading, with alarming consequences. 'Too late to worry about that now,' she muttered, having had them both cuddled together in the bed for hours.

As she had expected, someone knocked on the door within ten minutes of Christopher's departure. Cornelia stirred irritably and gave a single bark. 'I know,' said Simmy. 'I feel just the same.'

It was Nicholette, which was not much of a surprise. 'On your own?' she asked.

'Yes. Are you?'

'Not really. We were hoping you could come with us to Glenridding.'

'Well I can't. Robin's got a cold or something, and I'm not taking the baby out. Anyway, why do you want me? What's going on?'

'It's too complicated to explain. But first things first. The baby's going back to his mother. I'll take him to her now.'

'What? Where is she? What do you mean?' She looked over at the little bundle on the sofa and her heart throbbed violently. 'You can't.'

'She's at my house – my parents' house, I should say. With Celia. She's scared you'll call the police. She thinks they'll arrest her for the murder. She's in quite a mess, to be honest.'

'In no fit state to look after a baby, then. Tell her to come here. I won't call the police. They don't seriously think she did it, anyway. But they probably think she knows who did.'

'We'll come to that,' said Nicholette with a superior air that made Simmy clench her jaw. 'If she comes here, you have to promise not to cross-examine her. Just let her sit with the little one. Don't reproach her for abandoning him. Nothing like that.'

'Is Celia coming as well?'

'Oh yes. Diellza won't go anywhere without Celia. This whole business centres on her, after all.'

'Does it?' said Simmy weakly. 'Are you saying she killed Diellza's husband?'

'Of course I'm not. There you are, you see – that's the sort of thing I'm afraid of. You and those young friends of yours, making wild accusations and getting in everybody's way. It's no way to behave. I don't know how you've got away with it up to now.'

'You don't know what you're talking about.' Some of Simmy's recent thoughts about conforming to convention and doing everything by the book lurked in her mind. This self-satisfied Nicholette was overstepping a mark. 'You seem to be saying you've solved the murder and are now manipulating everyone from some weird plan that only you understand.'

'It's not a weird plan at all. As I'm sure even you will know, it's crucial to have evidence before charging anyone with murder. It's my intention to obtain some – which is not going to be easy.'

'So leave it to the police,' said Simmy tiredly. 'And let everyone get on with their lives.'

'The police have been hampered to the point where they are unlikely to be very appreciative or co-operative unless we can deliver something concrete.'

'Which is down to Celia,' said Simmy defensively.

'Indeed.' Nicholette smiled. 'We're not blaming you for anything.'

'Aren't you? You sounded pretty blaming just now, saying we've got in everyone's way.'

'Sorry. I was talking more about that boy detective, really. And his girlfriend. Lily filled me in about them. They seem very sure of themselves.'

'They're my friends,' said Simmy stiffly.

'Okay. So what do you want to do? Shall I go and get Diellza? I warn you, she's scared stiff that you'll yell at her for abandoning the kid.'

Simmy sighed. 'Just go and get her,' she said. Somewhere she was feeling she was owed some sort of consideration for her stalwart efforts as foster mother. Was it going to be all about Diellza, with her own contribution ignored? Her instinct to gather up the baby and run into the woods with him was quelled without too much difficulty. It would be a wrench to give him back, but her rational faculties were robust enough for it to be achieved without hysterics. 'Go,' she said again.

Nicholette went, and a very long ten minutes ensued in which nothing happened. She left the door slightly open, despite the cold and Cornelia's confusion. 'At least without Jerome, I can take you for a walk,' she told the dog, forgetting Robin's malady.

Then three women showed up and the day began in earnest.

Chapter Twenty-Two

The Albanian woman was indeed in 'a bit of a state'. Her eyes were swollen, her hair in a tangle and her coat muddy.

'Good God – you look awful!' said Simmy tactlessly. 'Come in quick and sit by the fire.'

Diellza simply stood where she was, staring around the room as if fearful of men with guns jumping out at her. Celia, at her side, gave her a gentle nudge. 'Go on,' she said. 'The baby's there, look.'

If anything this seemed to make things worse. Diellza actually took a step back. 'I can't,' she said.

'Here, let me fetch him,' said Simmy. She gathered up the little bundle and approached slowly. 'He's been absolutely brilliant,' she said. 'Doing all the right things. We think he might have come rather early, though. Is that right?'

Diellza said nothing, darting quick glances at the baby, then at the surrounding faces. 'Look at him,' Celia ordered her. 'Have a good long look.'

Instead, tears began to flow down her face, and she gave a great sob. 'I can't,' she said again.

'Sit down, all of you,' said Simmy. 'We've got to take it slowly. There's no need to do anything but just sit and calm down. We can take all morning if we have to.'

'We can't, though,' said Nicholette. 'We'll have to tell Aoife what's happening, for a start. She's waiting for us in Glenridding.'

'Let her wait, this is more important,' said Simmy firmly, on the basis of no information whatsoever.

'That's right,' said Celia.

'I suppose I can call her,' said Nicholette grudgingly. 'But she won't be happy. That wasn't the plan.'

'What *was* the plan, then?' asked Simmy.

The woman shook her head, her long face giving nothing away. 'It's too complicated to explain all in a minute.'

Simmy was already having to damp down her innumerable questions – all of them needing to be directed at Diellza. Guesses were popping up, more and more urgently needing confirmation. 'Here,' she said, suddenly decisive, and thrust Jerome at his mother. 'Let him lie on your lap for a bit. You've come this far, you can't just ignore him now.'

Celia and Nicholette both jerked forward as if to stop her, but then caught themselves up. 'It can't hurt, I suppose,' said Celia.

'Are you afraid you won't be allowed to keep him?' Simmy asked gently. She was still working on the assumption that the very fact of being Albanian made Diellza subject to harsh British rules that restricted her freedom.

'My husband is dead,' came the slightly startling reply. True, but stark, and obviously relevant. Yet somehow less so than the reality in the room.

'Yes,' said Simmy.

'He loved me.' The sobs returned, drowning any attempt to speak.

Celia and Nicholette had taken the two armchairs. Robin was frowning up from his rug, displeased at being overlooked so completely. He coughed ostentatiously. Then he sneezed. 'Did you say he's got a cold?' asked Nicholette. 'He looks a bit droopy.'

'I did. And Jerome's quite likely to get it,' said Simmy. 'The official line is that he and Diellza should both be given a medical check. If you ask me, her need is greater than his, but if he is premature, he should probably be looked over. There's that certificate thing they give you when a baby's born, for the registrar. You'll have to get that somehow.'

'All in good time,' said Nicholette, finally shattering Simmy's fragile patience.

'That's not good enough. You seem to have taken the whole thing over, for some reason, when you don't even *live* here. You don't know Celia or Diellza, even if you were at school with the others. What does any of it have to do with you?'

'I made it my business,' said Nicholette with dignity. 'I could see there were avenues to explore, and with Aoife's help, I quickly found these two.'

'How?' Simmy demanded.

'Aoife knew the car, for a start. She was sure Celia wouldn't go far with Diellza being so recently delivered, and it being Christmas. The options were really quite limited. All she did was text Celia to say we wanted to help, and to meet somewhere like Penruddock or Dacre, where there's warm pubs to sit and talk. It took a few attempts, but it worked.'

'My mother saw you in Keswick yesterday,' Simmy remembered. 'And you texted me,' she accused Celia.

'The police were looking for Diellza, but not for me,' said Celia. 'We were staying with an old friend of mine just outside Keswick – and I went to meet Nicholette and Aoife on my own.'

'Must be a very co-operative "old friend",' said Simmy suspiciously. 'Having you land on her – or him – all over Christmas at no notice.'

'If you must know, it's an elderly bachelor with two spare rooms and an old-fashioned idea about hospitality.'

The distraction of attention from Diellza was having quite a beneficial effect. When Simmy glanced her way, she witnessed a developing maternal instinct that gave her another pang. She looked away again quickly, and hoped the others would do the same. Perhaps some of her questions would be answered by Celia, if the conversation could be sustained. 'So you women got together and hatched a plan,' she prompted. 'What day was all this?'

'Yesterday,' said Celia. 'We didn't do anything or see anyone before that. Three days, during which Diellza did nothing but cry.'

'Annoying for your friend,' said Simmy.

'He coped.'

'And then Aoife ordered you to meet her at a pub and somehow everything fell into place.'

'I don't blame you for being cross,' said Celia. 'Anyone would be. But everything I did was for the best.'

Simmy remembered Nicholette saying everything centred on Celia. 'The whole business comes back to you, then,' she said. 'We assumed that you knew Diellza and her husband in Manchester, when they were first married. Did you bring them here? What about the Buntings? Where does Aoife fit in it all? And *who killed him?*' She almost shouted the final words, making Robin cry and Jerome whimper. Cornelia went to her young master for mutual reassurance. Simmy pulled them both to her, where she sat on one end of the sofa, with the Albanian woman and her baby at the other end.

'We have questions for you, too,' was Celia's infuriating reply. 'How much have you told the police? Or the Buntings? Who knows the baby's here? And can you keep him a bit longer?'

'We don't need to get into that now,' Nicholette interrupted. 'What are we going to do about Aoife? We said eleven o'clock at the Traveller's Rest. We can leave Diellza here, can't we?'

'Do you mean you want me to come as well?' asked Simmy. 'I can't imagine why, if so.'

'As witness,' said Celia shortly. 'The police will believe you more than they will us. You're probably the only person around who they *do* believe.'

'I wouldn't be so sure about that,' said Simmy. 'Especially if Moxon's not there.'

'Who?'

Simmy tried to explain, but ended by saying, 'Never mind. I'm not coming, anyway. I'd have to bring Robin, and he's already had enough of all this.'

'Leave him with Lily,' said Nicholette. 'I can get her to come and play with him, and keep an eye on Diellza.' She spoke as if this was almost too simple and obvious to be worth uttering, which made Simmy feel obstructive and petty.

'Is it just Aoife we're meeting?' she asked.

'Probably. We're to make it look casual. We'll walk up from the car park, and drop in for a hot chocolate or something.'

'That sounds very cloak and dagger,' said Simmy, taking a longer look at Diellza. 'I wish I knew what was going to happen.'

'Don't we all,' said Celia feelingly. 'If I'd only known a week ago . . . well, there's no point in that, is there.'

Diellza looked up, focusing on the pink-haired woman. 'It was all your fault,' she said, all the more shockingly for the clarity of her words. 'Everything is your fault.'

'Hey!' It was Nicholette protesting. 'Let's have none of that. We're going to get it all settled, you'll see. By the end of today, you'll have no more to worry about.'

Diellza narrowed her red eyes, and lifted her large head. 'My husband is *dead*,' she shouted. 'And he loved me. Can you not understand that? Alexander was a good, good man who loved me, and now he's dead. And you are the one to blame.' She spoke the last words to Celia, but she was clearly just as furious with Nicholette.

Celia spread her hands and heaved a sigh. 'I got it wrong, yes. I admit that, but only up to a point. You acted of your own free will, and don't you dare say otherwise. You agreed with me every step of the way. I was *helping* you, for heaven's sake.'

'We both got it wrong,' moaned Diellza, shedding more tears. 'You're right – I got it all much more wrong than you. Poor Alex. The poor man.'

Nicholette had gone to get Lily and was back with her within two minutes. The girl went first to Robin, who seemed inordinately glad to see her. 'Thanks, Lily,' said Simmy. 'I don't know how long I'll be. You probably know more about what's going on than I do.'

'No worries,' said the girl. 'If it gets to lunchtime, I'll find something for him in the fridge. Eggs? Cheese?'

'He's not very hungry today. He's got a cold or something. You might catch it.'

Lily shrugged. 'I probably won't.'

Nicholette was standing by the door. 'Come on – we've got to go. I'd better text Aoife to say we're late.'

Simmy opted not to resist any further. She could hear Ben in her mind's ear, telling her she ought to be grateful to be included. Robin was happy with Lily, as was Cornelia. 'I do hope we won't be very long,' she said. 'Jerome's going to want a bottle at twelve at the latest.'

Diellza registered this after a few seconds' delay. 'I will feed him,' said she flatly. 'I cannot do otherwise, can I?'

'There's a bottle in the fridge – sit it in a bowl of hot water for a bit to warm it up,' said Simmy. Further explanations could come later, if at all. Nicholette and Celia were already outside and Simmy hurried after them.

In the car, Simmy had to select from a long list of questions to consider. It was almost inevitable that Jerome would come close to the top. 'She wants him back, then?'

she asked the others. 'Doesn't she?'

Celia was driving, Nicholette next to her. Simmy was in the back, not strapped in because she wanted to lean into the space between them. Celia turned to answer her. 'Of course she does, but she can't see how. With Alex dead, the university accommodation isn't going to be available. She'll have to find somewhere to live. She's even thinking of going back to Albania, which is a ridiculous idea.'

'Who is Jerome's father?' Simmy blurted. 'The police have got his DNA, so they'll know any time now, so it's no good her trying to keep it a secret.'

'It's no secret anyway,' said Celia. 'It's the whole key to everything.'

'So . . .?' Simmy prompted.

'Honestly, I can't get into that now. We'll be at the car park in about three more minutes, and it'd take a lot longer than that to explain it all. You'll get the whole story soon enough, don't worry.'

'Just tell me – did Dan and Fran know that Diellza was pregnant? That's what everyone keeps asking. They talk as if they had no idea. Even on Wednesday, when I mentioned a baby, they didn't seem to make a connection.'

'Yes and no,' came the infuriating reply. 'Again – that'll become clear. You're jumping all over the place, which is only going to cause more confusion. You've done a brilliant job with him, and nobody's going to forget that.'

'Only because it was Christmas,' said Simmy, feeling the full force of that truth. 'Any other time, I'd have told you to get lost.'

'I know,' said Celia Parker. 'And that was the part nobody could possibly have planned for. He wasn't due until February.'

Simmy nodded to herself. 'Okay. Well, hadn't you better brief me as to what's happening next? Why exactly are we meeting Aoife? What about Fran? Does Louise know you're back? And—' She forgot what else she was meaning to say, as Nicholette interrupted her.

'Just don't say anything if you can help it. It's going to be tricky, that's for sure. Aoife's there for Fran, primarily. They're good friends, luckily. Basically, you're our link to the police. I said that already, didn't I? We'll tell you what to tell them, when the time comes.'

Simmy bristled. 'Oh, you will, will you? Can't I be trusted to know for myself? It sounds as if you're using me to cover someone's back.' Any thought of further concealment from Moxon was untenable. 'He's my friend – I can't tell him any lies.'

'You'll understand,' was all the woman said to that.

The walk up to the pub was the same from the one the Hendersons had done the Friday before, on their way to the Buntings' party, but went beyond their little close. Houses lined both sides of the little road, small and terraced on one side, larger with gardens on the other. Further up there were substantial grey-slate residences, well-spaced, facing south and west. Aoife's was the furthest and highest of them all. The pub was set at right angles to the road, its blackboard offering a range of food and their famous hot chocolate drink.

'Where's your house?' Simmy asked Celia.

'We just passed it. Right beside the car park,' came the ready answer. 'I'll show you on the way back.'

Simmy nodded, as if making a mental note. 'I came up here yesterday with Corinne,' Simmy said. 'We drove up to Rattlebeck and saw the place the man died.'

'Yes. Aoife told us,' said Celia. 'Your young friends were with you.'

'I've never actually been to this pub. It looks nice.'

'Caters mainly for hikers, needing to be warmed up. There's always a good fire.'

Simmy was mulling over the distances and connections between the few points she knew. The Buntings lived on the eastern side of Glenridding in a detached house, which turned out to be a very short distance from the Traveller's Rest pub. That in turn was not far from the Rattlebeck Bridge and Gillside Farm where Ben and Bonnie had readily located the scene of the murder. With Diellza firmly at the front of her mind, she calculated that it would not have been very difficult for the woman and her baby to totter down to Celia's house sometime on Sunday – although precisely where – or even *whether* – she might have hidden the baby remained to be discovered. Questions were again swarming insistently at her, and some of them had to be voiced to Celia.

'Did Diellza just leave the baby, as you said? Or did she stay with you all along? Was she there when you were at the pub with us in Patterdale? Were you telling outright lies all the time?'

'Hush!' said Nicholette. 'Not now.'

They went into the pub and took the door on the right leading to one of the two bars.

Aoife was sitting alone at a small table in the furthest corner. When she saw the others, she got up and moved to a bigger table by the window. 'At last!' she said crossly.

The woman at the bar squared her shoulders and stood ready for the newcomers' orders. 'Three hot chocolates, please,' said Celia.

'Put some Tia Maria in mine,' said Nicholette, without inviting the others to have the same. Simmy quailed at the scratchy atmosphere, recalling Aoife's sharp manner as well as the desperately serious topic about to be discussed. Her stomach started rippling with apprehension.

'Okay, then,' said Celia briskly. 'Let's get cracking.'

Aiofe had her phone in her hand. 'I'll text Nigel. Give him ten minutes or so.'

Nicholette gave a quick laugh. 'If this works, it'll be a miracle,' she said. 'If nothing else, I bet the technology's going to let us down.'

'Trust my Nige,' said Aoife. She smiled. 'This has been exactly what he needs to get him out of his hole. I was starting to think it was permanent.'

Simmy closed her eyes for a moment, wishing she had a hole to crawl into, away from this craziness. 'Ummm . . . ?' she said.

'Don't ask,' Celia advised her. 'It'll become clear soon enough, you'll see.'

'Meanwhile, we can settle one or two things for you,' said Aoife. 'You might find, when it's all brought into the open, that you'd guessed most of it already. You, of all people, have had the facts staring you in the face.'

Simmy blinked. 'Have I? That's not how it feels. Not at all.'

'Okay. Well, start with Celia. What do you know about her?'

Despite a sense of being played with, Simmy did not resist. 'She knew Diellza and her husband in Manchester. She brought the baby to me. She's been with Diellza ever since then. She works as a psychologist or something, and is fifty-six.' She caught Celia's gaze, which did not seem unhappy with what had been said.

Aoife made a silent clapping motion. 'Right so far. Anything else?'

'I'd be guessing – but perhaps there was something between her and Alex McGuire? Maybe before he married Diellza? It seems likely that she told him that Diellza was here with the Buntings, so he knew where to come and find her. And then she kept them – I mean Diellza and the baby – safe after he'd been killed. Either safe from the killers who might come after his wife and child, or safe from the police because they suspected she'd killed him.'

Nicholette gave an unladylike whistle. 'Wow! Jolly good,' she breathed.

'But which is it?' asked Simmy. 'Escaping from killers or the police?'

'Probably neither,' said Aoife. 'But that's what we're hoping to establish in another few minutes.'

'Diellza said it was all Celia's fault,' Simmy remembered. 'And Nicholette said it all centred on her. You,' she addressed the older woman directly. 'You knew there was going to be a baby – but he came early and threw everything off track. Is that right?'

'Sort of. There's a lot more to it than that.'

Aoife moaned softly. 'That's where poor old Fran comes

in,' she murmured. Then she looked at Celia and her tone changed. 'That's where I agree with Diellza. This really is all your fault.'

'Anything I say to that would be a cliché,' sighed Celia. 'But I'll say it anyway – I was only trying to help. It all felt perfectly logical at the time.'

'Because you thought you understood Fran. That was your big mistake.'

'Right,' said Nicholette.

Then Aoifes phone buzzed. 'Okay,' she said. 'Anything that goes wrong from here is down to me. Now please don't talk.' She looked round the table and everyone fell silent. Simmy wondered what would happen if people came in for a drink, as they well might.

Nicholette produced a lined notepad and pen, oddly reminiscent of Ben Harkness. She put it where anyone could reach it, and said, 'Write anything down you want to know.'

Aoife put her phone next to the pad. 'Just listen,' she ordered.

Half a minute later, a man's voice came through the phone. 'Here you go. Happy New Year and all that. Let's hope it's better than the last.'

'Cheers,' came a familiar voice in reply. Simmy's head went up and she almost said aloud – *Dan Bunting*.

'And here's to the womenfolk, bless 'em. They've had a lot to put up with, mine especially.'

'Yeah,' said Dan.

'So, here's the thing. Aoife's given us a deadline of this time next year. After that we give up the whole business, apply to adopt and brace ourselves for the nightmarish paperwork. Pity they're not throwing their girl babies out of China any more.'

'We were so close to deciding the same thing, before we found Diellza. It was a real godsend.'

'You'd got it all decided, then?'

'Not quite. I mean, *I* had and Diellza was thinking she'd got no alternative. But I wasn't quite sure enough to broach it with Fran. It's always been me that was keenest, anyway. I'm not even sure an adoption agency would ever have accepted us, the way she was. With her record it would always have been iffy.'

'So what went wrong?' The tone of the question was a lot less casual than the words. 'Something truly grim must have happened.'

'She had the baby, last weekend, and ran off with it. Simple.'

'No, Dan. That's not right, is it? You forget that we can see the beck from our bedroom – quite a big stretch of it, in fact. And the way I was that night, agitating about Christmas and not sleeping, and trying to get off the medication that was keeping me so zombified – couldn't even force myself to turn up at your party. Well, there I was, standing at the window at three in the morning, the moon as bright as day, and watching a man slash another much older man across the throat and shove him onto the rocks.' He stopped, and Simmy became aware that she had held her breath for far too long. She looked at the others, who were all looking at her.

'Hey! You must have been dreaming,' blustered Dan. 'Otherwise you'd have called the cops there and then.'

'I nearly did. Then I thought of Fran. My wife's best

friend. What would it do to her? And, idiotically, a voice kept reminding me that it was Christmas. All down the valley there were coloured lights, decorations and trees and goodwill to mankind. But I did see you, Dan, and I'd really like you to explain why you did it.'

'He wanted them back,' came an answer almost too low to be heard. 'He didn't care that it wasn't his baby. He said he couldn't live without Diellza, that it would make no difference.'

'So she knows you killed him.'

'No! She and Fran were both fast asleep. I made him stay outside and we talked in the lane. Nobody could have heard us. But it was all too late. He'd emailed Diellza to say he was coming, that he wanted to take her back. By the end of Saturday, she must have seen the news of the body and guessed it might be him. Fran was out somewhere, and Diellza came downstairs and asked me if I'd seen McGuire, because she was expecting him and had decided she should go back with him. She looked ill, deadly pale and panting. I wasn't in a much better state myself.'

'She'd had the baby by then, presumably. Did you see it?'

'That's the insane thing. I had it so firmly in my head that it was due in February, it never crossed my mind it might come early. I still don't know whether or not she'd had it by then – but I'm guessing not. I guess it was a slow labour, and she grabbed a lull to come and talk to me. I don't know anything about how it works, really. But I had to have that baby. I promised her ten thousand pounds if she'd stay with us and let us adopt it when it came. I said McGuire was far too old to take on a new baby, and she'd

307

be free to do whatever she liked once it was all over.'

'But she knew by then he was dead?'

'She knew *somebody* was. She was obviously scared, but she kept her cool, said she wasn't well, and would talk to me again in the morning.'

'Did she know you still hadn't told Fran there would be a baby?'

'Oh yes. She understood all that. She was very good at hiding it, and staying out of Fran's way. Celia had explained how it was, before she even moved in.'

'Dan – you are in very *very* deep trouble, my friend. Aoife – did you get all that?'

'Loud and clear. Well done you. We're coming through.' She got up quickly, waving to the others to do the same. There were still no other people in the bar. Simmy followed in a daze.

In the other bar there were four men, seated at two tables some distance apart. Simmy only recognised one of them, and that with difficulty. Dan Bunting was crouched over, holding his head in his hands, quietly weeping. Across the table a man in his thirties sat holding a phone. Two young hikers stared blankly from the other side of the room. Nothing that had been said had struck them as constituting a confession to murder.

'Simmy – call your friendly detective, okay,' said Nicholette. 'Tell him we have first-hand evidence that will solve his murder for him.'

Chapter Twenty-Three

The middle of Friday became lost in a cacophony of demands and conflicting priorities. Diellza, Robin, Ben, Christopher and poor bruised Moxon all had to be accorded proper attention. Everyone was throwing out questions with little immediate hope of answers. 'It was Dan,' said Simmy repeatedly. Every time, it became more obvious that it could only have been him all along. Details like the murder weapon, the motive and the remarkably skilful play-acting he presented afterwards went unaddressed for the moment.

Back in Hartsop, Nicholette took Lily home. Aoife had disappeared in search of Fran, who would shortly be utterly distraught. 'He told her on Monday that there would have been a baby for them to adopt, but that Diellza had changed her mind, probably after killing her husband,' Aoife explained in a rush. 'He was desperate to keep her on his side. But how stupid can a person be? She and I had figured out by the end of Boxing Day that the baby must have been born. She was stunned that he could have done all that without telling her. She'd been carrying on in absolute ignorance, poor thing.'

'That's why she'd been crying,' Simmy realised. 'Nothing to do with worrying about Diellza.' It might seem a minor detail to the others, but Simmy felt it to be significant. 'She must have thought she'd been living with a stranger. Horrible!' She shuddered. 'And now it's just got a whole lot worse.'

Celia took charge of Diellza and Jerome, only minimally consulting Simmy. 'She's going to take a while to recover,' she said.

'Obviously,' said Simmy impatiently. Celia was yet to explain just why everyone assumed the real fault lay with her, and Simmy was withholding goodwill until she knew it would not be misplaced. 'So what happens now?'

'Best they stay here with you. The police will show up any time now, don't you think?'

Diellza was still on the sofa, hugging her little son. She looked almost comatose. Celia had tried to convince her that she had nothing more to fear, that Dan Bunting had killed her husband and was in police custody. The news made little impression, and Simmy guessed that the woman's paralysing concern was with what happened next. A concern with which she could wholeheartedly sympathise. The death of Diellza's husband confronted her like a brick wall, removing all security and confidence. The result was a palpable despair. But it was a despair tempered by the joys and terrors of motherhood. Jerome was now the first consideration and Simmy knew she was never going to hold him again – nor should she. He was back in the rightful arms and whatever happened, mother and baby would be together.

Robin had wanted to go with Lily, and for a moment Simmy had been tempted to let him. But he was hers, and his place was with her. His nose was running and he seemed to have a headache. 'I bet he caught it at that party,' she muttered, all the time knowing it had been too long ago for that theory to work.

Christopher phoned her ten minutes after she'd got back, saying there was nothing much to do and he'd be coming home for a late lunch. 'You'll be lucky,' she told him. 'It's been quite a morning here.'

'I'll stop and get something, shall I?' he offered. 'The shop in Glenridding does takeaway pies and things.'

'They're not likely to be open this week, are they?' Mention of Glenridding did nothing for her mood. 'We've got eggs and tins and a few slices of bread. I can't really think about food, quite honestly. You've got a lot of catching up to do. You might even walk into a police interview.' She should have added *It's nice that you're coming home* but she couldn't form the words. Christopher would want explanations and recaps and that made her feel weak.

On top of all that there was Ben – and Bonnie. Their participation had been less than on previous occasions, but they were still very much concerned to follow developments. Simmy was tempted to send a curt text saying 'It was Dan' but she knew that would only elicit an avalanche of questions. Better to leave that until the next day, when she was supposed to open the shop with Bonnie. There should be more clarity by then, she thought optimistically. So the

311

text she finally sent said '*Case solved. Do NOT contact me. Wait until tomorrow.*' It might work, she told herself.

Moxon did not make an appearance, nor did he approach her directly. He had, however, responded with admirable alacrity to her call from the Traveller's Rest, dispatching two police cars from Penrith, which miraculously arrived in twenty minutes. Dan Bunting had been taken away with minimal drama, the second car proving to be redundant. Nigel, husband of Aoife, had gone too, brandishing his phone and saying a full confession had been recorded on it.

Christopher came home to find Celia and Diellza still ensconced in his living room. 'It was Dan,' said Simmy, half a minute after he came in. 'They've arrested him. Fran didn't know anything about anything, and most people are blaming Celia for the whole business.'

It appeared to satisfy him for the moment. He raised an eyebrow, smiled vaguely and focused on Robin. 'He doesn't look very good,' he observed.

'It's a cold. I can't think where he got it.'

'What does it matter? Let me take him. Has he had any lunch?' Simmy handed the child over and shook her head. 'Let's do dippy eggs then,' Christopher told his son. 'That's what my dad always gave us when we were poorly. With very very thin slices of bread and butter.'

'That'll be tricky. It's already sliced,' said Simmy, feeling a lot better all of a sudden.

Celia had flinched at the repeated casting of blame, but said nothing. Simmy supposed that both her visitors were probably hungry, and afraid to request nourishment. Jerome was awake and waving his hands jerkily on his mother's lap. Simmy wanted to ask whether he had been fed and if so how, but by the look of him, the answer was obvious. Diellza's clothes were loose at the front with faint patches of damp just visible. *It's such a miraculous system*, thought Simmy with a little pang.

'I'll make us some tea and find something to eat,' she said, feeling suddenly benign. 'We can have it in here by the fire.' Somehow the fire was still alive, but the log basket was empty.

'Lily kept it going, I suppose,' she said.

Diellza looked up. 'She did,' she said. 'That's a good girl.'

'Indeed,' Simmy agreed.

The tea worked well as a restorative, and Diellza finally found her voice. 'Will the police take him?' she asked.

'No!' It was Celia giving a forceful reassurance. 'They'll be more than happy that you're reunited. All they need now is a bit more background – how you and Dan are linked.' She pulled a face. 'And I can tell them all they want to know about that.'

'Tell me,' Simmy invited. 'Because most of what Dan told Nigel still doesn't make a lot of sense.'

Celia drained her mug of tea and put it down carefully. 'It goes back quite a way. I'll try to keep it short, but you deserve an explanation. Does your husband want to hear it as well?'

'I think he's happy to stay in the kitchen,' said Simmy. 'I can fill him in later – and, anyway, he can probably hear most of it from there.'

'Okay. So – to start at the beginning, Nigel and Dan were both in a support group that I was running, almost

313

a year ago now. It was for men who wanted children but for various reasons hadn't got any. You'd be surprised how many there are. A lot of them have wives or partners who can't or won't even consider parenthood until it's too late. Fran's thirty-five and was never medically eligible for IVF. Adoption seemed the last hope. I put them – him – in touch with Diellza. Alex and I were good friends, and he told me about the pregnancy.'

Diellza made a choked sound, half protest and half sob. Celia patted her leg and went on, 'It was never any secret about the baby's father. He was – is – Albanian, here illegally. Alex was trying to help him, but he was deported. He and Diellza got together because of their shared homeland. I think she was mainly just sorry for him . . . ?' She looked to her friend for confirmation and Diellza shrugged and flushed pink.

'Alex had never fathered any children, and assumed he was infertile. All the same, it was a real marriage, despite the age difference. Diellza settled in very well. But when she found she was pregnant, she was consumed with shame and insisted she couldn't let Alex raise a child that wasn't his. They argued about it for months, with her getting more and more upset. She arranged an abortion, but didn't go through with it.' Again, Celia patted Diellza's leg, seeking agreement with what she was saying. 'Say if I get any of it wrong,' she invited.

'It's all true,' said Diellza. 'I couldn't think what to do. It felt like a horrible bog that I was drowning in. A big stinking mess.'

Simmy tried to imagine it – the ageing academic and his distraught wife, facing a common yet cataclysmic problem.

'So you suggested that the Buntings adopt the baby,' she supplied.

'Right,' said Celia. 'Although it was nowhere near as simple as you make it sound. Dan's desperate desire for a child was obsessing him to the point of madness, I realise now. Fran had her job, and friends, and a nice house and plenty of money. She knew Dan wanted a baby and might one day leave her for a fertile woman. So Dan made the deal with Diellza, taking her into the house so Fran could be told gradually and made to feel part of it all. Diellza wanted to get away from Alex, dispose of the baby, then go back and take up where she left off.'

'"Dispose,"' Diellza murmured sadly. 'That sounds terrible.'

'Okay,' Simmy said. 'I get the picture. You don't have to say any more.'

'Except that we know now that neither Fran nor Diellza knew for sure that Dan had killed Alex. They didn't know he'd followed her here – which is my fault, because he got the address from me. Nobody knew the baby had been born until mother and child came to me on Sunday. By then it was dawning on us that Dan was going to make things very difficult for Diellza if she said she wanted to keep the baby, after all. So we took off until Christmas was done with, leaving the baby with you for safe keeping. My friend in Keswick has his limits, and a new baby would have crossed them big time.'

'Even so . . .' Simmy demurred. 'The note about his name . . . the *lies* you told.'

'I didn't really lie. We wrote the note just to give the story a bit more credibility. Diellza was in the most awful state, much worse than she was this morning. She wasn't capable of caring for him. Alex's letter – which she didn't read until Saturday even though it came on Friday afternoon with a Christmas card – threw her into a total tizzy, which combined with giving birth a month before it was due, nearly killed her. But she still had the sense to hide the birth from the Buntings and come to me for sanctuary.'

Simmy looked at Diellza and marvelled at the strength of endurance that must have been called into play.

'All right,' she said. 'I think I've got it now.'

From the kitchen, Christopher called, 'Looks like visitors.'

The knock on the door came fifteen seconds later. Simmy let the two detectives in, with a sense that there was really very little for them still to do.

There was equally little to convey to Ben and Bonnie in the shop next morning. She began with a tease: 'You two have really got competition in the shape of that Nicholette. She took charge just like you two would have done, and organised the whole thing.'

'She lives in Sheffield,' Ben pointed out.

'So she does,' laughed Simmy. 'So that's all right, then.'

Simmy's summary of Celia's explanation was reduced to a few sentences. 'They went back to her house once the police had gone,' she concluded. 'Diellza's got to have a doctor look her over, and see about registering the baby. I wouldn't be surprised if she takes him back to Albania and finds his father. Celia might have to give herself a talking to. And Fran's got Aoife and Nigel to console her.'

'Nigel's going to have to face charges for not reporting

a crime, remember. He actually *witnessed* the murder and did nothing about it,' said Ben.

'Gosh, yes – what'll happen to him?' wondered Simmy.

'Suspended sentence, probably. Given how helpful he turned out to be.'

'I can't bring myself to blame him,' Simmy admitted. 'I might have done the same, and I'm fairly sure Christopher would, as well.'

'What *about* the baby?' Bonnie asked timidly. 'I mean – weren't you upset to part with him?'

Simmy shook her head. 'You know more than most people how that goes. You've watched Corinne take tiny babies for a few days and then hand them back. It hurts, of course. Physically hurts. But you know it's right, and that feels good. Satisfying. A job well done. My hormones had a good shake-up in the process – but maybe that part isn't so easy to understand. I think that baby came at exactly the right moment for quite a few reasons.'

She did not mention that she and Christopher and Robin had celebrated and mourned in equal measure, their family home restored to them along with abiding images of an extremely memorable Christmas.

REBECCA TOPE is the author of three bestselling crime series, set in the Cotswolds, Lake District and West Country. She lives on a smallholding in rural Herefordshire, where she enjoys the silence and plants a lot of trees.

rebeccatope.com
@RebeccaTope